THE ACCIDENTAL SAVANT

A Novel

George Crowder

Chelsea Press
Los Angeles, CA

First Printing, 2021

ISBN 978-0-9979358-4-4 (paperback)
ISBN 978-0-9979358-5-1 (e-book)

This novel is a work of fiction. Any references to real people, events, establishments, organizations, or locales are intended only to give the fiction a sense of reality and authenticity, and are used fictitiously. All other names, characters, and places, and all dialogue and incidents portrayed in this book are the product of the author's imagination.

Printed in the United States of America

Book Cover Design by ebooklaunch.com
Page Layout by Polgarus Studio
Chelsea Press logo by Luis Contreras

For Liz,
with love and pizza

Belgrove Missionary Baptist Church
Indianola, Mississippi
May 30, 2015

AFTER MORE THAN 18,000 concerts, Riley B. King was about to play his last date. The air inside the venue was greenhouse heavy, sodden with Delta humidity and the aroma of fresh-cut flowers. Mourners gently stirred it with hand-fans decorated with B.B.'s likeness. It made me shake my head. Even now, they couldn't stop marketing.

Meanwhile, the headliner waited at center stage in a gleaming casket. Guests continued to ooze into pews, lulled by a languid organ. Some cast glances, recognizing me—or maybe wondering what a solo white boy was doing here.

Like everyone, I'd come to pay my respects to the King. But I'd also come *prospecting*—panning the waters of B.B.'s life, hoping for a nugget to guide me on my own. These folks had known the man better than me. What they had to say might be what I was looking for.

As the service began, testimonials to B.B.'s kind nature hit their mark. The man's warmth had been toasty as a wood stove on a frosty morning. But having shared the stage with him, I already knew that.

Ministers promised Mr. King's spirit would now take up residence with the Lord. He'd survive in the hearts of those he left behind, and his music would inspire souls yet to be born. Comforting words, but for me, they offered no revelation.

A wailing baby roused me when I nodded off. There were

1

disapproving looks, but I couldn't blame him. You had to either start screaming or start snoozing.

His momma had a third option, bouncing him on her horsey knee until his face ignited with joy. Entertained by his giggles, I watched and daydreamed. Who knew what that little boy might become? Possibly another Riley. Einstein. LeBron. Steve Jobs.

Since my accident, doctors probing the limits of human potential had probed *me*. They called it "the neurological equivalent of splitting the atom"—a release of enormous hidden power. No matter how they bled and scanned me, they couldn't figure it. Ignoring the evidence—uh, *me?*—some denied it was *possible*.

Well, it *was*. What I couldn't say—had wrestled with since the miracle occurred—was what it *meant*.

Part One

September-October 2012

Chapter One
Got it!

CALL ME FRIZ, not Frizzy. No fro, bro. Hair is short, brown, and straight. Unidirectional.

No, my name's short for *Frisbee*. Actually, *Frisbee Dog*. Weird nickname, but it suits me. Or at least it *did*.

A Frisbee dog is an alpha fetcher. Average pooches chase balls, bones, or toys tossed in their vicinity. Whatever. It's all good, dawg. But those pups know their place in the pack. They grovel at the feet of their gifted kin, who runs down the spinning disk and snares it in flight.

That was me. Like my namesake, I could track and catch any airborne object in Texas. *Thou shalt not land.*

Dad would hit me fly balls for hours, pounding fungoes to the depths of centerfield until his tanned face dripped sweat. We'd quit when I made a circus catch, going over the wall to steal a homer, or coming up with a diving, sliding grab. Those'll leave you lovin' life. Always said the same thing when I made one of those babies. *Got it!*

This being Texas, the love of my life was football. I got my nickname during Texas Youth tryouts. The coach, a welder from Waco named Bob Roberts, watched soberly, chewing a plug of tobacco. After studying me, he hawked a filthy loogie and proclaimed, "That kid catches footballs like a dog catches Frisbees!" Might have been expletives, too. With

Coach Two Bob, there usually were.

He ambled over and yelled, "Hey, you—Frisbee Dog—run a post." He barked at his son, the quarterback, "Zach, lead him good. I do not want the pass underthrown, ya hear?" Last, he hollered at the kid playing safety, "Goin' deep, Ferrell. See ya stop it."

We lined up and Zach took the snap. I juked past the linebacker, then loped down the sidelines. Ferrell fell in step with me and Zach let her fly.

Zach has an arm, and with his dad warning him, he wasn't going to leave it short. He put that sucker *out there*. I glanced over my shoulder, saw the ball still rising, and heard Coach Roberts already bawling out his son. "I toldja to *lead* him, not throw it to Juarez, for chrissake!"

A good dog doesn't quit on a fling and neither did I. Head down, I dug for the end zone, running like those whippets in Frisbee competitions. I'm built like one of them, too—long and lean, with thin fast legs. They shot me past Ferrell like he was trapped in tar and he plain quit. He didn't think I had any chance at that ball. Must have seemed like a waste of energy to chase me.

I'm not a conservationist. I let it all hang out, including my tongue, which dangled from my mouth like Michael Jordan, or, well, a Frisbee catchin' dog.

The whole play couldn't have lasted more than a few seconds. Hash marks flew by, and at the last moment I looked up to see the football plummeting in a spiral, just out of reach. I stuck out my long right arm, got palm and fingertips on it, then hauled it in without breaking stride. *Got it!*

People told me Two Bob was so thrilled he spit out his entire nasty cud. He whooped like he'd won the lottery, brown spittle showering anyone who had the bad luck to be nearby. "Friz, we are gonna hafta do something 'bout your flapping tongue or you're gonna be a half-tongue puppy 'fore the season's over!!"

I'd rather be The Rock. Magic. Snoop. The Mamba. *Such* cool names.

But I *coulda* been Half-Tongue Puppy.

So…Friz it is.

Chapter Two
The Hit

LIKE MOST TEXAS MOTHERS, Mom knows a thing or two about football. Together, we wrestled my jersey over shoulder pads before I put them on as a unit. We'd figured this out the hard way, sweating to get the jersey on *after* I put on the pads. That was like trying to stuff a hippo into a tutu.

We tugged the padded jersey over my head and down my torso, then Mom clapped me on the shoulders and sighed. She didn't let go and I looked up at her. She was still an inch taller than me, with the same kind of straight dark hair I've got, but longer. According to Dad, Mom could have been a model instead of a schoolteacher. When he says that, she just rolls her brown eyes and smiles. At the moment, she wasn't.

"Are you playing the thug today?"

Dad came around the corner, sipping a cup of coffee. "Oh, he's not so bad."

"Yes, he is," she insisted flatly. "What's his name?"

"Brody Pitts," I said. "He's just big, is all." I didn't want her to worry.

"The bigger they are…" said Dad.

"The harder they hit," Mom concluded.

Dad gave me a look, as if to say he'd done his best. Dad's a musician, but Mom says he looks more like the World's Hottest Male Librarian. He wears thick glasses and reads a lot. I guarantee he'd read about Brody. And he knew Mom was right.

If I was a whippet, Brody Pitts was a Rottweiler—big, fast, aggressive, and scary. We were in the Seniors, a division for twelve- and thirteen-year-olds. Though I'd turned fourteen a couple of weeks earlier, the deadline was August 1, so I'd maintained eligibility. I was probably older than Brody, but you wouldn't know it. He had a pituitary disorder and was likely doing steroids. Six-foot-two and growing fast, he tipped the scales at 205, all muscle. Pumping iron since he was ten, Brody was ripped and cut while the rest of us looked like string beans. He was the only player in the league to wear a cutaway jersey to show off his six-pack. It was like dropping a linebacker from the Longhorns among the kids.

Brody played for the Capital City Bearcats and my team was the Round Rock White Tigers. We were both undefeated. While we had a high-powered offense, they had the top defense in the Austin area, led by Brody. The irresistible blah-blah-blah meets the immovable yada-yada-yada. Today we'd see which would come out on top.

By the end of the third quarter we were locked up, fourteen-all. This sort of close contest was not to the liking of Coach Two Bob. When tension ramped up, so did his spitting. He aimed at a paper cup on the sideline grass, but he was no William Tell. The target was surrounded by a swamp of brown saliva. We looked at it with awe and high-stepped around it.

The fourth quarter was a grind, the score still tied. Finally, our running back, Tyrell Lee, broke one wide for fifteen yards, and it looked like we were in good shape. But he only picked up a couple on first down, and the Cats read a jet sweep, stopping it for a loss.

Third and long, and our passing game wasn't clicking.

Coach called time out and we huddled around him on the sidelines. José Hernandez, our center, plodded through the spit bog, and someone ooohed.

"Whoa—José stepped in it," said Tyrell.

That made us crack up. Sticking your foot in something foul is high comedy.

Coach's brow furrowed in wonder. "You boys're sure loose. Okay. Gonna run three cross."

"Not *two* cross?" asked Zach.

"*Three* cross. Shoot, you still no good at math," said Coach, and we all snickered. "Friz gonna line up right at flanker, Jamarie split. Jamarie's gonna take care of the corner so Friz can get off the line. Sanchez, you're wide left. Hesitate, then break downfield. Hit the twenty-five and angle in. Friz, you're front, Sanchez back. One of them's gonna be open, Zach. Put it on him."

I considered our chances as we broke huddle. In theory, crisscrossing receivers confuse defenders, leaving a man uncovered. It's up to the quarterback to make the read and hit him, easier said than done.

We lined up and the Cats took positions, with extra backs to stop the obvious pass play. To my relief, Brody was on the opposite side of the field, covering Sanchez.

Zach took the snap and the gears started rolling. Jamarie did the job on the corner. I sprinted ten yards upfield and broke left, losing my man.

The pass was already on its way, intended for me, but too high. So I went airborne and hauled it in. *Got it!*

Then something got *me*. I hit a brick wall—or at least, that's what it felt like. Flying across the field, Brody Pitts had clobbered me with a highlight reel hit. It stopped any forward momentum, except for my mouth guard, which wasn't wearing a seat belt and went flying.

I held onto the ball despite a vicious secondary hit from the safety. His helmet T-boned mine, which thunked like a melon.

I went down, and the referee whistled the play dead. The crowd cheered loudly but went silent when I didn't get up.

Chapter Three
Concussed

POPPING TO MY FEET and sprinting to the huddle would have been a tasty move, but it wasn't even on the menu. I just lay there, gazing at blue heavens, hugging the football to my side. I could hear more whistles, then teammates blocked the sky above.

"Can you move your finger?" asked Zach. I gave it a wiggle, as Coach Roberts joined the mob looming over me. "I don't believe his neck's broke, Dad."

"That's something," Coach allowed. He looked worried. He dug in his wallet and pulled out a card.

"What's that, Coach?" asked José. "Like, 'you have the right to remain silent'?"

"Dude, he caught a pass, he didn't rob a bank," snapped Tyrell.

"Dad's concussion cheat sheet," said Zach.

Two Bob scanned the card, then asked, "Know what day it is?"

Before I could answer, José blurted out, "Saturday."

The rest of the guys moaned, and a few laughed. Coach gave José a look. "Run on over to the bleachers and ask if anybody up there's a doctor. Get on, boy."

José ran off, and Coach turned to me with a sigh. "What's the score?"

"Fourteen-all," I answered.

"Good. What down is it?"

"Guess we just picked up a first and ten."

Coach couldn't help grinning. "Helluva catch. Y'all get knocked out on that hit?"

I twitched my head no.

He consulted the card. "How you feel? Dizzy? Nauseous? Blurred vision?"

"No, I'm okay, Coach. I can get up now."

He frowned and nodded. "All right then. But you're gonna sit a while."

Zach and Jamarie hauled me up. The crowd applauded while Coach Roberts put his arm around my shoulder and helped me to the sidelines.

Wobbling to the bench, I felt something below the belt. I glanced down and saw a stain. Lord, I'd *wet* myself! If it's possible to cross your legs while limping off the field, well, that's what I did, trying to hide my shame.

Coach grunted as he wrestled me the distance. "Boy, you sure got your bell rung. You're weavin' like a sailor on shore leave and you ain't had half the fun."

Taking a seat, I asked weakly, "Coach, can I have something to drink?"

He hitched his chin at Ricky Garcia, our perpetual benchwarmer. Ricky drew me a paper cup of Gatorade from the cooler. I hunched over and sipped, awaiting an opportunity.

It came a moment later when José Hernandez returned from the bleachers. "No doctors, Coach—but I found a plumber."

"That's good work, Hernandez. Plumber come in right handy if we clog a toilet," said Coach. "Go huddle with the rest of 'em. Burford, you get on in there for Friz."

José and Miles Burford ran to join the huddle, and Two Bob

grimaced. "It's a wonder that boy can snap on the right count."

With the distraction, I drenched my crotch with lime-green thirst quencher. "Oops," I said lamely.

Ricky burst into laughter, pointing at me. "Look there, Coach! Friz hydrated his privates!"

Coach's patience was waning. "He's not drinking it with his straw, Garcia! Get him another cup!" Then he gave me a look of disbelief. "Lord, boy, you hold onto a pass like that, then fumble the Ade? Sure you don't need nine-one-one?"

"Let's see how I do with the next cup," I said.

I wanted to see the end of the game. When Mom and Dad came to check on me, I convinced them I was all right…though I *wasn't*. I watched in a daze as we managed to rush for a touchdown just before the clock ran out. The Tigers were jubilant over our big victory, but I just sat on the bench and hung my head. I looked up to see Brody Pitts standing over me.

"Hey," I said.

"Hey," he said. "Sorry."

"S'okay. Was a clean hit."

"Sorry you held onto the ball. Shoulda hit you harder."

I tried for a wry smile, a real tough guy. "Next time."

Brody grinned and offered his fist. "You're all right, boy." We bumped, then I turned my head and vomited.

"That makes number four," he said, delighted. I looked up for explanation. "*Concussions*. Not on the stat sheet, but I keep track."

Chapter Four
Dr. Johnson's Report

Tamika Johnson, MD, Emergency Physician, St. David's

THIS CASE WAS NOT MEMORABLE. In the emergency room at St. David's Georgetown Hospital, we see hundreds of patients a day. It's the spectacular ones that stick with you—a construction worker impaled on rebar, horrific stab wounds, an unusually gruesome gunshot victim…

Gregory Collins was none of the above.

It's common to hear Round Rock referred to as the "Sports Capital of Texas." Boosterism. I call it the "sprains, broken bones, contusions, and concussions capital of Texas." He was one of those.

The boy presented with a mild concussion, no intracranial injury or skull fracture—my primary concern. A subdural hematoma or brain bleed can kill you in a hurry.

The patient had no retrograde or anterograde amnesia, cranial nerves II through XII intact without motor, sensory, or cerebellar deficits. No Battle's sign or raccoon eyes, indications of skull fracture we wouldn't expect to see for a least a day. No septal hematoma, no sublingual hematoma, no hemotympanum. No loss of consciousness, which is not surprising. Only ten percent of concussions are accompanied by LOC.

After all the hoopla, I pulled up the boy's paperwork. Based on his ER visit, no one could have seen this coming. We put him through a neurological exam—person, place, time, that sort of thing.

Touched his nose, walked a straight line, the usual. He passed it all.

His CT scan was clear. After the fact, I ran the films past three neurologists and they concurred: there'd been nothing there to see.

Usually this kind of soul searching is prompted by tragedy. A high school football player just died in California. Happily, that's not the case here.

The sole piece of information—and this is remarkable only in retrospect—was the location of impact, which is marked as "Left Temporal." But honestly, that's not unusual.

Neither are traumatic brain injuries in general. The Center for Disease Control pegs the frequency at about 1.7 million a year. Other estimates are higher.

So what happened to Gregory Collins last year was not one in a million.

A conservative estimate would put it at one in 1.7 million.

But of course, it was far rarer than that.

Chapter Five

From Marla Collins's Interview with the Austin American-Statesman, Sunday Edition

Did the trip to the emergency room worry you?
Not particularly. I'm a sports mom. Coping with injuries is part of the job description. And I had three brothers, so I've seen worse.

The doctors didn't find anything?
At first, things seemed okay. They sent us home with a checklist of symptoms to watch for. One of them was blood pouring out of his eyes or ears. Who wouldn't know *that's* bad? They also gave him a plan for returning to normal life. Which my son never made it through.

What activities did the doctors exclude?
Sports, of course. He took that in stride, so I knew he was sick as a dog. Video games, TV, electronic media...

They should prescribe that to *all* our children.
Yeah, right! Before he could fuss about it, they said he shouldn't go to school or do any homework, either. It was almost funny how confused he looked. He asked what he was supposed to do if he couldn't watch TV or play video games. They said, "Rest." "*Rest?*" he

said, like he'd never heard of such a thing. "Yeah," they said. "Just let your brain *rest*."

Did he follow doctor's orders?

Pretty much. But my son's brain had a mind of its own, you might say. Whatever it was doing, it wasn't just resting.

Chapter Six
Early Daze

DOING NOTHING IS HARDER than it sounds. No *Call of Duty*, no *Grand Theft Auto*, no *Assassins Creed*, no *Madden*. Shoot, no TV. They didn't even want me to read a book! First time they ever told me *that*. I just lay around…and *thought*…and *thought*…and *thought*…

That's supposed to rest your brain?

Mom took off work to keep an eye on me, but there was nothing to see. I managed to fall asleep out of boredom. Then the headache woke me up.

Adults complain about headaches, but I'd never had one. So I lay there experiencing it. It didn't take long to understand what all the griping was about.

In sixth grade, we read a story about Zeus, king of the gods, who came down with the mother of all migraines. He hollered so loud he could be heard all over the planet and was driving people crazy. They called in a blacksmith, who split Zeus's skull apart with a wedge— and out popped his full-grown daughter, Athena, wearing a suit of armor.

I was pretty sure I didn't have a goddess in my head, but it was hurting. Not enough to call in a blacksmith, but enough to tell Mom about.

The ER had a long line, but Mom made a scene and got me right in. I usually hate that and pretend I don't even know her, but this time I was glad she could be pushy.

They did another scan and it turned out my brain wasn't bleeding to death. We were relieved about that—and discouraged there was nothing they could do to make me feel better. They gave me Tylenol and sent me home to—you guessed it—get some rest.

Unfortunately, that headache rode back with us. Turns out it wasn't leaving any time soon. Light began to bother me, so Mom drew the blinds and made my room dark as a closet. I felt like heaving but couldn't. I just leaned over the wastebasket, panting.

I lay back down and Mom held my hand. I was so sick I let her.

In fact, only thing that made me feel a little better was having her there.

Chapter Seven
No Deposit, No Return

AFTER A HARD HIT in the old days, a player was expected to shake it off and get back in the game, long as no bones were broken. But when a few kids dropped dead and hefty lawsuits followed, folks got more careful. A rash of former NFL players killed themselves, which wasn't great publicity. Scientists cut open the skulls of the dead ballers and didn't like what they found. I guess no matter how rich and famous you are, it's hard to love life when your brain's been beat to mush.

Which is why no one was letting me go anywhere until my headaches let up. It was Wednesday and I'd been home all week, lying low in a dark room, resting just as hard as I could.

It was, at least, a safe place to shelter, under posters of football greats. One wall featured "The Catch" by Dwight Clark, in which the lumbering tight end leaped higher than anyone other than Joe Montana thought he could, making a two-handed grab in the back of the end zone. The play sent the 49ers to the Super Bowl and launched their dynasty.

On the next wall, Randy Moss made a one-handed snatch against the Steelers. The Vikings went on to lose the game—but Moss kept soaring to greatness, inspiring my own love for single-handed receptions.

My last poster featured David Tyree's "Helmet Catch," which helped the Giants destroy the Patriots' perfect season. Despite coverage that ripped one of Tyree's hands off the ball, he pinned it against his helmet with the other, maintaining control as he hit the ground.

Two-handed, one-handed, a hand-and-a-helmet. Until someone caught a ball in his mouth, like a true Frisbee dog, that about covered it. These plays and the men who made them had thrilled me for years. Worn silky soft from continuous tumbling in my mind, they had grown comfortable as old shirts. Now that I'd wound up on the disabled list, I hoped my heroes might have curative magic on top of their ability to inspire.

Mom took me to Doc Peterson today. I wore sunglasses and a baseball cap pulled low. She drove careful, taking it easy on turns. They made me dizzy anyhow, and we had to sit a minute before I could even get out of the car.

Doc Peterson still calls me "cowboy," like he did when I was four years old. Today it rubbed me the wrong way.

"I'm not a cowboy!" I snapped.

Doc Peterson blinked and reset.

"My mistake. Mind taking off the glasses?"

"Yeah, I mind. Light's too damn bright."

"Friz," my mother started, but Doc Peterson waved her quiet. He cut the overhead light and drew the shades.

"Better?" he asked. I nodded, and he carefully removed my dark glasses and started his exam.

When he finished, he said I was *not* okay to go back to school, much less to play football. He set up an appointment to see another doctor the next day.

Tyrell and Jamarie came over in the afternoon. Low as I felt, I was still glad to see them.

But I had to give them a hard time. "What, no flowers?"

Tyrell gave Jamarie a look. "Toldja he'd expect roses. But *you* said *no-o-o-o*."

"I just said he'd prefer those other ones..."

Tyrell smiled sarcastically. "*Lilies*. They what you bring to a funeral. Friz ain't dead. *Yet*."

I managed a brave chuckle. "Where's Zach?"

Jamarie smirked. "He was afraid he'd catch something."

I pointed out the obvious: "Concussions aren't infectious."

"Just tellin' you what he said. That, and get your ass outta bed. You ain't had but one concussion. Junior Seau had lots of 'em."

"And how'd that turn out for him?" said Tyrell. "Imagine how sick that man was. He had four little kids and still he shot himself dead."

"*I* didn't say it, Zach did," Jamarie protested. "We do have a big game on Saturday, though..."

"Any chance?" Tyrell asked, looking at me hopefully.

I sure couldn't help them. "I can hardly make it to the bathroom, let alone the end zone."

No one said anything for a minute.

"You lookin' a little scrawny, bro," said Jamarie. "The moms feedin' you?"

"She's tryin', but I keep blowin' chow."

"Anything we can do?" asked Tyrell. "Fetch over some protein bars, or something?"

"Nah, I'm good."

They looked at me dubiously.

"Homes, you ain't good—you *terrible*," said Jamarie.

"*Awful*."

"*Pitiful.*"

"You in the hurt locker."

"Without a key."

"And *no* combination."

I had to smile. "Sure am glad you guys came by to cheer me up."

Chapter Eight
Rah-Rah

NEW DAY, SAME SYMPTOMS. Headache pounding, nausea surging, appetite AWOL, and cringing from light like a scaredy-cat vampire. Today we'd see what the concussion doctor made of it.

When we walked into his office, they said it'd be a forty-five-minute wait and gave Mom a clipboard loaded with forms. She flipped through them with a sigh and we headed for a couch.

Across from us, a girl my age was paging through a magazine. She was wearing short-shorts and had slim, tanned legs. Her flip-flops showed off toenails that were such a shiny bright red, the polish still looked wet.

I had a moment of wonder I was noticing such things. It's never been like me to pay much attention to girls. I stopped wondering and got back to noticing.

Her hair was short and blonde—neat, pretty. Her face was, too, with full lips like slices of ripe fruit. As I was studying her, she looked up and smiled.

"Hey," she said.

"Hey," I said.

"Concussion?"

"Yeah."

"Football?"

"Yeah."

She nodded, like she knew it all along. "When?"

"Fourth quarter."

She snorted. "Not what I mean."

"Oh," I mumbled. "Saturday."

"Pretty fresh. Mine was three weeks ago." She smiled again, lips framing toothpaste-commercial teeth. *Wowza.* Oughta have a permit to open carry that mouth around.

Mom looked up from her papers. Her eyes swung from me to the girl and back to me. "I'm gonna get a cup of coffee," she said, exiting.

Mom's departure made me feel embarrassed, like this was more than just talking to a fellow concussion victim. I forced an awkward smile. "Mom loves her joe," I said, trying to cover.

"Oh, I know," said the girl. "I told mine she ought to stop fooling with those Starbucks cards, and go get her a franchise. She'd save money in the long run."

"Must have some habit."

"Drinks non-fat lattes *non-stop*," she said, pretending to guzzle one down.

I laughed, then held my head as a wave of pain coursed through me.

"Sorry," said the girl. "Only hurt when you laugh?"

"I *wish*. It always hurts."

She nodded like a wise veteran. After a moment, I recovered a bit. "How'd you get yours?" I asked.

"I'm a flyer."

"You are?" I said, stunned.

She studied me a moment. "Uh...you know what a flyer *is*?"

"*Thought* I did..."

"In cheerleading, a flyer's the person on top of the pyramid. We do the stunts."

"You're a *cheerleader?*" I sounded more disdainful than impressed.
"Um-hm."

"And you got hurt *cheerleading?*" I said, making it worse.

"Don't sound so surprised. You're more likely to get hurt cheerleading than playing football."

"Aw, you're making that up," I said, flopping back in my chair. But she stood her ground.

"Not me. It's what the doctor told me."

It didn't seem advisable to keep challenging her, but I couldn't help myself. "*I* just can't believe that."

Finally, her eyes sparked with annoyance. "Use your imagination. I don't wear any pads and I got girls throwing me twenty feet in the air. All I got between me and the hardwood floor is their skinny little arms."

"Never thought about it like that," I said, surrendering. "Can't say I've paid much attention to cheerleading."

"Well, maybe now you will," she said, with her best smile yet. Just then the door opened, and a nurse called her name. Samantha Lang.

"Good luck, Rah-Rah," I called after her, wondering what could have possessed me to tease her like that.

"Good luck, yourself," she said, with a little laugh.

I watched all the way, as her flip-flopping feet led her short-shorts through the door to what waited beyond. Looking at her was the kind of thing that *might* make me use my imagination.

Chapter Nine

Dr. Sugarman

WE WERE STILL WAITING when Rah-Rah came back through the door a while later, looking just as fine as I remembered.

"How'd it go?" I asked.

"Good," she said, grinning. "Cleared me to return to practice."

"Lucky you. I'm still out of school, so I'm a long way from football."

"Yeah, it sucks. But Dr. Sugarman's good. You'll like him."

The door to the inner office opened and a nurse called for us to enter. I stood slowly, getting my balance. Rah-Rah pulled out a cell phone.

"Why don't I get your number?"

Great idea. I mumbled digits while she pushed buttons.

"Do you go by Gregory?" she asked.

Huh? Oh, right, that's what the nurse called me. "Uh, well, everybody calls me Friz…"

"Okay, Friz. I'm Samantha. Most folks call me Sam."

"Okay, Rah-Rah," I said.

She appraised me with a squint. "I haven't decided whether I like you calling me that or not."

"Let me know when you make up your mind." It wasn't like me to be a smartass, but now it seemed to be coming naturally.

"I'm going to check up on you, Mr. Friz. You better follow doctor's orders."

"Once I find out what they are," I said as coolly as I could.

"Yeah," she said. "I'll see ya."

"See ya," I said, heading toward the inner office with Mom. We followed the nurse down a hall.

Mom leaned toward me and whispered, "I wonder if turning into a lady killer is a typical concussion symptom."

"*Please* don't ask him that," I pleaded, as we entered the doctor's office.

You know you've got a big shot doctor when his office has a desk, not an examining table. It was a large one, made of dark wood and covered with books and papers. Mom and I waited in cushy chairs while the doctor read the forms she had worked so hard on.

I inhaled deeply. Not a hint of alcohol or disinfectant. In fact, the room smelled like a library.

Dr. Sugarman looked up and smiled. "Football player?"

"Yeah," I said. "You?"

"Basketball."

"You *are* tall," I said, noticing how he loomed over the desk.

"Not tall enough," he said, amused. "Or quick enough. Not much of a shooter or ball handler. Couldn't rebound, either."

"Defense?" I suggested helpfully.

"Porous. So...MD, not NBA."

Dr. Sugarman had us tell him the story, starting with the game. He was mainly interested in how I got hit, acting it out with me. Mom and I described the symptoms of the last few days. Dr. Sugarman nodded often, occasionally asking a question.

"Good job," he said at the end. "Now we're going to take a look at your brain."

"Another scan?" asked Mom. She sounded a little frustrated.

"Not to start with. I've got films from the two ER visits. And imaging doesn't tell much unless it's extremely bad news," he said, trying to reassure her. "No, we're going to check Friz out six ways from Sunday, and that should give us clues about what we're looking at."

He picked up a clipboard and came out from behind the desk, taking a seat on a stool in front of me. "This test is called 'smooth pursuit.' Sounds like football, doesn't it?" He pulled a tongue depressor from his lab coat and I opened my mouth cooperatively. He laughed. "Good mouth reflex. But I'm not going to check your throat today. Also not going to take your blood."

"Yay," I said weakly.

He held up the stick again. "Without moving your head, follow this with your eyes. That's the 'pursuit.'"

He moved the stick slowly from side to side, up and down, then more quickly. He stopped to jot something on the clipboard.

We spent another ten minutes putting my eyes through their paces, making them look every which way but cross-eyed. Well, we actually did a test for that, too. Also for seeing double, which is normal if you look at something too close to your nose. Then he looked inside my eyes with a scope.

Next, he felt all around my head, finding sore spots. He checked muscles in my neck, and tested the strength in my arms and legs, making notes on the clipboard as he went. He had me walk the tightrope forwards and backwards, heel to toe, then feet spread apart. I fell off a couple of times, but he said most folks did unless they were ballerinas. He checked my hearing and made more notes. Then he tested my olfactory sense with a bunch of smelly markers and said I was cleared for dessert.

Finally, we returned to the cushy chairs for his assessment. "Well,

Friz, no doubt about it, you've got a concussion. That said, I've got bad news, and I've got good news. Which do you want first?"

"Bad news." 'Cause I can take it...

He shook his head sadly. "*Can't* put a cast on you. *Can't* sew you up. *Can't* inject you or give you a magic pill. Son, *I can't heal you.*"

We waited for him to add something, but Dr. Sugarman stood pat.

"Uh...what's the good news?" I asked doubtfully.

He gave me a confident smile. "Your *brain's* going to heal *itself.* It's doing it right now."

"How long's it going to take?"

"Somewhere between a week and a year."

"That's quite a range," said Mom, who'd been unusually quiet.

"I'd like to be more specific," he said apologetically. "But I can't have you getting impatient. Every brain's got its own timetable. I can't say what yours is going to be."

"Well, what *can* you do?" I was getting fed-up with the lack of assistance from the medical profession. No wonder folks didn't go to doctors even if they *had* insurance.

He leaned in. "Convince you not to do something stupid. Like I said, your brain will heal, given time. But if you play some football before you're ready and take another bad hit, we could have real trouble. Have you heard of 'second-impact syndrome'?"

Mom and I signaled we hadn't.

"Well, that's how we lose kids," he continued more gently. "When you injure a brain before it's healed, the damage can be a *lot* more serious—up to and including death. You have to take it easy, son, no matter how boring that might be."

Mom was convinced. "I'll make sure he does." She gave me a look that left no wiggle room.

Dr. Sugarman nodded. "Now I have to put you to work for a little while. You like computer games?"

"Yeah," I said, perking up.

"I thought he wasn't supposed to—" Mom started.

"He's *not*. But we have one called the ImPACT—'Immediate Post-Concussion Assessment and Cognitive Testing.' Your mom says you're a pretty good student…"

"I guess," I admitted. Before he could go on, I interrupted. "Can I ask *you* a question?"

Dr. Sugarman looked up from his notepad.

"Do cheerleaders get more concussions than football players?" I'd been dying to ask since we got in the office.

"No…" he began carefully.

"I *knew* she made that up!"

"—but there are a lot more football players than cheerleaders. The rate of concussions among cheerleaders *is* higher than the rate among football players."

"*Really?*" That left hook knocked my world view flat on its butt!

Dr. Sugarman gave me a knowing smile. "You must've met Samantha. May not look like it, but she is *one…tough…cookie.*" He said the last three words real slow, like he was trying to impress me. Or…scare me.

I couldn't help it. My eyes got big and I swallowed. When I looked over at Mom, she was smirking.

Chapter Ten
ImPACT

DR. SUGARMAN WALKED us to the hall, where he introduced me to Nurse Gina.

"She'll help you get started on the ImPACT. Better if your mom waits in reception."

"Oh?" said Mom, ready to defend her turf...er...*son*.

"Hard for kids to take a test with Mom breathing down their neck," he explained. To me, he added, under his breath, "Or play computer games, right?"

Gina led me to another office, not as nice as Dr. Sugarman's— just a table with a few chairs and a computer. We took seats and Gina unfolded the laptop. She clicked buttons, and the screen opened a portal to the ImPACT website.

"I just need to log you in," she said. Then she spun the laptop to face me.

"This test is real simple. Read the directions and you'll understand what to do. I'm going to leave so I don't distract you. When you're done, come get me and I'll close the session. Any questions?"

"Is it open book?"

Gina laughed. "Wouldn't help you on this one. Just do your best," she said. She got up and left. The door closed with a soft click.

I inhaled and sat up tall. I like tests. I'm good at them. Figured I'd do fine on this one.

The first section flashed words on the screen, and none of them were hard. Then, one at a time, it showed a word and asked me to identify whether it was one that had been flashed. "Frequent." Yes. "Child." No. And so it went. Oddly, I wasn't sure about a couple. Maybe I hadn't been paying good attention.

The next part was the same, except with squiggly line drawings. This was more difficult. I sat up straighter. I studied the first one for a long time, trying to remember if they'd flashed it. For the life of me, I didn't know. I had the same problem on all the rest of the questions. I just had to guess.

I took a break and walked around the room. I did exercises to get more air to my head and sat back down.

The next couple of games had matching patterns. One part of me could tell that normally I wouldn't have trouble doing these. But the part that was clicking the mouse was moving in slow-mo. Nausea was kicking in and my head was hurting.

I tried to speed up on the color match test and I might have made mistakes. By now I hardly cared and just wanted to get through it. Even if I was trying my best, well, my best wasn't very good today.

The test finished with identifying letter combinations, which made me feel like I ought to go back to kindergarten and relearn the alphabet. I walked out to find Gina.

"All done?" she asked.

"Yeah," I muttered. "I am. All done."

"Little hard?"

I nodded wearily.

"Well, I'm sure you did fine." Which is what teachers say when they know you *didn't*. She was looking at me with concern. "Are you okay?" she asked.

"Not hardly."

So I followed Gina to *another* room with a skinny little bed, like the nurse's office at school. I lay down and she turned out the lights.

Chapter Eleven
ImPACTed

I STEWED in the waiting room for what felt like a long time while Friz took his test. With no success, I tried not to brood over my son. He couldn't take drugs, but I could sure use some. No more caffeine, though. I felt like prey on high alert, scenting the air for signs of danger. My head snapped up every time a patient entered the office, or the nurse came looking for the next victim. I should have been grading papers, but I would have been harsh with the red pen. Instead, I just sat there.

The interior office door opened and Nurse Gina looked at me. "Ms. Collins? Dr. Sugarman would like to see you for a moment."

Anxiety spiked. "Is my son all right?"

Gina's lips smiled, but the rest of her frowned. "He's fine, just a little worn out. He's lying down for a few minutes."

I followed her down the hallway, re-entered Dr. Sugarman's office, and took a chair in front of the desk. Dr. Sugarman looked up from the papers and gave me a tight smile. "I wanted to see you before you left, Ms. Collins. Just you and me."

"Of course," I said. "What are you looking at?"

"These are the results from your son's ImPACT. Normally, we like athletes to take the test pre-season so we have baseline data. If injury occurs, we can compare the post-test to the baseline."

"What if you don't *have* baseline data?"

The doctor nodded. "We compare to statistical averages. But it sounds like Friz is above average."

"At most things. Not at cleaning his room, but I doubt that was on the test." Dr. Sugarman's beating-around-the-bush was scaring me, so I fell back on a lifelong habit: make a joke to alleviate my fear. It didn't work.

The doctor forced a laugh. "No. A good thing for most of us guys."

"So how'd he do?" I asked, coming to the point.

"Well, I'm concerned." He pushed the graphs toward me.

I looked at the headings: verbal memory, visual memory, processing speed, reaction time, and impulse control. The bars were short and stubby. "This is the raw score, isn't it? That doesn't tell me much."

"Good point," he conceded. "You want to know how he compared to the norm." He read from a notepad. "Verbal memory, eighth percentile. Visual mem—"

"*Eighth?*" I interrupted. Not *eightieth?*"

"Eighth," he emphasized. "The rest of the test scores are first percentile."

"*First percentile?*" I slumped in my chair. This exceeded my worst fears.

"You understand it's not percent—" he began.

"I'm a teacher," I snapped. "I *know* about percentiles. You're telling me that out of a hundred kids, Friz scored worse than ninety-nine of them. Except on verbal, where he beat out seven."

The doctor nodded somberly. "Not that I want you to feel competitive about these results."

"Well, I *don't*. It's not *him* I'm disappointed in, it's his *brain*. Could this be a mistake?"

The doctor pursed his lips. "I doubt it."

"Do other people score this low?" I asked, grasping at straws.

Dr. Sugarman was choosing his words carefully, trying not to trigger further Mom DEFCON escalation.

"We often see significant decrease following a concussion," he said. "Big drops. But these results concern me." He paused, then solemnly delivered my marching orders. "You need to make sure your son's body gets every chance to heal itself."

"Trust me, Doctor. I will chop off his legs if that's what it takes to save his head."

Chapter Twelve
Stale Oreo

THEY DIDN'T EVEN let me walk to the car. They took me in a
wheelchair—like my back was broken, not my brain. Wiggled me
into the Honda and Mom drove home. I must have fallen asleep,
because the next thing I knew, she was waking me at our house.
Think I leaned on her as we walked to the front door.

I woke in my bed to the cell phone ringing. Still half-asleep, I
answered it.

"Yeah," I whispered.

"Is this Friz?" said a voice. A girl.

"Friz *who*?"

"I don't know your last name." The voice sounded irritated.

"Who is this?"

Irritation progressed to annoyance. "*Samantha*."

That woke me up. "Rah-Rah?"

"If you insist on calling me that, yes. But it's not accurate. I don't care
who wins a damn football game. I just like doing tumbling routines."

"So…I shouldn't call you Rah-Rah?"

The other end went silent a moment. "Depends on how you mean
it."

"I mean it nice." I couldn't have said such a thing if I hadn't been
in a deep concussion fog.

"In that case, I don't mind." Her tone was getting more friendly.

"You know, I'm not supposed to be talking to you," I teased.

"Oh?"

"Dr. Sugarman said no electronics. Doesn't that include cell phones?"

"Not when it's used for talking. But no texting."

"Thank you, Dr. Rah-Rah."

"You joke, but I just might wind up pre-med. How'd it go with Dr. Sugarman?"

"He called you a stale Oreo."

"*What?*"

"Well, 'tough cookie' were his exact words."

"Are you always like this?" she asked, laughing.

"Afraid not. At the moment, I'm brain-damaged."

"Well, are you okay to keep talking?" she said sarcastically.

"I'll let you know if you make me nauseous."

"Tell me more about Dr. Sugarman."

I gave her the details of my exam. She asked questions and kept saying that Dr. Sugarman did the same thing with her. I guess he recycled his jokes.

"Did you do the ImPACT?" she asked.

"Man, it was hard. I bombed it."

"Doesn't count on your GPA, anyway," she said. I laughed, then moaned. "I should let you go…" she said hesitantly.

"Probably," I said, but didn't want her to.

"Okay if I call you again?" she asked. "Like, to check up on you?"

"Sure," I said.

"You have my number, too. Add the contact."

"Then I can screen."

"You better *not*," she said. "Are you sure you're not always like this?"

"We've been through that. Once I'm feeling better, I won't be any fun at all."

"Let's hope that's not the case," she said. "I like you this way."

"You *do*?" I was glad she couldn't see me blush.

"Not saying it again. I don't want to swell your head any more than it is."

"It could swell more," I protested weakly.

"Goodbye, Mr. Friz. I'll talk to you tomorrow."

"Bye, Rah-Rah."

I pushed the red "end call" button and closed my eyes. This concussion cloud just *might* have a silver lining.

Chapter Thirteen
Later Daze

THE CLOUD DIDN'T LIFT. I slept most of the time, with Mom and Dad waking me to eat chicken broth. Mom insisted she wasn't feeding me: she was feeding my brain, and the rest of my body was just the delivery system. My stomach rejected the plan, along with solid food.

The guys came over after the game Saturday with a pepperoni pizza. They tiptoed in while I was sleeping, and Jamarie waved a piece under my nose. I reacted like it was smelling salts. My eyes slammed open, I bolted upright, and vomited a pale stream over the slice. No extra charge for *that* topping.

Man, they roared, laughing so loud Mom came to see what was going on. She called them idiots and threatened to throw them out if they tried another stunt. It was comical listening to them apologize and promising to be good. Even Mom, who has always found it easy to like boys, couldn't keep from smiling.

As soon as she left, they abandoned their vows.

"Okay, bro," said Tyrell. "Let's do it again." He turned to Zach and Jamarie. "Roll tape when I say, 'Action!'"

"What are you, a director?" I said.

He peered at me through framed fingers, as if setting up the shot. "Why not? Tyrell Spielberg," he said.

"If anyone's a director, it's me—I'm the quarterback," said Zach.

"What you know about cinema?" said Tyrell. "Only movie you seen is *Little Mermaid*."

"Tell me about the game," I interrupted.

"Played Buda," said Jamarie. "Kicked their butt."

"Without you, had to hitch up to *this* hoss," said Tyrell, poking his chest with a finger.

"Ground game, huh? Gimme the highlights."

That kept them busy, interrupting each other while they ate pizza and wiped greasy hands on their pants. No wonder the guys were high. Nothing like winning to lift your spirits.

It didn't lift mine, though. As if I were two people, old Friz nodded and asked questions, while another part of me couldn't wait for my friends to leave me in peace and quiet. I was actually relieved when Mom shooed them out.

On Sunday, I got brave and called Rah-Rah. When she answered, I said in a formal voice, "This is Mr. Collins's assistant calling for Miss Lang. Is she available?"

"Uh…yeah," she said doubtfully.

I tried to sound bossy. "Could you put her on the line, please?"

"This is *she*."

"Please hold for Mr. Collins." I changed to my normal voice and said, "Rah-Rah?"

"Duh-duh. What are you, a multiple personality?"

"Not yet. But my mom calls me a character."

"Yeah, looney tunes," she teased.

"My football team won yesterday," I said, veering to a comfortable topic.

"Good for them." She didn't sound impressed. More like disapproving.

"*I* didn't play," I clarified.

"Good for *you*. Dr. Sugarman would be pleased."

"How about you? Back to the rah-rah-sis-boom-bah?"

"Not yet." She sounded kind of down.

"I thought you were cleared for practice."

"I *was*—I *am*—but I'm…I've been practicing on my own."

"How do you do that?" I asked, bewildered.

"Well, I need to stay stretched and practice my moves. I'm working on a scorpion."

I didn't know what to say to that. I thought for a moment but couldn't come up with anything.

"Are you there?" she asked.

"Yeah, but…I don't get this. I thought you'd be memorizing cheers, or something. 'Our team is red hot. Your team is pig snot.'"

"I'm not a *pompom* cheerleader," she said, clearly annoyed. I'd taken a misstep. "I'm an All Star cheerleader."

I fumbled to understand. "Like, you're the best?"

"That's not what 'All Star' means in cheerleading. Are you even from Texas?"

"Yeah, but I went to Hawaii once."

"That's no excuse," she said, barely amused. "Look. There are two kinds of cheerleading, pompom and All Star. Pompom cheers for teams. All Star *is* the team. It's like gymnastics, but with more makeup and bows."

This conjured a pretty repulsive image, but I tried not to sound judgmental. "Do you like that stuff?"

"The gymnastics, yes. The makeup, yes, but not too much or you look like the Joker. Hate the bow. I keep my hair short and wear a headband. That's what Maddie Gardner does."

"And she would be…"

"You *are* clueless. Ultimate cheerlebrity. She's, like, the Tom Brady of cheerleading."

"You mean she's old?" I said.

"No, well, yeah, she *is*, but that's not what I mean. She's won a lot of competitions, like Tom Brady. She would've been an MVP, if there were such a thing in cheer."

The football reference brought to mind the Dallas Cowboy cheerleaders, whose routines provoked Mom to change channels when Dad began to drool. They *had* to be pompom, and I'd catch hell for bringing them up. "Uh...do you guys do tumbling and stuff?"

"*Now* you're getting it. Roundoffs, handsprings, flips. You oughta watch *Bring It On*."

"No TV, remember?"

"When you get better. Or google 'All Star cheerleading videos.'"

"No computer, remem—"

"*Yes*, I remember. Or..."

"What?"

Her voice dropped lower. "Come to a practice. If you want..."

"Are you...inviting me?" It sure sounded that way.

"Yeah, well, sort of..."

"I don't know if I can," I said. "I mean, I don't know if my mom'll let me." I face-palmed after that one! Truth or not, it made me sound like a little kid.

"It's no biggie."

"Do you want me to come?" I asked, hoping she'd say yes.

"Yeah, I guess, I think...you'd...well..." she stammered. I closed my eyes and waited. "I keep seeing the stunt where I got hurt," she finally said. "You know what I mean?"

Even I could appreciate the enormity of this admission. Rah-Rah was going way out on an emotional limb, and I didn't want to knock her off it. "Yeah, I do," I said. "I must've felt Brody hit me a hundred times. Not sure how I'll go up to catch a pass with that thought in my head."

"That's what I mean," she said. "I'm scared to have them throw me."

"Bet they're scared, too."

"Yeah." She didn't sound reassured.

"I guess you gotta get back on the horse, right?"

"I guess..."

I kept blundering forward, trying to be supportive. "Probably once you're into it you'll be fine. I'm sure they'll be double careful not to drop you again."

"Hope you're right," she said. "I just...don't feel like much of a stale Oreo, right now..."

It came out before I had time to filter. "Well, I think you're definitely the driest, hardest, crustiest, most horriblest Oreo I know."

"You're just saying that," she giggled.

"You're so rock-hard you might be petrified," I said. "And I'm pretty sure my mom'll let me go. 'Cause I wanta see a cookie fly."

Chapter Fourteen
Flying

MOM DIDN'T GIVE ME a hard time when I asked to go to Rah-Rah's practice. Naturally she asked the obligatory who, what, when, and where—totally leaving out the why. She gave me a hard Doctor Mom look and asked if I really thought it was a wise decision. I said *absolutely*—it might even make me feel better. She repressed a smile and said okay.

Rah-Rah and Ma Rah picked me up Monday afternoon. Rah-Rah and I rode in the back seat as we made our way through traffic. Ma Rah—who I called "Mrs. Lang" like the disgustingly polite kid I was raised to be—drove with an aggressiveness that bordered on road rage. The last time I'd been on a ride this wild I was a five-year-old hostage on one of my grandpa's frantic NASCAR sprints in search of a bathroom. While he had managed not to wet himself, I *hadn't*. The recollection did not help me relax.

"Uh…are we late?" I asked, attempting to tighten my seat belt.

"Right on time," Mrs. Lang answered. I gripped the seat and fought inertia as she nearly mowed down a bicycle rider with a hard right turn.

I might have gasped. Rah-Rah looked over and pursed her lips. "Mom, ease up. Friz is turning green."

"Not his normal shade, I take it."

"He's got a concussion!"

"Right, right…" she answered. "Sorry, Friz. State of your mind slipped *mine*."

"Perfectly understandable," I said, cringing as the words left my mouth. Rah-Rah was looking at me with distaste.

"I like to get the most out of my vehicle," Mrs. Lang explained, punching the gas to scoot through a yellow light.

"As long as you provide air sickness bags on this flight," I said under my breath.

"Excuse me?" said Mrs. Lang.

"That was to me, Mom," said Rah-Rah, giving me a wink.

Mrs. Lang moved on to a new topic. "Speaking of concussions—"

"We *weren't*," Rah-Rah interjected.

"Does your mother want you to give up football?"

"Uh…I don't know."

Mrs. Lang grunted disdainfully. "I imagine she would, don't you think?"

Most likely, but I said, "The topic hasn't come up." Rah-Rah gave me a small nod.

"It's sure come up at our house," said Mrs. Lang, her voice rising. "Hasn't it, Sam?"

"Um-hm."

"I believe one concussion is one too many," said Mrs. Lang. "Isn't that right, Samantha?"

"Sure is, Mom." Her tone suggested pretty much any other topic would be preferable.

But Mrs. Lang was undeterred. "I developed new respect when I watched Dr. Sugarman perform that exam. You had that too, didn't you, Friz?"

"Yup." Rah-Rah pretended to gag.

We halted at a four-way stop and Mrs. Lang twisted to look at me. No longer consumed with eating up the road, she seemed now to be ignoring it.

"Your brain controls your senses—eyesight, hearing, smell, taste, touch. Processes your emotions. Guides your movements. To say nothing of your thinking and your learning…"

The car behind us honked, and Mrs. Lang casually turned around and proceeded through the intersection. As she continued in this vein, I made the appropriate respectful noises, but Rah-Rah was making Charlie Brown *wah wah wah* with her talking hand. I couldn't help snickering.

"Mom, Friz knows this stuff!" Rah-Rah interrupted. "And he hasn't even been cleared to go back to school. He's not thinking about playing football. He's worried about winding up on the short bus, and you're making him feel worse."

"Well, that was not my intention, dear."

"Of course, not, Mrs. Lang," I said. My voice took on an embarrassing vibrato as she let the car wheels drift to the rumble strip on the side of the road.

"Thank you, Friz."

"I *am* concerned. I don't want to drop fifty IQ points."

"Impossible," Rah-Rah scoffed. "You can't go below zero."

"Samantha!"

"That's harsh," I said. "You think I have a two-digit IQ?"

"*Low* two-digits."

"It's *three* digits. Maybe four," I said.

"Yeah, with two decimal places," she came back.

"Samantha!" Mrs. Lang chided again.

"Just keepin' it real," she said. "Friz don't know an IQ from a bowling score."

"*Doesn't*," Mrs. Lang corrected.

"Hell I doesn't!" I said, and they both laughed.

Cheer Athletics didn't look like much from the outside—a big warehouse. Parents were dropping off kids, a few our age, though most older. Some were parking their own cars and hopping out.

"I hope they don't think I'm a cheerleader," I said.

"Not much chance of that," Rah-Rah sniffed.

"Why? I see some guys."

Her eyes narrowed scornfully. "Wait'll you see what *they* can do."

I guess the money they saved on the exterior they spent on the interior. As big as a basketball court, the floor was covered with blue tumbling mats. The walls were painted a neutral grey and royal blue banners hanging from the rafters proclaimed the different championship teams. An endless string of trophies lined a ledge that ran around the room. They looked identical, each featuring a big gold megaphone on top of a gold cup.

"Did you win any of those?" I asked, gesturing upward.

"Not yet," she admitted. "Workin' on it." Meanwhile she stripped off her sweats. Underneath were tight black shorts and a tiny top with the letters "CA."

"Are you a California team?" I asked innocently.

"*California?*" exclaimed Ma Rah.

"I mean no disrespect," I said in a rush. To some Texans, "California" is about the dirtiest four-letter word you can say. "But your shirt says 'CA'…"

"*Cheer Athletics,*" said Rah-Rah. "C…A."

"Ooooooooh…"

"Negative IQ," she said, shaking her head sadly.

"Nah, I just know the state abbreviations. Try me."

"Alabama."

"AL."

"Alaska."

"AK."

"Ari—"

"Samantha," interrupted her mother. The other cheerfolk were taking places on the mats.

"To be continued," said Rah-Rah, as she hustled to fall in line.

I was surprised that Mrs. Lang and I were the only civilians left in the building. "Where is everybody?" I asked. Sports events, even practices, featured large-scale family participation on the sidelines.

"Not invited," she said. "Don't want trouble from CSPs."

"CSPs?"

"*Crazy Sports Parents*. Thought you knew your abbreviations." Mrs. Lang's look of disapproval suggested where Rah-Rah might have learned hers.

"Only for the states," I admitted.

"CSP's a state of *mind*. Don't know about you, but I'm not going there."

I was quick to surrender. "Me neither."

"Good." She gave me a pointed look. "We got special permission 'cause of Sam's concussion, and I wouldn't want any misbehavior."

"I'll follow your lead, Mrs. Lang," I promised.

"Let's take a seat," she said, leading the way to a bench on the wall.

I relaxed as the cheerleaders warmed up. They did calisthenics, ran around the gym, and did stuff on all fours that made them look like uncoordinated dogs.

Then came stretching. I expected them to be limber, but those girls might have joined the circus as contortionists—and the guys, too. If Two Bob were to put our football team through the drills they were doing, there'd be screaming and torn ligaments all over the field.

Next was tumbling practice. It seemed more like the Olympics than cheerleading, with all the flips, cartwheels, roundoffs, handsprings, and such they were doing. Though Rah-Rah was one of the youngest, she was very good. A muscular kid named Dre stood out as exceptional.

Rah-Rah came to see us during a break. "What do you think?" she asked.

"Not what I expected, I tell you that."

She seemed satisfied with my response. With the assurance of a poker player about to lay down a winning hand, she hitched her chin at the mats and ordered, "Watch this."

The space was cleared for Dre, as he launched a pass from the far end of the gym. He took several powerful steps, then exploded into a tumbling sequence that seemed it would never end. He flew across the mats and just kept going, with hoots and whistles rising from the others as his pass went on and on. Close to the far wall, he concluded the routine and stuck the landing. He pivoted to set his back against the wall and slid down it, crumpling to the floor.

"Still afraid they'll take you for a cheerleader?" she asked.

"Not likely."

She harrumphed and ran back to join the group.

Now came stunt work. Some of the cheerleaders were bases, and helped hoist the smaller flyers into the air, where they'd strike flexible poses.

Ma Rah and I had been quiet, just watching. She nudged me and said, "This is how Sam made the team. She's got the other skills—you have to. They make you test at every level. But being younger and smaller is a big advantage to a flyer. Otherwise she's got no business with these older kids."

"Something wrong with them?" I asked.

She nodded somberly. "They throw her too high."

In a few minutes, I saw what she was talking about. They started to work on a different kind of stunt. Instead of hoisting the flyer into the air and forming a pedestal, the bases kept their arms accelerating upward, propelling the lighter girls high into the air. This was more dangerous, and the groups performed one at a time under the watchful eye of the coach.

Rah-Rah's group went last. When the bases launched her, she flew twenty feet into the air, scissor-kicked a leg to her upstretched arm, then lengthened into a plank as she rotated a full turn. She landed on her back on the outstretched arms of the bases, like a baseball settling into an outfielder's mitt. Popping to her feet, she flipped us a smile and turned back to her teammates.

Ma Rah blew out her breath in a rush. The stunt was so pretty I hadn't had time to worry. But I wasn't a mother.

This "cheerleading" world had exactly nothing to do with my preconceived notions. The people on the floor were athletes, performing stunts I'd never dare attempt, and it was a humbling experience to spectate instead of participate. It was even odder that I was here to support a *girl*. Somehow, under orders to do nothing, my life was expanding into new frontiers.

Practice dragged on for hours, but I didn't see much more of it. Next thing I knew, Ma Rah was shaking me awake and helping me to the car. Rah-Rah might be flying again, but I wasn't.

Chapter Fifteen
Rebooting

MOM HAD USED her sick leave, so we worked out a new plan. My father set up an air mattress in his store's tiny office. I lay on it in a comatose haze, with Dad looking in occasionally to make sure I was alive. That went on for days.

Dad owned a small brick-and-mortar that sold sheet music and instruments, specializing in guitars and the like. It was more a labor of love than profit, since most of the "shoppers" ended up buying online, where they could save a few bucks. The real revenue came from music lessons, which he taught in a small room next to his office. The lessons provided a painful soundtrack to the horror film I was living.

Music was in Dad's blood. His grandfather was a Kentucky fiddler, and his father played bluegrass banjo in Austin clubs until he passed. Dad picked up the guitar as a boy, and growing up in the eighties, he worshipped at the altar of classic rock. After years of striving, he'd had to acknowledge that his ambition outstripped his ability. There's a reason those guys are gods and the rest of us mortals.

Dad *was* a good teacher, though, and stayed busy with his students. I'd never been one of them. He'd done his best to sign me up, pitching for the guitar, as well as piano, violin, trumpet, flute— even the drums. No musical instrument in Dad's store had the allure of a ball in flight, so I couldn't be persuaded.

Lying on my mattress day after day, serenaded by rank beginners, I reflected on Dad's attempts to recruit me and felt I'd made a good decision. Though playing the cello probably wouldn't have laid me up for weeks with a concussion…

But one day I woke from a troubled sleep and felt different. Better, yeah…but extremely…*different*.

Chapter Sixteen
Twinkle, Twinkle

THE DOOR TO MY STUDIO slammed open so hard it smacked the wall. My student, a fourth grader named Josh, jumped from his chair, wide-eyed. I almost dropped the guitar I was tuning for him.

I watched what happened unfold like a movie. Friz stomped into the room. Without a word, he snatched the guitar from me, a Green Beret disarming a civilian.

"What the—" I started. "What're you doing?"

"Tuning it."

"I just did," I protested. "It's in tune."

"Not," he answered, his brow knitted in concentration.

I gawked as he plucked strings and adjusted pegs. I hadn't seen my son so much as hold a guitar before, and he was handling this one like a veteran player. He strummed the open strings.

"*That's* tuned," he judged. "Wasn't hard, was it?" He sounded sarcastic.

Josh and I exchanged a glance. "My son hasn't been himself lately."

"Feeling better now," Friz said. Instead of handing the instrument back, he plucked strings.

"Been listening to this darn 'Twinkle, Twinkle' for a week," he mumbled.

He didn't know how to play it. How *could* he?

While Josh and I watched, my son taught himself. I've never seen the like! He slid his left hand from fret to fret while thumbing the high E-string. He played the chromatic scale, nodding to himself. Then he found the "Twinkle, Twinkle" melody.

As I would have taught him, he adjusted his fretting to smooth out the rhythm. He played it again, speeding up.

"*Damn*," murmured Josh.

"Could do this on any string, couldn't you?" He worked his way from the high E to the B to the G, all the way to the low E string. He cocked his head, listened, then went back to the high E string. "These strings have the same notes," he said. "But there's a difference…"

"An octave," I suggested. "*Two* octaves, actually."

"Doesn't sound the same to me," Josh objected.

Friz was perplexed, too. "Not exactly. Why is that, Dad?"

"Pitch is different. But you're right, they *are* the same notes."

He wasn't listening. He'd figured out how to play the tune using notes on the G and B strings together.

"You haven't showed me that way," Josh complained.

"We'll get to it," I said, my eyes still glued to my son.

Suddenly losing interest, he handed the guitar back to Josh and looked at me.

"I'm starved," he said matter-of-factly. "Can I have a few bucks?"

It was the first sign of appetite he'd shown in weeks. Apart from what he'd just done with the guitar—as if you could ignore *that*—he seemed okay. Back to being a teenager.

I extracted a couple of fives from my billfold. "Take her easy, though. You've been way off your feed." Texas understatement.

"'Kay," he said, walking out.

Josh glared at me accusingly. "You said he didn't play the guitar."

"Yeah. He *doesn't*."

He gave me a look of utter disgust. "I'd like to *not* play that damn good."

"Language, Josh," I reprimanded mildly. "But you've got a point."

Chapter Seventeen
Slowhand

I WALKED DOWN THE BLOCK to a chain burger place. Not the one where you have it your way, or you're lovin' it, or they don't make it 'til you order it, or that's what a hamburger's all about, or it's just like you like it. The one where the food's the star. Or so they say.

I ordered a hefty burger combo with fries, supersized it, moved to the soda station, and filled my cup with ice and Coke. I took a seat at a table and waited for my order.

Pulling on the drink, I had a moment to think. Something very weird had just happened. With all of Dad's guitars lying around, I had never picked one up. No reason to think I could make music with one, any more than I could locate water with a dowsing rod.

Music had never interested me in the slightest. Most of my friends had iPods or iPhones loaded with tunes, and it took a surgical operation to remove buds from their ears. Some of the girls thought they were Taylor Swift, cut their hair just so, and knew all the lyrics to her songs. It was kinda sickening. I even knew a few who went to church just to sing in the choir, a choice I couldn't fathom.

My food came and I dug in. I couldn't remember anything ever tasting this good, and I wondered if it was me, or whether the food really *was* the star.

There was a burst of noise from the next table. A guy eating fries silenced his phone.

"Sorry, man." He was in his forties, dressed in a coat and tie.

"Sounded good. Let's hear more."

He restarted the song. An electric guitar wailed, and I gazed into space.

"I can *see* the music," I said, amazed. Shapes and colors scudded across my mental landscape, like clouds driven before a gale. The visual had patterns and repetitions.

"*Righteous.* That's 'Layla.'"

"Heard it before. Who's playing?"

He shook his head in disgust at my ignorance. "Slowhand."

Still baffled, I gave an excuse. "I'm Generation Z."

"Generation don't-know-*shit.* Good thing we're out of letters. *Eric Clapton.*"

"Pretty good."

He stabbed an offended finger at my burger. "That there's pretty good. Clapton's a forty-dollar-grass-fed ribeye."

"Are you saying you like Clapton, or you like steak?"

"Both. 'Specially after a little of *this.*" He mimed taking a hit off a joint. Holding his breath like a stoner, he wheezed out, "Little herb and *I* can see the notes, too, man."

I didn't try to explain.

"Can't fool me. Not in school, you're *seeing* the music, and you got the munchies. Eyes don't give you away, though. What's your trick?"

"Couldn't tell ya," I said. I took another bite, closed my eyes, and experienced a rush of colors, shapes, and textures.

Yeah, my head felt better—but I had *no* idea what it was doing.

Chapter Eighteen
Dead Stop

AS A GUITAR TEACHER, I prefer to tune by ear. Old school. Like working wood by hand, no power tools. Helps you feel the spirit of creation.

But if I want to make sure an instrument's dead-on-the-money, I turn to a device. The Peterson 490 strobe tuner's as good as you can get. To be taken as a serious tech, you gotta have one. That's not why I got mine, though. Won it in a poker game, kings full of eights.

The interval between any two semitones—say a B and a C—is divided into a hundred smaller increments called "cents." A hundred cents to a dollar; a hundred cents to a semi-tone. The Peterson claims an accuracy of one *tenth* of a cent. I can't hear a difference of any less than five cents, but I had a hunch my son's new dog ears heard things mine couldn't.

Friz came in after Josh's lesson and bolted for the bathroom to retch up his lunch. I thought better of saying, "I told you so." Also thought better of what I had in mind.

"How you feel?" I asked. Despite vomiting, he looked fine.

"Good."

"Yeah?" He was standing tall and his eyes were clear for a change.

"Guess I ate too much, but it felt good going down. My head's all right."

"No headache?"

"Nope."

I'd have felt foolish asking him to touch his nose or wiggle his ears or whatnot. I tried to think of what my wife would say. "How 'bout you lie down?"

He eyed me sideways. "Been doing that for three weeks, Dad."

He seemed to know the calendar, anyway. "Feel up to an experiment?" I asked tentatively.

He looked at me with interest. Another good sign. "What you got in mind?"

"You did a nice job tuning Josh's guitar. Thinking you might want to match wits with a machine." I gestured at the Peterson 490 on the table.

His face lit up. "Like John Henry?"

"Uh, yeah…just don't tune 'til you have yourself a heart attack."

He guffawed. Seemed to be his old self. "Bring it on, Dad."

I sat him down so he couldn't see the face of the tuner and picked up my guitar. "If the note's too low, you say *flat,* and if it's too high, you say *sharp.*"

"Okay. What's the machine say?"

"Not much."

"Seriously. How's it tell you're in tune?"

I angled the Peterson to show him the dial. "It's got a wheel on the display, spins to the left for flat, to the right for sharp." I plucked a string and demonstrated, showing him how the wheel changed direction. "When it stops spinning, you're in tune."

"Hasn't stopped yet," he pointed out.

I nodded. "Plenty hard to get to a dead stop. I settle for a slow spin."

I angled the tuner away from him and plucked the A string.

"Way low," he said. "I mean, *flat.*"

I made an adjustment and plucked again.

"Still flat."

Another adjustment.

"Little flat."

The wheel on the Peterson was spinning slowly to the left. Normally I'd stop tuning at this point. I gave my son a look.

"It *is*," he insisted. "It's a little flat."

I made an adjustment, plucked again.

"Too much," he said. "A little sharp."

Sure enough, the strobe wheel was spinning slowly to the right. I made another adjustment.

"Flat."

Adjustment.

"Sharp."

Adjustment.

"Still sharp."

Adjustment.

"Little flat."

Adjustment.

When I plucked this time, he gave me a condescending look and held out his hands. I surrendered the guitar.

As mentioned, I've got a good poker face, and didn't give anything away. He kept tuning and I watched the wheel nudge one way, then the other, slower than I'd ever seen it move.

After a few moments, he plucked the string and declared, "There. *That's* the note." He looked at me awaiting the verdict.

"Dead stop," I ruled. I turned the Peterson to show him the display. He plucked the note again and the strobe wheel hardly wavered.

"Well, take *that*, you old steam engine!" He grinned at me. "I guess we're not obsolete yet, huh, Dad?"

"Well, *one* of us isn't," I said, playing it low-key.

Somehow, along with his concussion, my boy had caught himself a case of pitch so perfect he was accurate to a tenth of a cent.

Chapter Nineteen
Deliverance

WHEN BILL CALLED to tell me Friz was better, my first impulse was to rush to the music store and squeeze him in relief. But if I did, I'd burst into tears, and my men wouldn't want that. They can't stand strong emotions unless it's a ballgame. If their team isn't winning, stay out of their way. They regress all the way back to tantrummy two-year-olds.

Instead, I went to the H-E-B and picked up what I needed for my son's favorite dinner. He'd lost weight in the last month, but Bill said Friz's appetite was back. We'd give it the meat-loaf-and-mashed-potatoes test.

I set to peeling spuds and tried to keep my mind from racing. Knowing my boy, he'd want to get out on the field and chase a ball. Fortunately, I figured I could count on Dr. Sugarman to veto any quick return to tackle football. It might be the Texas religion, but after what we'd been through, count me among the heretics.

They walked in carrying guitars. Both of them. I gave Bill a look. He shrugged an answer that after eighteen years of marriage I should have been able to interpret, but couldn't.

"Is that meatloaf?" exclaimed Friz, sniffing the air.

"I guess somebody's feeling better," I said, pleased.

At the table, my son helped himself to four slabs of meat. Bill cleared his throat.

"Remember lunch? Might want to slow-up."

"Uh, yeah…" He forked half of it back to the platter.

"Seems reasonable," Bill said.

"But chew every bite—" I started.

"—Forty times," said Friz.

"No," I said. "That's *me*, to lose weight. By the time you've puréed something into baby food, you wish you'd never put it in your mouth. *You* can stop at nine or ten chews. That's about three times your normal."

That kept him busy finding his pace. He caught me looking and opened his full mouth for inspection.

"Yuck!"

"Think I'm goin' vegan," said Bill.

Struck by a random thought, Friz declared, "Hey, you know that 'Layla' song? I wanta play that." His tone was blasé, as if he'd just declared a notion to scramble some eggs.

I did a take and looked at Bill.

"Friz has conceived an interest in the guitar," he said mildly.

This news was as startling as my son's recovery. Absorbing it, I dispensed a mother's cautionary advice. "That song's *advanced*. Might want to give yourself a few years before you tackle that one."

Friz grunted and kept eating. My son was not *that* dense. I looked to Bill again. He didn't meet my eyes.

After clearing dishes, I had a pile of essays to correct and my two men got out guitars. This was something wildly new.

"Honey, you remember that tune from *Deliverance*?" Bill asked. "'Dueling Banjos?'"

"What's *Deliverance*?" asked Friz, curious.

"An old movie," Bill answered, deflecting. "You're a little young for it still."

Now Friz was hooked. "I'm not that young."

"Some parts were not PG," I said.

He blew out a long-suffering sigh. "What about the song? Can you teach it to me?"

"We could give her a try," said Bill. "I'll play something, and you see if you can play it, too."

The film is about a group of men getting into trouble on a rafting trip to the backwoods of Georgia. In this scene, one of them, a guitar player, meets a country boy playing banjo. Wordlessly, the guitar player "calls" to the banjo player, who "responds" in kind. What ensues is a duet that won legions of fans to bluegrass music.

I watched my husband engage my innocent son in a re-enactment of the scene. Bill played chords which Friz copied. Then he played a short melody of individual notes. Friz repeated them—same string, same cadence.

In the movie, the guitar player "tests" the banjo player to gauge the level of his skill. With growing wonder, I realized my husband was doing the same thing with my son.

But Friz had never—*ever*—played the guitar.

He was doing it now. Bill played the same notes on other strings, and Friz followed without faltering. Bill led him through the song, building chords and melody, until they were making music together.

How do you make sense of something that defies all reason?! I *tried* to. Could my husband have been teaching him behind my back—for the last *how many years*? The notion was as inconceivable as what I was seeing: neither could keep a secret for ten minutes, let alone one this big.

They traded phrases, the pace quickening, creating a complex song. Then they brought it to a close.

Bill and I exchanged a look of shock—but Friz was blissfully unaware of our reaction.

"Have you been teaching him?!" I mouthed silently. Bill shook his head firmly no.

That did it. What I had just witnessed was incredible. *Impossible.*
No one can pick up a musical instrument and play like that
without years of practice. I bitterly regretted we hadn't filmed it—
because nobody would believe this without seeing it! In the morning,
I wasn't sure *I'd* believe it.

"That was fun, Dad!" he exclaimed. "Now, what about 'Layla'?
Can you teach me that?"

"Uh... I guess," Bill said doubtfully. "Let's get out the Strat and
an amp."

"Do you mind if I video this?" I asked, trying for an offhand tone.

"What do you think?" Bill asked Friz.

"Nah," he said.

"Why not?" I said, ready to argue.

"Bad hair day, Mom," he teased. "Sure, knock yourself out."

Chapter Twenty
On the Stairway

I HAD WORRIED about the boy. While the concussion he'd suffered was not exceptional, his recovery had been slow. I'd given my standard lecture that each brain has its own timetable. But sooner is better. Longer recoveries suggest more damage. Friz had been out of school for weeks. The prognosis was troubling.

So my first reaction was relief when I saw him for re-examination. Even at a glance, he looked dramatically improved. The boy presented as alert, responsive, and cheerful. I conducted a standard neurological exam.

"Looks good," I admitted. "Let's have Friz retake the ImPACT and see how that goes."

Gina led the boy down the hall. Instead of exiting to the waiting room, his parents lingered.

"We'd like to show you something while he's taking his test," his mother said. Oddly, she seemed shook-up, not relieved by her son's improvement. Her face was haggard and there were rings around her eyes. Her husband looked like he was going into an audit with the IRS.

She pulled an iPad from her purse. "I recorded this last night."

She pushed a button, and I savored a minute or so of Mr. Collins teaching his son to play the opening licks on Clapton's greatest hit.

"'Layla,'" I said, looking up. "What's your concern?" I tried for a reassuring tone.

"Keep watching," Mrs. Collins answered, frowning.

For another minute, Mr. Collins taught his son the first section of "Stairway to Heaven." What followed was an extended take of the boy playing the *entire song*! I glanced at the parents. Mr. Collins had his eyes closed, listening. Mrs. Collins was studying me, her lips pursed.

I returned the iPad, still puzzled. "I didn't realize your son was such a musician. How long has he been playing?"

Mrs. Collins glanced at her husband. She took a breath and sighed, "That'd be just under twenty-four hours."

"*What?*" I stared at them, looking for clues.

"Before yesterday, our son did *not* play the guitar." She underlined the words, trying to convince herself along with me.

I fell back in the chair, stunned. *Now* their anxiety made sense.

"Doctor, I've taught guitar to hundreds of students," said Mr. Collins. He gestured expansively. "Some pretty good. I have *never* had one make it all the way through that song. He did it in *one night.*" He rubbed his jaw, more troubled than thrilled by his son's achievement.

"We know it's impossible…" Mrs. Collins started.

"It's not—" I broke off. "*Impossible.*"

Chapter Twenty-One
Savant

MAN, THE SECOND TIME that ImPACT was a breeze. I must've been knocked silly to have thought it was hard.

My parents were still in Dr. Sugarman's office. Gina gave him the results with a little nod.

It was like watching your folks go over your report card. You want to be cool, but you can't help noticing every little thing about their reaction. Dr. Sugarman nodded to himself.

Mom was studying the doctor's face just as carefully as I was. "Did we break the eighth percentile?" she asked nervously.

"Above the ninety-fifth across the board," said Dr. Sugarman. "Return to school." He looked at me. "But don't try to catch up in a hurry. Don't overdo the studying. Your brain still needs rest."

I saw an opening and took it. "You're saying not to do much homework, right?"

"I don't believe the doctor said that," said Mom, jumping in quickly.

"He kind of did," I insisted. We looked to the doctor, who smiled, amused.

"Half an hour to start."

"*Half an hour?*" Mom wouldn't have it.

The doctor made a conciliatory gesture. "An hour. My final offer."

"Done," said Mom, sealing the deal. She was sure giving in easy.

Dad cleared his throat. "What about football?"

The doctor hesitated.

"I don't want to play." *Did I just say that?*

"Come again?" said Dad, his eyes wide with disbelief.

Everyone was looking at me. "Are you afraid you'll get hurt?" asked Mom.

"No—maybe—I don't know. I just don't feel like playing."

"You don't feel like playing football?" said Dad, unconvinced.

"Rather play the guitar." *And now I said that?*

"Is that a new interest?" asked Dr. Sugarman. His tone was casual, but he was studying me as if this were another cognitive test.

"Yeah," I said. "Didn't know it was so easy or I might've paid attention before. Fingers are killing me, though."

"Mind if I take a look?"

I offered my hand. "It's the left one that hurts," I said.

He examined it briefly, then looked up. "Red and tender, but no blisters," he said, releasing my hand. "Give them time and they'll toughen up like your father's."

Dad held out his hand and I felt the tips of his fingers. They were callused and hard as stiff leather.

"That comes from years of pressing frets and strings," said Dr. Sugarman. He looked at me soberly. "Friz, do you know what a savant is?"

It didn't sound like a football word. I shook my head.

"In the world of neurology, a savant is someone with an extraordinary gift—often in music or art. For example, Mozart was a savant."

"Yeah, okay." Where was this going?

Mom jumped in. "Dear, Dr. Sugarman thinks *you* may be a savant."

"*Me?* I'm no Mozart," I protested. "I've never even *liked* music."

"Before yesterday," said Dad quietly.

"Yeah…"

"And now you want to do nothing but play the guitar," said Mom.

"Yeah…"

"Doesn't that strike you as odd?" said Dr. Sugarman gently.

I looked at the three of them and felt tired. I didn't know what to say. After a moment, the doctor went on.

"It's rare, but there are people who experience brain injury and develop a new ability. Like what you did yesterday."

"That was not a big deal," I objected.

"Yeah, it was," said Dad. The look on his face was your-grampa-died serious. "We didn't make a thing out of it. Wanted to talk to the doctor first. But I tell you, I didn't sleep a wink last night."

"Neither did I," said Mom.

They were starting to scare me. "I just tried to play like the video you showed me of that hippy," I stammered.

My dad sighed. He wasn't mad, he was just…I don't know.

"That hippy was Jimmy Page," he said. "*Rolling Stone* magazine rates him the number three rock guitarist. Of all time."

"You don't sound as good as him," said Dr. Sugarman, amused.

I hadn't grasped what they were telling me. All I could say was, "Guess I've got to practice."

Chapter Twenty-Two
Other Savants

THAT NIGHT WE DID research as Dr. Sugarman suggested. He told us information was available online, though he was also contacting a doctor who was an expert on this sort of thing. Getting a brain injury and developing special abilities instead of a crippling mental condition was so rare that few doctors ever saw a case like mine.

Weird, I kept thinking. That's what I'd thought at first, but since Mom and Dad hadn't made a fuss, I'd let it slide, figuring I was a late bloomer or something. Beginner's luck, maybe. I hadn't understood that picking up the guitar and playing like a rock star was, uh, not totally normal. All right, it's totally *not* normal. But so much had happened in the last twenty-four hours I hadn't had time to make sense of it.

The Internet had no mention of anyone who got hurt and developed guitar-playing powers. However, there *were* a couple of guys who had brain injuries and wound up being able to play the piano. One dove into the pool and smashed his head—ouch!—and *voilà*, he could tickle the ivories. The other guy got struck by lightning! Compared to them, I'd gotten off easy.

Several others had developed the ability to paint, and samples of their work were shown online. It was colorful, though I wasn't sure it was Leonardo da Vinci or anything. But what do I know?

Another guy got hurt so bad he couldn't even tie his shoelaces anymore—but he *could* make sculptures of animals so lifelike you'd swear they'd run away if you startled them. After I read that, I made sure I could still lace up my Converse.

We found a record of a sports injury—a guy who got hit in the head by a baseball when he was ten years old. After that, he could tell you bizarre things about the calendar, including the weather for every single day since he'd gotten injured. I was glad I hadn't developed a useless ability like that. If he could *predict* the weather, that'd be worth knowing. He might've become the world's greatest weatherman. But who cares that it rained Wednesday three years ago?

I also looked up people who were just born savants. Man, the stuff these folks could do was unreal. One guy had read 12,000 books and could remember every word in each of them. That's a book-a-day for thirty-three years! Doable, since he could read two pages at a time—one with each eye. In three seconds!

I gave that a try, and I could hardly turn pages that fast. I can't imagine how he did, either, since he couldn't even button a shirt. Seems like many savants could do with a valet.

This fast reader guy—Kim Peek—fascinated me. If I could read a book in five minutes, I might not be too picky about what I read. On the other hand, remembering every word could be as much of a burden as a blessing. Who wants to remember every word of a boring book? Was this special power one of those fairy tale curses, like the Midas touch?

Another guy could take a helicopter ride over a city—any city, like London, or New York—then paint a picture of what he'd seen. Not just a little picture—a thirty-foot landscape, filled with hundreds of detailed buildings and landmarks—without ever taking a photo from the helicopter. He didn't need to—he had a high-resolution camera in his brain.

We were all jacked-up on this world of mutant-brained people, but after a while Mom and Dad started to wilt. I guess they hadn't gotten much sleep the night before.

I lay awake thinking about going back to school the next day. I'd had the chickenpox once and had missed a couple of weeks. Then I'd been nervous returning to school, but within an hour, it was just like normal. This'd probably be the same.

We agreed it might be best to maintain a low profile on the guitar thing. Mom and Dad didn't even want me to tell Rah-Rah what was going on, and I hadn't had a chance to call her yet. Considering how much media attention there'd been for other acquired savants, I might want to take some time before becoming a celebrity. *Yeah, right*, I thought, as I drifted off to sleep. *Me, a celebrity.*

Chapter Twenty-Three
School Daze

THE INTERVALS OUTSIDE of class are all some kids live for at school. They enjoy free time with friends so much they can endure academic drudgery, and will probably look back on middle school incarceration with nostalgia.

The students who are targets of ostracism or scapegoating, however, dread these periods when the inmates are released from their cells. These kids don't fit neatly into any of the prison cliques—the populars, jocks, mean girls, gossip girls, trouble-makers, or too-cool-for-schools. It's a safe bet none of these kids will recall this experience favorably. They'll just be glad they got out alive.

Because I was not a masochist, I'd slipped into a niche group: "jocks the girls don't notice." The guys were glad to see me when I moseyed over to join them.

"Yo, look who it is! Homes, I thought you was getting *homes*-schooled," said Bill Ballard. He had greenish blond dreads and talked street.

Before I could respond, José Mireles jumped in. "Where you been, Ballard? Friz just following concussion protocol. Going to school is hazardous to your brain's health."

"True dat," said Ballard.

Sam Conner, who sat right behind me in our alphabetically-ordered classes, clapped me on the shoulder. "*Not* glad to see you back, man. Nice view without you, know what I mean?"

I did, because I sat behind Rebecca Collard. Gazing at her flowing black hair was a lot better than looking at a teacher's face.

"Dude, you been gone so long I thought you died," Jack Rucker said.

"For reals, you might be a zombie, Friz!"

"Yeah, *Dawn of the Dead.*"

"*Shaun of the Dead.*"

"*Evil Dead.*"

"*Walking Dead.*"

"*Alien Dead.*"

The guys were obsessed with zombies and could go on and on one-upping each other. The only rule was that each title cited had to have a word from the preceding title. Sticking with the word "dead"—the most common word in the zombie dictionary—ensured the game would continue for some time.

So far, I hadn't said anything to my friends, which was fine with me. I was feeling odd, and I wondered if it was because I hadn't seen them for weeks. The warning bell rang and we all ran to first period.

That was science class for me. Mr. Pennington said he was glad to have me back, then turned to the board to prepare for the day's lesson on food webs. He meticulously wrote up the vocabulary: "producers," "consumers," "decomposers," "diurnal," "nocturnal," "predator," and so on.

Franklin Thompson audibly groaned, earning a glare from Mr. Pennington. But we all understood. This was the same stuff we'd studied in fifth, sixth, and seventh grades, and even the worst students knew it backwards and forwards.

Lori Marsh saw an opening when Mr. Pennington started with producers, who got their energy from the sun. "You mean they use *solar* energy?" she asked in an innocent tone.

"Why, yes, they do," said Mr. Pennington.

"Do they get a subsidy for that?" asked Franklin, which drew a laugh because it was comical to think of a head of cabbage applying for government aid. It did the trick. Mr. Pennington veered from the lesson to a topic he found far more interesting: the liberal bias against the oil industry, about which he could, and did, pontificate for the rest of the period. Several kids played hacky sack with Mr. Pennington's head to keep him digressing, while the rest just zoned out. I zoned.

Social studies was equally enthralling. Eighth grade focused on the history of Texas, as indoctrination into our state cult became more academic. Lone Star is *not* just a beer.

In my absence, the class had arrived at the guts of the legend: Unit 3, Mexican Texas. Woo hoo. My mother had fortified me with her thumbnail version of events: Mexico, hard-up for colonists, foolishly invited Anglo-Americans to settle the land provided they convert to Catholicism and learn Spanish. Americans have never tolerated anyone telling them what to believe, and they're notoriously bad at foreign languages, so they didn't do either. There was also the issue of slaves, owned by many Anglos, though slavery had been banned in Mexico. One thing led to another, and soon you had rebellion, the Alamo, Sam Houston's amazing victory at the Battle of San Jacinto, and the Lone Star Republic. And, eventually, the beer.

Now that's something the mind could grasp, unlike our ridiculous textbook. They sold these books by the pound, and the publisher loaded them with color pictures, captions, timelines, more captions, sidebars, big self-important titles in high alert colors, graphic organizers of every variety, maps with more captions, review questions, web links, and practice items for our silly high-stakes state test. Even Kim Peek would have needed three or four more eyes to read this thing. Let alone to understand it.

We started with a reading assignment, otherwise known as "naptime." I briefly stayed awake, contemplating this pearl of wisdom: "As Moses Austin left Governor Antonio Martinez's office, he happened to meet an old friend, a Dutchman known to the Spanish as the **Baron de Bastrop,** though his real name was Phil Hendrik Nering Bögel." In one sentence the author had included four names, two of them for the same person, and zero that anyone could possibly need to know.

As I put my head down for a little rest, I realized I could fall back on my post-concussion frailty if Ms. Kirk gave me a hard time. Shut-eye napping was discouraged, so students had learned to sleep like snakes, with their eyes open. I guess that included Ms. Kirk, who also seemed unnaturally still.

Next came math, where the class had moved on to something called "proportions." As far as I could tell, these were just equivalent fractions. Maybe it was like calling Phil Hendrik Nering Bögel the **Baron de Bastrop**, or repackaging the same zombie movie with a different title. In any case, we spent the hour solving problems about flagpoles and shadows. You never know when that skill could come in handy, right?

The high point was when Kenneth Udall worked a problem on the board and determined the man casting the shadow was a foot and a half tall. Ms. Niswonger harped on us to consider whether the answer we come up with is reasonable, since if you set up a proportion wrong, you won't be a little off, you'll be way off.

But Kenny was not one to surrender easily, and he argued that a foot-and-a-half-tall human being was not out of the ordinary. He finally hollered uncle when Ms. Niswonger got out a ruler to show him what that height looked like. Kenny had confused his units of measurement, thinking a foot was a yard.

That brings us to English class. I had already been admitted to the Conjugator's Hall of Fame—which is not Cooperstown or anything. Mr. Henson gave a test every week on the principal parts of the verb—like, "I **go**, I **went**, I have **gone**." According to Mr. Henson, you have to memorize these in order to be a good writer. Hall of Famers like myself were entitled to skip daily drills and weekly tests and instead do a little in-class reading of whatever literary work was assigned.

With my usual skepticism, I confronted the paperback I was handed: *Hatchet*, by Gary Paulsen. Survival story, according to the back cover. Easy to read, I discovered when I started the book. Within a few pages I was lost in the tale.

The main character, a thirteen-year-old boy named Brian, has to take the controls of a small plane when the pilot dies of a heart attack. Brian somehow survives a crash landing and winds up alone in the middle of a forest in Canada. He knows nothing about living in the wild and has only a hatchet to help him do it.

After lunch I went to PE, where I gave the coach my excuse. I sat on the bench with the other lepers, a couple of kids in casts and one who couldn't stop coughing. We all moved as far from the plague dude as possible. I pulled out *Hatchet* and kept reading.

As the bell rang to end the period, it occurred to me why I was enjoying this story. Brian had to figure out how to make his way in a completely new world. Everything that was familiar and comfortable had been taken from him. He would be forced to develop new abilities in order to survive the harsh environment.

Now that the day was nearly over, I had to be honest with myself. Returning to school hadn't been like going back after I'd had the chickenpox. Something was very, very different, and it wasn't James Garland Walsh Middle School.

It was me.

Until now, I'd attended school on "mute," or with wads of cotton stuffed in my ears. Today I experienced school in a completely different way. I heard the students and teachers—unfortunately—but *what* they said was not as interesting as *how* they said it. The rhythms of speech, the timbre of voices, emphasis, inflection—the jangled sounds of excited teenagers surging through halls, punctuated by chimes of texts received. In moments of relative silence, coughs, sneezes, sighs, burps, suppressed giggles, pens drumming on the desk, were still audible.

The symphony of school.

Not Mozart, but musical, somehow, to the ears of a boy who had never cared the least bit about music.

Without going anywhere, I found myself immersed in a completely new environment.

To survive, I would need a tool.

My hatchet would be a guitar.

Part Two

October-November 2012

Chapter Twenty-Four
In Theory

RAH-RAH HAD LEFT MESSAGES, and despite pangs of guilt, I hadn't called her back. I was bursting to tell her everything, but apprehensive. My newfound ability was such a big change it might alter things between us. Maybe she'd welcome such amazing news. But the thought that she might *not* kept me paralyzed for the moment.

My football buddies were also on the phone, bugging me to play. I held them at arm's length, blaming my over-protective doctor. But I did promise to at least come to the game on Saturday.

Not playing ball, talking to Rah-Rah, or doing homework opened extra time during which my brain was supposed to rest. I figured it could kick back while I was on the guitar. The steel-stringed acoustic was rough on the fingertips, which Dad assured me would toughen up. Meanwhile, he brought home a nylon-stringed acoustic and an electric, which were easier on the digits. It's a great advantage to the budding savant to have a father who owns a guitar shop.

We practiced every day and Dad began to teach me theory. My hands seemed to naturally know *what* to do, but he insisted that knowing *why* they were doing it would give me more power in the long run. Dad made a lot more sense than my history textbook.

"You're making it easy," I said.

"If *only*. I'll take that much credit," he said, holding his thumb and forefinger half an inch apart. He looked at me a moment and set down his guitar. I put mine on its stand, too.

"Friz, in one day, you pick up what it takes a normal person months to learn." It seemed like a compliment, but Dad sounded disturbed.

"Well, I don't think I'll keep that up," I said, trying to reassure him. "That'd be Kim Peeky freeky."

Dad chuckled nervously. "In less than a week you've memorized the fret board, mastered bar chords, extended bar chords, and voicings all over the neck."

"I wouldn't say 'mastered.' Bar chords are hard."

Dad twitched his head in agreement. "Most folks don't even try them until they've been playing a year or two. Grab your axe." I picked it up. "Play me a C major off the E string." I did. "Make it minor. Make it a seventh. Make it a minor seventh. Make it a major seventh."

I found each chord and arpeggiated the strum so Dad could hear every string ring out. The last was tough—the major seventh off the E-string was a contortion. Dad smiled and nodded. "Find a better voicing."

I shifted up the neck to base the chord off the A-string, a more comfortable position for my left hand, and the chord rang true.

"Beautiful sound, isn't it?"

"One of my favorites," I agreed.

"What color is it?" he asked curiously.

I thought of a box of crayons and tried to find a match. "Kinda blue—guess you'd call it aqua."

"You know who else can see these sounds?" Dad asked. "Duke Ellington. Stevie Wonder. Kanye West. Billy Joel. Leonard Bernstein."

"Never heard of 'em."

Dad smiled at my ignorance. "'Cause they're not ballplayers—but they're good company."

"If you say so, Dad."

"Did all right for themselves. Looks like you could, too." He gave me an appraising look to see what I thought of the idea.

"I like it fine, so far," I said.

He seemed to have something else to say. Finally, he gave a little nod, like he had it. "You used to have a friend, think his name was Jake…"

"Jake McGrath? The one with the father?"

"*That's* the one."

My eyebrows shot up at the thought of the man. "Ultimate CSP." Dad gave me a questioning look. "Crazy Sports Parent."

He laughed the way he always did when I told him something kids knew that he didn't. "You think Jake even liked football?"

"In the beginning, yeah. But his dad liked it too much for both of 'em. After a while, Jake wasn't sure his dad liked *him*."

"We're not doing that," Dad said. "Gotta be *you* first, guitar *second*."

I nodded, agreeing—though it was starting to feel impossible to separate the two.

Chapter Twenty-Five
Dos Equis

THE MISCHIEVOUS GLINT in Mom's eye when she fetched me from my room should have been a tip-off. But I'm too trusting, and the visitor downstairs chatting with Dad took me by complete surprise.

"Rah-Rah." I tried for a casual tone, but to my ears, I sounded guilty as a thief caught hotwiring a pickup.

"*Bah*-Rah to you," she said, scowling. "You don't call, you don't text, you better be dying."

"Not unless I have an undiagnosed disease…"

She had me on my heels and weighed in, swinging. "Then you got some explaining to do."

My parents were enjoying this. "Are you sure you're fourteen years old?" my mother asked Rah-Rah.

"Honey, it's a *dos equis* thing," said Dad.

"*Beer*?"

"No. *Chromosomes*. When you're born with two x's, you naturally know how to put those of us with a 'y' on the defensive."

"Watch yourself, sir," Mom warned. Dad clapped a hand over his mouth and we all laughed. The distraction helped me get off the ropes.

"Go for a walk?" I suggested, looking for more privacy.

"*Can* you?" asked Rah-Rah.

"Think I'm up to a stroll…"

I grabbed a jacket and we headed out the door. The heat had held into the fall, but now that we were well into October, the late afternoon air had a chill. Or maybe I was nervous. I stuck hands in jacket pockets and we ambled up the street under a canopy of oak and dogwood trees cloaked in red foliage.

"So, how the hell are you?" Rah-Rah asked.

"Well, I'm better…"

"That's *good*." Her tone suggested sarcasm-free surprise, so I thought I'd share a little more.

"Doc Sugarman cleared me for school."

"Awesome! When you going back?"

"I've *been* back. For three days."

Uh-oh. Silence.

"Take a deep breath," I suggested. She gave me one of those "if looks could kill" glares. "Or *don't*."

"Let me get this straight. You've been at school for three days and you haven't returned my calls?"

"Technically that's true, but—"

"But *what*?"

"I've had conversations with you…in my head."

"You must be brain-dead if you think those count!"

"I meant to call you, but…" I trailed off, hoping for a miracle. I didn't get one.

"I know you don't have much homework—Dr. Sugarman probably has you on a one-hour limit!"

"Would you believe my hour takes me *longer*?"

She almost laughed despite herself. "For *you*, I might. Understand, the last I heard, you were on your deathbed. Thought the next news might be your funeral." She gave me a look to drive her point home. Meeting her eyes, a realization dawned on me.

"Wait. Were you…worried about me?"

"*Dos equis*, remember? That's what we do!"

The possibility had not remotely crossed my mind. In my limited life experience, friends' angst was reserved for truly important concerns, like football games. I was aware that my mother worried, but I chalked that up to her parental role rather than to her gender. Now that I glimpsed the gulf of my ignorance about women, I could do little but beg forgiveness.

"Well, all I can say is, I'm sorry. I honestly had no idea. It was an awful thing to do and I won't do it again."

This didn't go over as well as my infrequent trips to the Catholic confessional. She glowered at me, my *mea culpa* falling flat on its face.

"You're just a little too good at apologizing to be trustworthy."

"Please. Give me a boatload of Hail Marys and let's get past this."

"Don't think so. You're goin' to hell."

"Whoooooaaa…" I guess I got the right inflection on the moan, because Rah-Rah busted up. She elbowed me in the ribs.

"All right, I want the whole story."

She got some of it. I left out the best part, not sure how to handle it. I *wanted* to tell her. I was *dying* to tell her…

We passed a guy working in the garage with a radio blaring, which prompted an off-topic question. "Hey, what was that I heard at your house?" Rah-Rah asked.

"The music?"

"Yeah. What was that song?"

Seemed like a safe one to answer. "Oh, that was Eric Clapton's version of 'Crossroads.'"

"Man, you've got some system. Sounded awesome."

"Well, it wasn't a recording." She was looking at me. I *had* to finish the thought... "Uh...that was *me*."

Rah-Rah stopped and gaped. "*You* were playing that. On the guitar." It sounded like an accusation.

I bit my lip and nodded. She was looking at me with bewildered awe. "And I thought you were just a dumbass jock."

"Well, I *am*."

"Not if you can play guitar like that, you're not!"

"I never did that before."

"You mean you haven't played that song?"

"No, I've played it through a couple of times..."

It was like floundering in quicksand—the harder I struggled, the faster I sank. I tried speed walking, like I could outrun the questions, but Rah-Rah wasn't going anywhere. She'd come to a dead stop—and she was a lot harder to outwit than that tuning wheel.

"What are you trying to say?" she demanded.

So I ground to a halt and told her. Grudgingly, like a guilty suspect being interrogated. With crimson leaves fluttering down on us, she worked me over until she got it all. It took so long I thought the red oak we were standing under might be nothing but bare limbs by the time we got done.

They say confession is good for the soul—and after telling my tale, I *was* relieved to be on the same page with Rah-Rah. It was instructive to see how she was taking this, since she was the first to hear it. She was somewhat peeved, but mostly amazed.

"Man..." she said, "I went back to flyin', but *you're* gonna take off."

"Mom and Dad don't want me to tell anybody," I said. "That's why I didn't call you."

"Well, you wouldn't have had to tell me."

"Are you kidding? Look how fast you wormed the whole chapter and verse out of me!"

She looked pleased with herself for that one. "All right, you're forgiven and you're not going to hell. Probably."

"Thank you."

"Just don't tell anyone else. Media'd be campin' out in front of your house."

"Nah…"

"It is not every day someone gets hit in the head and turns into a git-tar hero!" Rah-Rah was practically yelling.

"Shhh," I said, looking around for neighbors. "I'm no git-tar hero."

"You *will* be."

I raked leaves with my foot, clearing off a place under the tree. We sat and leaned against the trunk, digesting this momentous prediction.

"Well, enough about me…" I said lightly.

Rah-Rah laughed. I looked over and grinned. She twisted, leaned up, and kissed me on the lips. It was the first time ever for me, and I can tell you, it was somewhat better than a concussion—though it knocked me for as much of a loop. After a few moments, she pulled away and smiled at me.

"Really?" I said.

"Oh, yeah," she said. "By next week you'll be too famous for *me*."

So we huddled-up, she called the same play, and we ran it again.

And again.

And again.

Chapter Twenty-Six
Triple H

I WOKE EARLY, plugged a preamp gizmo into the electric, and played it with headphones so I didn't disturb Mom and Dad. They liked to sleep late and there was no rush for them to get up. Even though it was Saturday, I wouldn't be getting into my football uniform today.

The world of music was more thrilling than my trip to the Magic Kingdom had been when I was eight. Just like Orlando, with so much to see and do, I wanted to experience it all. So far, the blues were my favorite ride, though I'm not sure why. A lot of the notes were off-pitch, which offended my newly-tuned ears—yet the music called to other parts of me.

Mom and Dad got up, pried the headphones from me, and we took off for the game against "Triple H" on their turf. We drove past the giant hippo sculpture in front of Hutto High and headed for the school's stadium.

"Triple H" stands for the "Hutto Hustlin' Hippos"—not to be confused with their other youth football team, the "Hutto Fightin' Hippos." The high school teams also took the hippo for their mascot. In fact, the whole town is hippo crazy, decorating the streets with hundreds of gape-jawed hippo statues.

Far as I know, Hutto is the only place in the US to have the hippo as its mascot. It's not a typical animal you'd choose to strike fear into an opponent's heart. But to be fair, the state features plenty of other odd mascots, such as the Pied Pipers of Hamlin, the Grandville Zebras, and the New Braunfels Unicorns. I believe the most outrageous is the Hockaday Daisies. Lord, I'd rather be pushin' up daisies than be called a "hockadaisie." Their games must have some awful trash talking.

Mom and Dad headed for the bleachers and I walked over to join my teammates, who were stretching, jogging, and tossing footballs. Zach saw me coming and whipped a bullet at my gut. I pivoted and caught the ball over my hip. Easy-peasy. I lobbed the ball back to him.

"Go long," he said, with a wave at the end zone. I looked over at my folks, who were engrossed in conversation, so I broke down the sidelines.

I started in a lope, and it felt so good I took it up a gear. Still no ill effects. I glanced back at Zach as he let her rip.

Instantly, I knew where that ball was going and what I'd have to do to get under it. I turned my head upfield and kicked the throttle open, thinking back to the very first pass Zach had sent my way. We'd hooked up for a good many completions in the years since, and gauging the trajectory of his bombs had become second nature.

I could've caught the ball with two hands, but where's the sport in that? Instead, I stretched out my right arm and plucked it from the sky one-handed without breaking stride, the same way I did that first time. Gotta admit, it felt good, as did the cheer several buddies sent my way when I sped toward the goal line.

I entered the end zone, spiked the ball, and did a little dirty bird dance for the fellas. Enjoy it, guys, 'cause I'm not gonna be doing it during regulation any time soon.

I retrieved the ball and jogged back to Zach.

"Still got it, bro. Go suit up," he said.

Jamarie joined in. "For reals, man. You'll never get hit by no Hippo."

"Maybe not, but I'd get clobbered by Mom and Dad. I'm just a spectator today."

I headed for the bench and took a seat next to Coach Roberts. He gave me a cockeyed look and took a big spit in the direction of a Starbucks cup. Missed.

"Reports of your demise have been greatly exaggerated," he offered. "And I was fixin' to make a speech over your corpse..."

"Glad to hear it, Coach."

He flashed a brown-toothed grin and clapped me on the back. "You are a good ol' dog, Friz. A good ol' dog."

Before I could respond, an errant football shot toward Coach's head. I reached out and intercepted it.

Coach spun to identify the guilty party.

"Oops," said José Hernandez. He was still bent over in the position from which he'd hiked the football many feet over the head of our punter, Alex Calderon.

"Dammit, Hernandez!" yelled Coach, windmilling his arms. "There's centers can long snap without lookin' but you ain't one of 'em! Like to give *me* a concussion!"

"Sorry, Coach," said José, but he was snickering, as was everyone else.

"Yeah, you *are*," said Two Bob, punctuating his sentiments with another errant spit at the coffee cup.

The game was close—for about a minute. Well, not even. Tyrell received the kickoff and ran it back for a touchdown. Two of the Hippos missed him, but tackled each other—which is not an infraction, though it's frowned upon.

It's not just that we were playing well, it's that the opponent was playing poorly. Triple H merited one more H. They were the *Horrible* Hutto Hustlin' Hippos.

But you have to say they were good sports about it. No Hutto player got down on a teammate for a bad play—and they made plenty. They even congratulated *us* for good plays, which had Coach Roberts shaking his head at the impropriety of it all. If a Tiger had helped an opponent off the sod the way the Hippos were hoisting us, I believe Coach might have swallowed his chaw. I could hear him rumbling, "What is this 'jolly good old chap' crap?"

Coach jumped up and called a timeout. The team huddled around him, waiting for a play. Instead, he eyed the players accusingly. "What's goin' on out there? Y'all look like you're gonna start bowin' and curtsyin' to one another!"

"Coach, I don't know how to curtsy," said José Hernandez with sincerity. Several players laughed.

"Hernandez!" Coach started, then took a deep breath. "That's *right* you don't. Curtsyin's for girls!"

"Oh," said José, pleased. "No wonder."

"From now on, none of y'all letta Hippa hep ya up. Ya hear me?" Coach got twangier as he got angrier.

"But Coach, it'll hurt their feelin's," José objected.

"Yeah, they're holding out a Hippo helping hand," added Ricky Garcia, egging on Two Bob.

"Hippa heppin' han', my ass!" said Coach. "This is football, not kindy-goddamn-garden!"

After the timeout, Tyrell went up the middle for twenty, when he pretty much allowed himself to be tackled. Instead of taking a Hippa heppin' han', he wagged a finger at it and said something. The Hippo player glanced toward the sideline at Coach Roberts, then jogged back to his team.

Our team huddled to get the next play. When Zach called, "Break!" the players stood erect and snapped a crisp bow to the center of the huddle. Problem was, they were standing too close to one another, and several knocked helmets. José Hernandez lost his balance and fell on his butt. He was laughing hard and could barely get to his feet. Even Coach hung his head and grinned.

By halftime all our subs were playing, and we were doing our best not to run the score to the century mark. Coach believed in at least that much sportsmanship. The Hutto cheerleaders had no quit in them, no matter what happened on the field, and continued to lead the crowd in boisterous chants of, "When we say Hut-to, you say hip-po!!"

Meanwhile, several kids were hawking T-shirts to benefit the Hutto Youth Football and Cheer Association, and a lot of people were buying. The shirt was a fabric thesaurus of niceness, with a jumble of commendable adjectives in various fonts assembled above the Hutto motto—"INSTILLING GOOD CHARACTER, ONE CHARACTER AT A TIME."

Maybe it was the one-sidedness, but the game wasn't holding my attention. I went for a walk to the bathroom to lose some of the Gatorade I'd drunk. Before I could reach my destination, I heard something that brought me up short.

A duo was set up near the concession stand, an electric guitarist with a portable amp, and a drummer. What they were playing raised the hair on the back of my neck.

The guitarist was a tall, lean black man, dressed in a kind of vaquero outfit. He wore fringed pants and a wide-brimmed hat shaded his face. With the guitar slung low, he looked like a gunslinger spitting lead in red hot bursts.

What a lead he was playing! It rose and soared and ranged far and wide before coming back to the theme, which it developed and expanded. It was melodic, rhythmic, deeply propulsive—the most exciting thing I'd ever heard. I crept toward him, like a wolf slinking to fire.

When the song ended, the guitarist looked at me and nodded. I glanced around and realized I was the only person listening. "What...*was* that?" I managed to ask.

He seemed pleased at my reaction. "Baby, that's Hendrix, SRV, and *me*. Thetis Redford. Black sheep brother of Robert."

"You're Robert Redford's brother?"

"I got the looks, he got the bucks. Song called 'Little Wing.' You like?"

"Yeah. Can you play it again?"

He laughed. "Yeah, *can* I, but *will* I...?" He nodded at an open guitar case lying on the ground with a few bucks in it. I dug in my pockets, threw what I had in the case, and looked up at him. He gave a look to the drummer and launched into the song a second time.

I listened differently, still under the spell, but watching and learning. It was just as exciting, but this time I felt like a passenger on the "Little Wing," not a grounded observer. When Thetis wound up, I was still the only spectator.

He raised his eyebrows to the drummer. "Tough house, Jackson." He took a pull from a paper-bag-wrapped longneck, wiped his brow, and considered me. "You play, man?"

"Yeah."

"Little bit, huh?"

I nodded uncertainly. He smiled at me. "You wanta play something?" he asked. "I gotta take a leak."

I'd never played anything in public—which was the plan. *Low profile.* I shoved my hands in my pockets and shook my head. "I don't know too many songs."

"All you need's one, little brother. You got *one?*"

Maybe I put too much money in the case. Thetis was encouraging me. I shrugged. He took that for yes.

"All right, then," he said, unstrapping the guitar. "We gonna hafta shorten this strap a little…" He handed the guitar to me and secured the strap to a pin on the guitar's butt. "How's that feel?"

I strummed a few chords, ran through a scale—and dropped the pick on the ground. The drummer chuckled.

"Don't worry, baby—happen to everybody. Lemme recover that fumble for you." Thetis plucked the pick off the ground and handed it to me. "You look good, man. Axe suits you. Now, what you want to play?"

I looked around. Nobody was paying attention. "'Little Wing,'" I murmured.

"*Thas* the song you know?" exclaimed Thetis, jerking his head back.

I shuffled my feet and studied the asphalt. "Know a couple more—but that's the one I want to play."

"Shit, I started on 'Walk the Line,' which wasn't but strummin' A and E chords…" he muttered.

"I don't know that one."

He rubbed his jaw, then said, "Play what you know, baby. You don't have to count this one off. Jackson'll come in when it's time."

He backed off and headed for the bathroom.

I took a deep breath and began to tap out the beat. I started to play.

It was the greatest feeling I'd ever had. Better than running, jumping, and catching a ball. I don't know if I was riding the wind, or if I *was* the wind itself—blowing—swirling—flying. But I was soaring, higher than I'd ever been.

The song was playing *me*.

I noticed that Thetis had resisted the call of nature and was gaping at me like he just might wet his pants!

A few other people were drifting over, which I knew was not good. But I couldn't help myself. I played on.

I finished the song and held the vibrato on the last note to a smattering of applause and a couple of whistles. Thetis approached and lifted the guitar over my head. He leaned in and whispered in my ear.

In a low voice, he demanded, "Who the fuck *are* you, man?"

Chapter Twenty-Seven
Jackson Greens

PEOPLE WERE THROWING BILLS into the guitar case. Thetis gave me a glare.

"That shit's mine," he warned.

"Yeah, no worries."

"Rock on, dude!" one guy called.

"Give the kid back the guitar," said an old guy with a hat so big it covered his ears down to the lobes.

"Uh…it's *my* guitar," objected Thetis.

"So what?" said the man. "Let him play some."

Others called out similar comments. They were getting antagonistic and their faces weren't friendly. Thetis looked flummoxed and I thought I'd better do something.

"We're gonna take a short break," I said.

"Yeah," Thetis said. "Back in a few, folks. Plentya game left."

The mini crowd dispersed with a collective grumble. Thetis set the guitar in the case with the money, flipped the lid, and latched it shut.

"Pack up," he told the drummer in a low voice.

"You're leaving?" I asked.

He gave me a tight nod as he coiled the wire to his amp. I felt bad about it.

"Thanks for letting me play, Thetis," I said. "I'm sorry if I screwed things up for you."

He stopped what he was doing and grinned at me. "Baby, I be all right. Plenty other joints where they ain't heard *you*."

He unzipped a backpack and pulled something out. He flung it at me and I caught it. It was one of the Hutto Youth T-shirts.

"These Hippo cats crazy, anyway. One of 'em tossed that in the case."

"You don't want it?" I asked.

He took on a pained expression. "*That?* How I 'sposed to drink *that?*"

"You could wear it…"

"Not my style." He slung the pack over a shoulder, hefted the guitar in one hand and the amp in the other, and gestured toward the drummer. "Y'all give Jackson a hand with his kit."

The drummer was carefully breaking down his set. He had the biggest drum lying face down in a large bag that fit it like a glove. That drum had no head on one side, and the other drums, which were smaller, fit inside. It reminded me of those Russian nesting dolls, where an extended family all cuddled into one big mamma. The drummer looked up at me.

"You know your percussion, son?"

I'd been focused on the guitarist and hadn't paid attention to this man. He was old, with a face that showed his years like rings on a tree trunk. Concentric wrinkles creased his brow and cheeks, rippling like the waters of a dark pond disturbed by something hidden beneath the surface.

"No, sir," I said.

"Big one's the bass. This kit packs up real nice. Toms and snare go inside. Stands and cymbals got their own tote." He gestured with his chin. "Go ahead, take the wing nut off the hi-hats. Watch you don't drop 'em. Good cymbal costs more'n a drum."

"I'll be careful."

"B'lieve you will." He extended his hand to shake mine. "Jackson Greens."

"Friz Collins."

"*Friz?*" I nodded. He made a face and said, "Okay."

I took the hi-hats apart and flipped one of the cymbals so they nested together. The drummer zipped a bag and took the cymbals from me.

"You thread the wing back on the stem?"

"Yessir."

"Good boy," he approved. "I'll get the rest. You watch and learn. Just how you learned that song." He looked up from what he was doing and cocked his eye at me. "Young man, I seen a few things. Nothing like that."

I didn't know what to say. Jackson was studying me like a golfer trying to read a tricky putt. "How long you been playin'?"

"A while…"

"Long's that?" he insisted. I licked my lips but didn't answer. Jackson's eyes narrowed. "Thetis been playing twenty-five years—and you ain't be alive much more'n half that. When you start, boy?"

"You don't want to know, Mr. Green."

"*Greens.* The name's *Greens.* Plural. And I *do* want to know. *Tell* me." He gave me a look that said he wasn't going to let it drop.

"Last week," I mumbled, looking down.

"Last week," he chuckled. "Y'all be playing for a *week*, and you made Thetis Redford look like cowpie in bad pasture."

Quick as a snake, his arm lashed out and grabbed hold of my left wrist. With his other hand, he ran a finger lightly over the tips of mine. When I looked up, he was no longer smiling. He looked shaken, even afraid.

"Shit," he said, "Y'all musta made a deal with the devil."

I took a step back and stared at him. It sounded like he meant it.

"Greens, c'mon!" It was Thetis yelling from the driver's seat of a pickup. He revved the engine.

"S'my ride, son." He pulled a card from his wallet and handed it to me. "Most nights you find me there. Could be I help you with ol' Scratch."

"I didn't sell my soul!"

Frown lines split his eyes like exclamation points. "Thas what *you* think."

On the ride home, Mom and Dad chatted about acquaintances they hadn't seen since I'd been injured. I was lost in my own thoughts.

"You all right back there?" asked Dad.

"Uh-huh."

"Frustrated you couldn't play?" asked Mom.

"Uh-uh."

"You're *not*?" asked Dad.

"Uh-uh."

"Huh," said Dad.

"Huh," said Mom.

"You making fun of me?"

"Uh-uh," said Mom.

"Uh-uh," said Dad.

I was quiet a moment, then I asked, "Can someone sell their soul to the devil?"

"You offering?" joked Dad.

"Bill!" said Mom. "That's a good question, Friz, so you ought to—"

"I *know*, google it—but just this once would you mind telling me the answer?"

"Weee-llll," teased Mom. "I don't know if you *can*, or if you *can't*. But it has been the subject of lots of books, plays, movies—"

"Songs," said Dad. "That Clapton piece, 'Crossroads.' That goes back to Robert Johnson, one of the early blues players. They say his ability was not natural—that he met the devil at the crossroads, and afterward, he made music no mortal man could."

"*Who* says that?" I asked.

"Jealous people, honey," said Mom. "Tryin' to tear him down."

"Or," said Dad, "it might have been Johnson himself who came up with the story to enhance his legend."

"People *believed* that stuff?" I asked. It seemed absurd.

"Folks took talk of the devil very seriously," said Dad.

"Still *do*," said Mom. "Why this sudden interest in selling your soul?"

"I'm not selling *mine*, if that's what you're worried about," I snapped.

I lay awake that night. For as long as I could remember, I'd fallen asleep thinking of whatever balls I'd caught that day. I'd relive highlights, watching the movie in my mind. Running the field, wind in my face, the impact of the ball in my mitt or on my palms—I never tired of these thoughts. Mom said I even ran in my sleep, legs twitching like a dog having a cat-chasing dream.

Since my injury those visions had deserted me. Instead, I relived "Little Wing," how playing that song had lifted me high above a landscape whose colors were a visual representation of sound.

Even as I savored the memory, discomfort crept in, emotions I had difficulty identifying. Sadness...for the way new experiences were rocking the foundation on which my life was built.

Maybe worse, shame. I'd learned to identify the feeling from early crimes—shoplifting a candy bar or getting caught shooting peas at passing cars. Yet this shame was worse than any I'd self-inventoried to date. I tossed in bed, trying to pin down what I'd done to trigger it.

Try as I might, I couldn't get it. My understanding lay just out of reach, a pass I couldn't quite catch up to no matter how hard I ran. I wondered if it had something to do with what Jackson Greens had said about selling my soul to the devil.

I clicked on the bedside light. My jeans lay in a heap on the floor. I dug in the pockets, hoping I hadn't lost it…yes! I still had the card he'd given me.

I examined it now. An address, a phone number, a couple of musical notes, a martini glass with a sexy girl in it…and the name of a club.

The King Lounge in Austin.

Chapter Twenty-Eight
Of Birds and Bees and Mice and Men

"WE'RE GONNA DO HOMEWORK," Rah-Rah informed her mother as she towed me through their living room. Mrs. Lang was glued to the television, surrounded by sections of the Sunday *New York Times*.

"Um-hm," she said without looking up. "Keep your door open."

Rah-Rah took the stairs two at a time as I ascended more cautiously, toting my backpack. *So this is what they mean by the Stairway to Heaven*, I thought. I hadn't been in her house before. Whatever we did together was a first for me—exciting, but nerve-racking, too.

I followed Rah-Rah into the first bedroom at the top of the landing. She swung the door closed, prompting me to remind her of what her mother had just said. A long kiss shut me up good.

When she pulled away, I said, "So…we're *not* going to do homework?"

I hadn't meant it to be funny, but she thought it was. She gave me a look and laughed. Then she said, "Eventually." *Wow.* She gave that word a syrupy spin you won't find in the dictionary, as she plucked the backpack from my grip and slung it across the room. "Try using your hands a little."

"Your mom?"

"Take an earthquake to shake her off her Sunday shows. Mom's very political. What about your folks?"

"Well, they vote…"

"Democrat or Republican?" I gave her a look to suggest the question was out of bounds, but Rah-Rah was not easily put-off. "I like to know what kind of mouth I'm puttin' my tongue in."

"An Independent one," I said, recalling Mom and Dad's party affiliation. Dinner table conversation was dominated by talk of sports, classrooms, and local affairs that weren't especially partisan.

Rah-Rah made a face, but allowed, "Could be worse." She pulled my head down for more oral distraction and I ran my fingers through her hair. Despite sensory overload, it occurred to me that Rah-Rah seemed to know a lot more about this activity than I did.

"I guess I'm not the first boy you've kissed…" *Damn—did I really say that?*

"Uh-oh," she said, grimacing. She pulled away and flopped on the bed. "Can your ego handle it if I say, 'No, you're not'?"

I tried to be casual, though I wasn't sure how I felt about the information. "Possibly. Could be good one of us knows what they're doing."

I searched for anything I could find to change the subject, and noticed her room for the first time. I raised my eyebrows. The walls were a light grey. "It's not pink."

"You thought my room'd be *pink*?" Her tone was indignant, but I ignored the warning.

"That's kind of the girl color, isn't it?"

"Well, let's see," she said. "My friend Janelle's room is peach. LaShonda's room is white. Amber's is…guess you'd call it mauve, though I don't expect you'll know what that is. Brianne's is yellow, ugh. Juana's is white." She ticked the counterarguments off on her fingers and paused when she'd submitted a handful.

"Well, I'm clueless," I said. "I even thought you'd have a big picture of Maddie Gardner on the wall."

Rah-Rah gave me a long look and went to her closet. She opened the door and extracted a cardboard cylinder from a chaotic jumble. She gave the tube a shake to release a rolled-up poster, unfurling it for me to see.

"Is that her?" I asked, thinking I was one-for-two, sort of. A petite blonde girl posed high atop the upstretched arms of her cheerleading team. Her radiant smile contrasted with the contorted posture of her body.

"You're a lot prettier than her."

"It's not all about how you look," Rah-Rah snapped. "Her form is perfect."

I raised my hands defensively. "I shouldn't have said that."

She sighed. "What I mean is, *thank you*." After a moment she added, "And unfortunately a lot of it *is* about how you look."

She hopped up and walked over to her desk, clicking on the light. "C'mere," she said. "Look there."

I examined a spot on the wall where the paint had worn. "Is that pink?"

"Painted over it a couple of years ago." I had to laugh. "But I'm fighting the stereotypes!"

Two-for-two, if you include the past, anyway. Continuing my investigation, I noticed a picture of a handsome man with a camera posed atop a rugged mountain. "Your dad?" She acknowledged with a nod. I scanned the rest of the shelves. "No picture of your mom."

"I see *her* every day."

"Uh...divorced?"

"Deceased. Killed in Afghanistan."

That set me back. The cause of death was surprising. "Your dad was in the military?"

Rah-Rah threw herself on the bed and leaned on a stack of pillows.

"Journalist. War's dangerous for them, too."

I nodded and didn't say anything.

"Think I'd get over it. I was only four, so..." She laughed, recalling a memory. "He used to try to teach me to catch a football. He'd have loved *you*."

"How'd your folks get together?" I asked gently.

"College. Mom was in graduate school and he was teaching a class. One thing led to another."

"He was older than her?"

"Quite a bit. Mom used to call him 'Grampa.' It confused me, 'cause I had two other grampas. But Mom said you couldn't have too many of them. Still, I couldn't figure out how your mother could marry your grandfather. I told it to my preschool teacher, and she couldn't, either. Mom had to come explain that one to her."

We traded stories about being little. How we'd found out Santa Claus wasn't responsible for all those Christmas presents, and the tooth fairy wasn't the one who left cash under our pillows. The betrayal we'd felt at having our bubbles burst had given way to realization that our parents did even more for us than we'd thought.

Eventually, blathering on about infancy reminded us we'd grown up. Rah-Rah gave me one of her irresistible smiles and we got back to the business of being teenagers. The details of further activities are highly classified.

After a while, we did try to do some studying, but it wasn't easy: being alone with a pretty girl isn't conducive to academics. Still, I took the armchair and cracked my history book. The only thing that kept me awake was watching Rah-Rah writhe at her desk. Looked like her essay on *To Kill a Mockingbird* was killing *her*.

Finally, she threw down her pen and turned her chair to me. "Will it bother you if I put on some music?"

I stifled a yawn and said, "I certainly hope so. Got any blues?"

"Nope. How 'bout polkas?"

I made a face. "If you had a cat, we could just pull his tail instead."

"That's mean as hell. Would you do such a thing?" she said, laughing despite herself.

"'Course not. But I wouldn't listen to a polka, either."

"Don't make fun," she said. "Mom's from New Braunfels, sixth generation."

Apparently Mah-Rah hailed from the hotbed of German settlement in the hill country not far to our south. Mom and Dad had taken me for the annual sausage fest a couple of times, and to float down the Comal River on inner tubes. With difficulty, I wrenched my mind from fantasies of "Fräulein Rah-Rah."

"There *must* be some other German music with less oompah. Why don't you surprise me?"

"Love to." She dialed up something on her phone and moments later a piano intro came out of a pair of small speakers. The vocal began—a woman's soprano voice, which held a single word, a wave of inflections rippling through the drawn-out vowel: "*Bluuuuuuuuuuuuuuuuuuuuue.*"

I smiled at Rah-Rah's joke, which pleased her. "Not the *blues*, but…"

"Who is it?" I asked.

"Joni Mitchell." My eyes narrowed at the unfamiliar name. "Girl thing, like the color pink. I'll take it off."

"No, I like it. Leave it."

We listened as the singer spilled her guts to simple piano accompaniment. I had to keep wiping the corner of my eyes. Rah-Rah smiled at me, her own eyes gleaming.

"Another," I requested.

She made a selection. A moment later a guitar and laid-back drum were prelude to a raspy female vocalist who, again, held a single word until it was painful: "*Summertime.*"

"Joni?" I asked, though the voice was completely different.

"*Janis*. Joplin." I looked at her blankly. "Don't you know *anything?*"

That was the blues. Without ever raising her voice, the singer wrung every drop of emotion from what seemed the saddest, most desperate lullaby ever sung. I was snuffling and coughing as Rah-Rah passed me a box of tissue. When the song ended, I blew my nose and took a shaky breath. I was embarrassed by my weepy response. Dialing up the waterworks is not in the Texas Ranger manual.

"Think I'm ready for a polka," I mumbled.

Rah-Rah looked at me like a birthday girl opening a present and finding something she never expected. "You have a very emotional reaction to music."

"Since my injury. Sorry about that." I looked away, hoping she wouldn't laugh in my face.

Instead, she wrapped her arms around me soothingly. "You were kind of looking up at the ceiling. Your eyes were moving like you were seeing something."

"Yeah," I said. "I *do* see things when I hear music—all kinds of shapes and colors. 'Synesthesia,' I guess it's called. They're only in my head, but...seems my eyes haven't gotten the message yet."

She looked puzzled, trying to work it out. "So...the shapes and colors tell you what notes to play?"

"Pretty much."

"And your fingers just know how to do that on the guitar?"

"I can't explain it any better than that."

"Well, I think it's easier to believe in Santa Claus." She started to tickle me and I wriggled away from her. My escape carried me to the bookcase. I took in the titles, shocked at how extensive they were. I hadn't seen a collection like this outside of the library, which I hadn't been to for years.

"Have you read all these?"

She winced. "You thought I was just a dumbass cheerleader?"

"No, but…who are these people? Marie Curie, Frida Kahlo, Jane Goodall?"

"Famous women. Please don't tell me you've never heard of Eleanor Roosevelt."

"Barely. Wow! You've got a lot of these."

"Haven't you ever read a biography?" I could see I was losing the ground I'd gained from my weepy ways. On this topic, my cards were low.

"Sure. Willie Mays, Ted Williams, Gale Sayers…"

"Athletes." Her voice was just short of scornful.

"They're famous, too, you know."

"More than they should be. Folks care more about sports and reality TV than anything else in this country."

This wasn't a point of view I was prepared to dispute, especially since I was one of the individuals it applied to. But maybe she was bluffing. "You've got a lot of novels, too. Why, I can't believe you've read all these."

"Read 'em and remember 'em. Try me."

I selected a volume at random and pulled it from the shelf. I examined the cover. "Who's Algernon?"

"A mouse who gets real smart."

I did what I usually do when perusing a book—flipped to the end to see how long it was. "Over three hundred pages about a smart mouse?"

"It's really about this man named Charlie. They give him the same operation they did on Algernon, and he goes from being super learning-disabled to a total genius."

That startled me and I looked up from the book. "Sort of like me."

"Well, you didn't get an operation."

"And I didn't get smart," I joked. "Do man and mouse live happily ever after?"

"No! It made me cry," she said. She took the book from me and reshelved it. "It wasn't actually that good."

I didn't read books, but I could sure read evasion. "What happened?"

"I forget." As *if.* She was studying her bookcase like a librarian, not meeting my eyes.

"Might as well tell me—I'll just google it," I said.

She turned to me. "The operation wore off and Charlie went back to the way he was," she said sadly, then added, "But it was worse..."

"'Cause he'd had a taste of something better." I tried to look cool, but I wasn't.

"Friz, it's just fiction. There's no such operation. What happened to you is different."

"Is it? We don't even *know* what happened to me."

I crumpled onto the bed, depressed. Rah-Rah sat down next to me. "All I know," she said, "is that I like you. Idiot or savant." Before I could respond, she added, "But you *should* read more. If I'd known you were so ignorant, I wouldn't have teased about your IQ. I thought you got good grades."

"I *do*," I said. "But that doesn't mean I've *learned* anything."

Chapter Twenty-Nine
Dr. Monaghan

DR. SUGARMAN'S EXAMS were getting less intensive. He finished this one quickly, smiled, and gave me the thumbs-up.

"What are the details to that, Doctor?" asked Mom.

"Well," he started, "caution's advisable. I'd ramp up the homework gradually."

"*Gradually*," I emphasized. Get in the first punch, even with Mom. *Especially* with Mom.

"We're at one hour," said Mom. "Why not double it?"

"*Mom…*"

"Let's go to an hour and a half for now," suggested the doctor. *My hero*.

Mom acquiesced with a nod. "Football?"

"I'd rather not," he said.

"For *now*, or forever?" I asked.

The doctor gave me a rueful look. "My neurologist hemisphere conflicts with my sports fan hemisphere. The neurologist prefers 'forever,' but the sports fan says 'for *now*.'"

I nodded to the doctor's proposal. "It's cool."

Mom gave me a suspicious "mom look," as if I were running a game on her.

"Good," said Dr. Sugarman. "Before you go, I've contacted a

colleague who'd like to meet you. Dr. Monaghan knows more about savants than anyone in the world."

Mom frowned at the proposal. "Is he covered under our plan?"

"No charge."

She tilted her head and said, "Call him in."

"That's what I propose. He's in Wisconsin," said Dr. Sugarman. "I set up a camera and a monitor to Skype him.

We said hellos to a white-haired man with wire spectacles who smiled back at us, crisp and clear on Dr. Sugarman's big TV set. Dr. Monaghan was even older than Jackson Greens, but he was chipper. He wore a white lab coat with a bow tie popping out the top of it.

"I'm eighty-five and I'm Skyping!" he crowed. "And thrilled to talk to you, young man. Dr. Sugarman tells me you've developed new cognitive capacity after your concussion."

This made me feel foolish, like when folks gush about how big you've gotten. "Could be," I admitted.

Dr. Monaghan smiled. "Friz, I propose an experiment. I've got a colleague here who's a guitar player herself. If you're willing, she'll play a composition and we'll see if you can replicate it. Would that be all right?"

First my dad, now Dr. Monahan. Seems I was a guinea pig with a guitar. I shrugged agreement.

Dr. Monaghan nodded off-camera, and a middle-aged woman entered the shot. She was pretty, with curly dark hair and oversized eyeglasses. She held an acoustic guitar with mother-of-pearl inlays that glittered through the camera link.

"That's some guitar!" I exclaimed.

"What about the *woman?*" chided Dr. Monaghan. "She's my daughter, Molly!"

"Oops. She's nice, too."

Molly laughed, made herself comfortable, and began to play.

It was a folk song with a melody I didn't recognize—pretty, and not difficult. When Molly finished, I was eager for my turn. I took my guitar from its case and settled myself. Everybody got quiet.

I was getting more used to this experience, but it was slightly different each time. Today it felt like plunging into a pool of water— yet I was still above the surface, watching as I swam deeper and deeper.

I wasn't moving like a clumsy human, but like a nimble fish, darting through reefs of brightly colored coral. As I played, choices could be made, passages explored—but I ignored them to stick to the path Molly had chosen.

I concluded and looked to see how everyone was taking it.

"Wonderful!" exclaimed Dr. Monaghan, as if he'd just netted a Dotted Skipper for his butterfly collection. "It sounded flawless to me."

"I heard two mistakes," said Molly, raising a cautious hand.

"Oh?" said Dr. Monaghan. "Perhaps you're being overly critical, dear."

"One on the chorus, one on the last verse," she insisted.

Dr. Monaghan's lips squeezed tight. "Still, we can agree that Friz gave a remarkable performance. And wasn't that an original composition?"

"True, Papa. He played it cold."

"Bravo!"

"But I want to come back to the mistakes," Molly pressed.

"Dear—"

"*I* made them when *I* played the song," Molly said.

"Oh," said Dr. Monaghan, taken aback.

Mom and Dr. Sugarman looked at me. "You said to play it the same way," I apologized.

"And so you did. Well done, young man," said Dr. Monaghan.

"It's harder to make intentional errors than to play something correctly," added Molly. "Papa, it makes me think of Leslie Lemke."

"Quite. And Blind Tom."

Chapter Thirty
Blind Tom

"I THINK BLIND TOM is the most amazing," said Molly.

"Perhaps," agreed Dr. Monaghan. "You see, Blind Tom was a slave. His parents were sold to a Georgia lawyer when Tom was a baby. Tom was, you might say, a lagniappe."

"A *what?*" I said.

"A thirteenth donut. Something given for free because you buy a dozen—in this case, his mother and father."

"That's offensive, Papa," said Molly sharply. "We're talking about slavery, not donuts."

Rebuked, he adjusted his tone. "I don't mean to make light of it, dear. But it's not every day one gets to use the word lagniappe."

"For which we can all be grateful," she judged.

Dr. Monaghan gave a long-suffering sigh. "I simply mean to underline the irony that this boy, considered of no value, would go on to earn a sum estimated at fifteen million in current dollars."

The money got my attention. "How did he do that?" I asked. "Not by working the fields."

Dr. Monahan continued, assuming the tone of a professor delivering a favorite lecture. "You are correct. Because he was blind, Tom was not expected to do any labor. He was ignored and allowed to roam the plantation and the Big House.

"Tom also suffered from what are now termed 'speech and motor delays'—he had hardly any spoken language. Yet he showed interest in sounds of all kinds—a rooster's crow, rain on the tin roof, screams of pain when he'd pull the hair of his sisters. Especially the piano. He would often be found in the music room where the Bethune daughters practiced. As a slave, it would have been unthinkable for him to touch the instrument himself, but he was permitted to listen."

Dr. Monahan knew the story so well he sounded like he was reading it from a book.

"One day, as the Bethunes enjoyed lunch, strains of the piano came to their ears. They looked around the table, taking a headcount. All players were present and accounted for."

"Papa, you don't *know* they did that," objected Molly.

"I have it on good authority they *did*," insisted Dr. Monaghan.

"*What* authority?"

"My imagination," Dr. Monaghan sniffed. "Now stop interrupting my embellishments." He went on with his story.

"They lowered their forks and listened. The song was a composition the eldest girl had played before lunch—a Chopin nocturne, quite difficult."

Molly looked exasperated. "Not an etude or sonata?" she taunted.

Her father ignored her. "Who could the performer be? Had a piano-playing intruder snuck into the mansion? A ghost, even? The family crept toward the music room to find out."

The doc was so worked-up his specs were steamed.

"Muffling his footsteps, the General led the way. Imagine his astonishment as he turned the final corner and regarded the performer.

"For there, seated at the pianoforte, was Tom—a three-year-old slave. This blind boy, who had not been allowed to even touch the instrument—whose arms could hardly reach the extremities of the keyboard—was playing Chopin as well as they'd ever heard. We can hardly imagine the shock of such a revelation—particularly in light of the widespread belief in the inferiority of Negroes," said Dr. Monaghan.

I managed to squeeze in a question. "Did they...whip him?"

"You might expect that," said Dr. Monaghan, wiping his lenses with his lab coat. "However, the Bethunes held more humane views on their chattel. And the General was no slouch as a businessman. It became evident that, like Friz, Blind Tom could reproduce complex musical pieces, with no instruction whatsoever, after hearing them a single time. Thus, he was able to assemble an extensive repertoire of songs within a few years.

"At that point, the General took young Tom on the road for a string of concerts. In one year, he earned $100,000—which now would be twenty times that sum."

"What was Tom's cut?" I asked. Dad says musicians always get cheated.

"Sadly, none," said Dr. Monaghan. "Though Tom was an extraordinary individual, he was, after all, the Bethune's slave. His earnings were not *his* earnings."

"*None* of it?" I should have known, but still I was jolted.

Dr. Sugarman put his hand on my shoulder. "It's one tiny stone in a mountain of injustice, son."

I didn't know what to say, and neither did anyone else. We were quiet a moment.

"Dr. Monaghan," I began. "I understand the concussion changed my brain. But how did it change my *hands*? How do they know what notes to play—and to do it so quickly?"

Dr. Monaghan cocked his head. "How, indeed? How can an individual who could draw no more than stick figures transform into a photorealist painter? How can lips and tongue speak a language they never learned—perhaps never even *heard*? Yet there are documented cases of savants performing these feats."

"Yeah, but this is different," I began to protest. "Muscle memory—"

"Has a strong genetic component," he interrupted. "Children of professional athletes often enjoy greater athletic success than their peers with less-gifted parents. In your case, I believe injury allowed access to brain sectors previously off-limits. We can only imagine what was stored there—conceivably, an inheritance from your ancestors. Wouldn't it be wonderful if we could pass on not just money and possessions, but all that we know and can do? I can't prove it—*yet*—but that's my explanation."

I stared at him and swallowed hard. "It sounds like science fiction."

When Dr. Monaghan grinned, he looked a lot younger than eighty-five. "It *is* science—but the cases of Blind Tom and Leslie Lemke are well-documented facts—and you do not appear to be a fictional character, Friz."

I had to laugh at that. I hesitated, then asked, "Are there more...people like me?"

"Some. Not a lot."

"Do you know them all?"

"Most of them, yes."

I had a sudden thought. "You kind of remind me of Professor Xavier."

"I've not heard of him." His brow furrowed at the unfamiliar name. "Which institution is he with?"

"*The X-Men*," I said. "He rounds up mutants and helps them learn to use their special powers."

Dr. Monaghan looked baffled. "It's a comic book, Papa," explained Molly.

"Ahhh. Popular culture," he said in a mournful voice. "Young man, I hope no one calls you names—though I fear they may. Correct them. You are a *savant*—not a *mutant*, or any similar epithet they should bestow upon you. You may tell them I said so."

"That'll strike fear into their hearts, Papa," Molly teased.

"Quite," he agreed.

On the way home, I tried to process what I'd heard.

The miracle—which had felt like fantasy—was becoming reality. Dr. Monaghan had anchored it with historical and scientific fact.

There'd been others. There *were* others.

I'd read about them on the Internet, but hearing firsthand—from a doctor whose lifework was studying savants—was different.

In a way, it was reassuring. I was not the only one of my kind. There were other mutants.

Or…*aliens*. Weren't we a bit like people from another planet?

No. We were indisputably Earthlings. So that would make us…*freaks*.

But that didn't fit. What I'd suffered was no deformity. It was a gift.

Then, in a moment, it came upon me again—the overwhelming feeling of shame—for a crime I could not identify, that I didn't remember committing…

"Mom…"

"Um-hm."

"I feel bad about something."

"Oh?" Mom glanced over at me. Unlike Mrs. Lang, she made a habit of watching the road when she was driving. "What?"

"I don't know." She was quiet, so I continued. "I can't think of anything…but something's bothering me. Like I did something wrong, but I don't know what."

We stopped at a light, and Mom turned her full attention to me. She gave me a little smile and waited. Finally, she said, "Give it time, honey. It'll come to you."

Chapter Thirty-One
Día de los Muertos

FOURTEEN WAS TOO OLD for trick-or-treating. I would miss the candy—but *not* the costumes. They were hot, uncomfortable, and embarrassing. While I knew people who enjoyed them, playing dress-up was not my idea of a good time.

This was frustrating for my mother, who had missed her true calling as a fashion designer. Mom was tolerant of my typical outfit of jeans and T-shirts. But when October rolled around, she stopped looking at me as her son, and instead considered me a model—or maybe just a seamstress's dummy. She'd squint her eyes and nod, or shake her head in disapproval. I'd learned not to take it personally.

This year, however, she'd turn her head my way and emit a woeful sigh. "They grow up so fast," she'd moan. "People say that—but you can't imagine until it happens to you." It made me feel bad I wasn't endowed with eternal youth like Peter Pan.

Mom perked up when I asked to go to a Day of the Dead party with Rah-Rah. Some rich friends from the cheerleading world were having a no-holds-barred fiesta on their estate, and Rah-Rah had scored an invitation. It was on a Saturday night, so there'd be no conflict with school, but I was still uncertain what my parents' response would be.

Dad looked to Mom for her reaction. She was smiling broadly, already lost in a world of her own imagining. Dad gave me a mournful look.

"You're in for it now, bud."

Mom turned her gaze to me. She appeared no longer in control of her actions, like the undead in zombie movies.

"Exactly when is this party?"

Since it was less than a week away, Mom had no time to waste. A blessing. It altered the objective from "creating the greatest *Día de los Muertos* costume in the history of the world" to "creating the greatest *Día de los Muertos* costume under severe time constraints." Something to remember when you deal with a perfectionist. A limited time frame ratchets the obsession down a notch.

First, she went to the thrift store and picked up a used tuxedo. I had to try it on, followed by lots of pinning and altering. Jacked-up on coffee, she'd stay up most of the night, tromping around the house and laughing at old movies that kept her company while she worked on her creation. Dad and I put in earplugs and tried our best to ride out her mania.

Mom reverted to teacher mode to school me on the significance of Day of the Dead. It seems the Aztec festival shares a superficial resemblance to Halloween, what with scary costumes and sugared-up kids—but Mexicans take their end-of-October celebration a good deal more seriously than we take our commercialized version of All Hallows' Eve. *Día* is a chance to taunt death by joyfully greeting the spirits of departed relatives, who get a twenty-four-hour hall pass from the afterlife to visit earthbound relatives. Cemeteries are packed with families tidying up graves, and homes are filled with shrines offering treats to ancestors.

Mom's respect did not dampen her creativity. She ripped out the black piping on the tuxedo and replaced it with ghoulish green satin. She found punk rocker boots with three-inch heels that were precarious for me to stand in, but had the intended effect of lengthening my legs. "Just don't go out for any passes," she advised.

She couldn't bear to deface her handiwork by painting a gaudy skeleton all over it, as was often done. But the outfit needed a touch of the macabre and Mom came up with something "inspired" for the neckwear. She created an elegant red-and-black satin noose, which stood out against a wing tip collar shirt, one of those fancy jobs people wear to give you a good look at their bow tie. In this case, it showed off what she termed her "ultimate fashion statement."

Mom fastened the noose securely around my neck like cinching a saddle on a recalcitrant horse. "Not so tight," I protested.

"Looks better tight."

"Will that be your excuse when you identify me at the morgue?" I asked.

She gave the necktie a little slack. "How's that?"

"Less lethal."

We were running late. When Rah-Rah rang the bell, Mom hadn't even started the all-important makeup. I ran to get the door and stood in shock at what I beheld.

It was *Día de los Sexy Muertos*! Brilliant red flowers were woven into Rah-Rah's flowing dark hair, which I supposed must be a wig. Her top was low-cut to accentuate a figure I had been very aware of, but it got more of my attention now. Lacy sleeves went all the way to elegant black gloves, and a long skirt was slit way up the thigh. Somehow, revealing a select portion of her beautiful legs was more provocative than seeing all of them in a cheer outfit.

"Oh, my lord," I said in a low voice.

"How you like me now?" She pirouetted on her stiletto-heeled shoes to give me the full effect. Her cadaverously made-up face grinned horribly, stretching suture lines on her lips.

"I've been thinking about something for a while," I began.

"Um-hm," she purred.

"And seeing you like this…"

"*Yes?*"

"I believe I might start calling you 'Samantha.'"

She snorted. "That's *so* much more than I expected."

"Maybe not all the time."

She gave me a dismissive wave. "You look great—but where's your makeup?"

"We're a little behind."

"I'll help," she said.

I suppose painting my face was a bonding experience for my mother and Samantha, with one or the other hissing at me to stay still. Dad came in and shook his head. "*Quatro equis*," he counted. "Doesn't get much worse, bud."

They finally let me see myself in the mirror, and it was a shock! I was no more recognizable than Samantha. I looked taller and older, transformed into a dapper cadaver-about-town. I'd not have been out of place at the Academy Awards for the deceased, and it made me blush under my makeup. Mom and Samantha seemed pleased by my stunned reaction and spent several minutes taking photos.

"Their chariot awaits," said Dad, trying to get things moving.

"Don't be home late, Cinderella," said Mom.

"Oh, we won't," said Samantha. "My mother dislikes turning into a pumpkin."

The reference to pumpkins suited the fall night we stepped into, a sweet spot between central Texas extremes of scalding summer and bone-chilling winter. Mrs. Lang glanced at us from the driver's seat and stiff-armed us like a cop halting traffic. I looked questioningly at Samantha. She heaved a sigh of immense resignation.

"She's gotta finish the chapter on her audiobook. We could be here a while."

But within a minute, I heard a click as Mrs. Lang popped the locks to admit us. Like the dead gentleman I was, I opened the door for Samantha to slide in.

Mrs. Lang looked at me appraisingly. "You clean up nicely, Friz," she said. "Seems like a ridiculous thing to say to a paira *muertos*, but fasten your seat belts."

Recalling my last ride with her, that advice struck me as gratuitous. Samantha elbowed me in the side when she buckled her belt. She caught me unprepared and I let out a whoop.

"Settle down, you two. Don't want to have an accident and end up deader'n you already are," said Mrs. Lang.

We were quiet while she navigated the southbound on-ramp to Texas Route 1. Then Mrs. Lang put pedal to the metal and carved a decisive swath across the lanes, grabbing pole position in the fastest one. I may have blanched, though my makeup would have hidden it. I'm pretty sure my eyes bugged-out. I looked over at Samantha, who was enjoying my discomfort.

"That's what Mom calls 'the swoop.'"

I nodded sagely. "Very hawk-like." My torso compressed the seatback as Mrs. Lang continued to accelerate. Then, cruising speed attained, the g-forces receded. Attempting to distract myself from her driving, I took a stab at polite conversation.

"Uh...are you enjoying your book?"

"Oh, yes," she said. "John Grisham. Have you read any of his novels?"

"Friz is allergic to bound forms of paper," sneered Samantha.

Ignoring her daughter, Mrs. Lang warmed to her subject. "I don't expect they're on the school lists, but they're wonderful. The lawyerin' part is interesting—much better to read about the legal system than to be victimized by it."

"That's what my parents say," I concurred.

"Bet they do. Wait'll they get divorced."

"Mom!" said Samantha.

"That didn't come out right. I didn't mean to imply that they were going to separate, though statistically, it's not unlikely."

"Mom, you're making it worse!"

"That could be. Lemme try again. Just saying that once lawyers get hold of two decent folks who have decided to split, they can turn a sad thing into a genuine tragedy. Seen it happen a time or two. That's my point. Take a bad thing and make it a lot worse."

The mention of "tragedy" was disconcerting. We were flicking by cars at a rate that was far from safe. I plunged on with the small talk. "Is the novel about divorce?"

"No," said Mrs. Lang, brightening. "This book is set in the jungles of Brazil. One thing I love about John Grisham is that his novels usually inform you regarding a topic about which you're ignorant."

"Which, for you, is a lot of things," Samantha muttered under her breath.

Her mother seemed not to have heard and continued. "Such as mass torts, one of his favorite subjects. He oughta take on the oil lobby. Plenty to write about there. No shortage of villains."

"My science teacher is a big fan of fossil fuels," I said.

"Popular point of view here in Texas," she sniffed.

"Mom says our state is the epicenter of climate change denial," said Samantha, rolling her eyes at me.

"Yes, I do say that. And don't roll your eyes."

"Mom, how did you see that? You should be watching the road."

"I *am*, dear. Don't have to see your face to know what you're doing with it."

Mrs. Lang held forth on Grisham's novel in detail. I found it interesting, though Samantha did not. She had a remarkable gift for expressing frustration non-verbally. Her mother was just as gifted at ignoring her.

I held up my end of the conversation, while somehow managing to reflect on the strange direction my life was taking. Here I was, dressed in a tux, flying down the highway at bank-robber-getaway speed—a spectacular girl at my side. A year ago I'd been knocking-up the neighborhood, hoping for Snickers, not suckers.

As we passed Austin, Mrs. Lang altered trajectory and made a swoop all the way to the far-right lane. I held my breath as she barely made the exit. She took a couple of turns on surface streets and we entered a ritzy neighborhood.

"Don't know how you scored an invite to Westlake," she said suspiciously.

"I *told* you, Mom. It's a cheerleading friend."

"Guess they're good for something," said Mrs. Lang. "That came out a little different than I meant it. I *am* impressed with the company you're keeping."

Mrs. Lang transitioned to sightseeing mode and drove slowly for several blocks, her head swiveling from side to side. Finally, she turned into a driveway, passing between large wrought iron gates that were open to traffic.

We followed cars as they slowly moved up a long brick road. The front lawn alone looked large enough for an entire subdivision in my neck of the woods. Finally, we got to the main house, a mansion fit for royalty.

"Nice place," said Samantha. "French prudential, I'd call it."

"*Provincial*, dear. Like us," her mother corrected. "I'd say it's 'Mediterranean.'"

"I agree," I said. Samantha gave me a scowl.

"Pick us up at midnight," she ordered her mother.

"Ten o'clock, dear." As Samantha began to howl, her mother amended. "*Eleven.*"

"On this very spot," said Samantha. She opened the door, jumped out, and slammed it shut. Following suit, I got out my side.

"Thanks for driving us, Mrs. Lang," I said, careful not to slam the door. Mrs. Lang pulled away.

Samantha regarded me like a dog who'd just dropped a steaming pile on the living room rug. "Are you planning to go to college?" she demanded.

The question took me by surprise, and I answered reflexively. "Yeah, I guess…"

"I can't imagine why. You already got a PhD in brown nosing my mom."

Chapter Thirty-Two
Noche de los Muertos

WE PASSED THROUGH massive front doors along with several other ghouls and entered a palatial foyer. It featured enough marble to have emptied a small quarry, with pedestals set up to display artworks that looked plenty expensive. I reverted to the habit of infancy, stuffing hands in pockets to avoid accidentally breaking anything.

Samantha and I flitted through the house, like flies looking for a place to land. It was filled with people dressed-to-impress in *Noche de los Muertos* fashion. With outfits and makeup concealing identities, the scene had an eerie vibe that was disturbing.

There were plenty of clues this gala was not targeted at the teenage demographic. The women's outfits made Samantha's racy attire look prudish, showing more skin than an undertaker would see in a lifetime. The men loomed over me, and they didn't need lifts to attain their height. Then there was the booze.

Wine and beer flowed freely, and liquor bottles of every type were on display. A crowd massed around a margarita fountain decorated with daisies and marigolds, shooting up streams of yellow-orange-green liquid to splatter down in a giant cauldron. The air was thick with lime-scented fog, and I thought I might get a buzz just from breathing. Nearby stood a large display of all kinds of tequila, presided over by a skeleton man wearing a sombrero so big it looked like a flattened umbrella balanced on his skull.

"Are you sure we're supposed to be here?" I asked nervously.

"Chill, dude. We just have to find my people. Let's try outside," said Samantha.

I followed her through French doors to an enormous swimming pool, whose far edge fell into space, appearing to meld with the Colorado River flowing toward the skyline of Austin in the distance. Skeletons took their ease on chaise lounges. An actual skiff floated in the pool, manned by a fisherman in Mexican peasant dress, who rhythmically raised and lowered a large net into the water.

I wandered toward a couple sitting on a lounge. The man's tuxedo was covered in a gush of crimson from his severed jugular, while the woman next to him wore a headdress of brilliant plumage, like a deathly Vegas dancer. They looked up at me expectantly.

"What's that guy doing?" I asked, gesturing to the boatman in the pool.

"Fishing," said the man, stating the obvious.

"For *what*?"

"Souls, darling. Have you got one he could catch?" teased the woman, bursting into a throaty laughter that chilled me.

"I don't think so."

"Don't be shy. I'm sure he'd negotiate. We all have our price."

Samantha led me away, with the woman's spooky laughter ringing in my ears.

I don't know what was most troubling about all of this—the nightmare setting, the ridiculous wealth, the feeling that I was totally out of place—or this creepy reference to selling my soul. There it was again, haunting me.

We roamed from the fisher of souls to the surrounding grounds. Fictitious tombstones had been set up, transforming the expansive lawns into a graveyard for prominent Texans and Mexicans—Sam

Houston, Lyndon Johnson, Ima Hogg, Buddy Holly, Pancho Villa, Diego Rivera, and the like. I had run out of superlatives and fell back on my trademark, "wow."

I couldn't help saying it again as we caught sight of several partygoers who had not received Mom's memo on the cultural significance of the event. They were urinating at the foot of one of the tombstones.

"Too much beer or something weirder?" asked Samantha when we went to investigate.

"Gotta do it, man, says to," said a tall guy who had a pair of scissors sticking out of his neck.

We bent over to read the tombstone, which identified it as the resting place of the number one Texas boogeyman, the Mexican General Santa Anna, who led the assault on the Alamo.

The epitaph read: "I shit on y'all. Now y'all piss on me."

"I'll pass, not piss," said Samantha.

"How about you, bro?" invited a skull-masked guy, tucking himself back in. "Join the party."

"I'll be back," I said. "Gotta load the shotgun."

"Good call, bro! Mine's a Mossberg. I'm giving it both barrels," said a third guy, relieving himself liberally. He had a Frankenstein bolt coming out of his neck.

"Mossberg? Shit, I got a Bellini," said scissor neck.

"No way your johnson's Italian," retorted skull mask.

"*Mine* is. It's a Guerini. Better than a Bellini," said Frankenstein bolt.

"Not *better*—just five times as expensive," said scissor neck.

"If you have to ask the price, you can't afford it. Am I right, babe?" said Frankenstein bolt, shaking his crotch at Samantha.

"Whatever," she growled, repulsed, pulling me away. When we got clear, she observed, "Exhibit one that firearms are phallic symbols."

"I assume you're in favor of gun control?" I replied.

She cackled and we continued to wander. Eventually we came to a flatter expanse of lawn. There, illuminated by the full moon, we found Samantha's tribe. Several skeletons were doing tumbling passes through the grass, and I thought I recognized the transcendent moves of Dre as he soared high into the air.

"Finally!" exclaimed Samantha, bursting from me to greet them. I approached more leisurely, and by the time I arrived, Samantha had found who she was looking for. She rushed to introduce me to a petite girl whose face was etched with makeup cobwebs. Spiders dangled from her earlobes, and she had a choker of skeleton hands clutching her neck.

"Friz, this is my friend Jordan. It's her party."

"Nice to meet you," I said. "Thanks for inviting us."

"Glad you could come."

"This is…incredible," I said. "I've never been to a place like this."

She gestured at the grounds dismissively. "The house that Rebo built."

"Rebo?" asked Samantha.

"A boring little program no one's heard of, but everyone uses," she said. "That's how Daddy puts it. Says it's the second-best way to become a billionaire."

"I'll bite," I said. "What's the *best* way?"

She batted her eyelashes playfully. "Be *born* one." She gave her head a little shake, and the spiders' eyes glittered as they caught the moonlight.

"Are those diamonds in your earrings?" I asked.

"I expect so," she replied off-handedly. "Are you a cheerleader, too?"

"No, Friz is a civilian," Samantha answered for me. She seemed a little curt, and I realized that Jordan might be flirting with me, a bizarre occurrence.

"Won't hold that against you," she said, with a smile that leapfrogged friendly. I looked away, but she grabbed me by the noose. "Nice neckware, Friz."

Startled, I met her gaze. She measured me like a trout on the line. I didn't pass the legal limit, so she threw me back with a smirk. "Mind shooting pictures?" she asked cooly. "We're gonna do some routines." She handed me her iPhone and cartwheeled away.

Having a job calmed me down. Photographing the creepy cheerleaders was the most comfortable I'd been all night. For the next half hour, I shot stills and video as they did their routines.

Time after time, Samantha flew high into the air, spinning and landing in a skeleton-armed basket. Jordan was a flyer, too, and side-by-side she performed the same tricks as Samantha atop a second pyramid. They did a sequence of poses, the girls alternately calling them out—"*Arabesque!*" "*Scorpion!*" "*Bow and Arrow!*" "*Needle!*" "*Chin Chin!*" I snapped furiously, hoping I was getting good stuff. Unlikely there'd ever been such a cheerleading display, or ever would be again.

They took a break, popping water bottles from a cooler out on the grass. As they caught their breaths, a familiar guitar riff filled the air.

"Is that...?" one of the cheerleaders started.

"ZZ Top?" Jordan finished. "Uh-huh. Must be starting up." This came as a surprise to everyone, who just stared at her. "They're at the bandstand down yonder," she added, gesturing.

The pack of cheerleaders lit out in that direction, running, handspringing, and flipping to cover the distance. I returned Jordan's phone and Samantha grabbed my hand as we jogged toward the music.

By the time we got there, a crowd of partygoers had assembled around a stage. Spotlights illuminated three musicians. The guitarists looked like odd twins, with identical flowing beards, dark glasses, and fedoras. They wore skeleton tuxedos to get with the night's theme, but no makeup, since beards and glasses covered their entire faces. The drummer had only a moustache and was made up like the rest of the *Noche de los Muertos* crowd, presiding over his kit with the energy of the undead.

They made a lot of noise for a trio, cranking out a string of tunes that were well-known, even to me. Talking was out of the question, so Samantha and I communicated by smiles, nods, and gestures.

One of the guitarists took extended solos on each song, and those got my attention.

During a break between songs, I asked Samantha, "Who's playing lead?"

"ZZ Top's all I know," she answered.

A guy nearby overheard. "That's Billy Gibbons, man."

"Pretty good," I said.

Samantha leaned in close and whispered a question in my ear. "Can *you* play like that?"

I considered—and nodded. What he was doing was catchy, but not that technically difficult.

Her eyes got wide. "*Like ZZ Top?*"

"Yeah. No biggie."

"Uh-huh. Yeah, right."

Her tone surprised me. The words didn't sound like the teasing I'd become accustomed to, but something different. Dismissive. *She didn't believe me.*

The band started the next number, a slow blues song. Billy Gibbons's lead work was soulful and understated. I liked it. Admired it.

And I could sure play it.

Samantha's scorn cut me. I had no idea how this strange power

138

had come to me, whether it was a freak of nature or a bargain with the devil.

But it was time to collect on my end of the deal.

Chapter Thirty-Three
The King Lounge

I'LL TAKE THE RAP for what happened next, though at the time I had no clue. Lord, I *hate* it when Mom is right! She's always railing about men's fragile egos—and, damn, it's *so*. Turns out a woman's scorn stings, even at fourteen. It's not that I didn't believe Friz—though it *was* unbelievable. Mainly I was reacting to Jordan giving him the eye. I was feeling hurt, so I hurt him.

I'm also gonna blame it on the costumes we were wearing. Criminals put on masks to hide identities—but being disguised has got to affect their behavior as well. Make them act even worse than they normally would. It's done that to me.

I had a pal named Marcie when I was little. She'd come over to play and we'd dress up in Mom's clothes, put on jewelry, clomp around in heels, do fashion shows. Folks thought we were cute.

We'd pack suitcases and roll from room to room, pretending we were going on a grand tour of Europe. On the way to Italy, we'd layover in the kitchen and have a snack. We'd put on bikinis and go out to the French Riviera, our patio.

One day I took twenty bucks from Mom's purse so we'd have spending money for our spree abroad. It was the make-believe made me do it. Think that's what happened to me and Friz that night.

One minute we were standing with the crowd, listening to

music—and the next minute he was fumbling out his wallet and pulling a card from it. He turned away from the band and began to fight his way through the mob. I followed after.

"What are you doing?" I yelled when we got clear.

"Going."

"Obviously. But why?" He seemed more determined than angry.

"Gotta see a guy. Jackson Greens."

"*Where?*"

"King Lounge," he said. He handed me the card. I paused to read it by moonlight. The address was in Austin.

He stopped to wait for me. "C'mon," he yelled, and I ran to catch up.

"Do you even know where this is?" I objected.

"Good point." He pulled out his phone. "Gimme the address."

I read it to him while he typed into his cell. "Twelve minutes away. That's close. Do you have an Uber account?"

"Yeah…it's on my mom's Visa." I added, "*For emergencies.*"

He considered a moment. "This is an emergency."

Friz started walking, but I didn't. Sometimes a girl's just gotta dig in her heels and say, "Whoa, there, boy." After a moment my hoss trotted back. "Are you sure about this?" I asked as calmly as I could.

"Yes," he answered. I waited for details. "It's only eight. We have time to see this guy, get some answers, and be back before your mom comes to pick us up."

I weighed the proposition. "Hey, we're already dead," he added. "What else could happen to us?"

I had to laugh. "All right," I agreed. "But we have to leave by ten-thirty."

"Sure."

"At the *latest*." I gave him a hard look for emphasis.

"Does your mom check her bill?" *Now* he sounded worried.

I thought about Mom going over her statements with a calculator and a glass of wine. "Obsessive-compulsively. And sometimes, drunkenly."

"What're you gonna tell her?"

I'd gotten away with that twenty. Figured I could get away with this.

"She just paid it. The Uber won't show up 'til next month, and I'll think of something by then," I said.

It took longer than twelve minutes to get there. Friz and I sat in silence, exchanging nervous glances as we got farther from where we were supposed to be. I took his hand. The night was shaping up to be even more adventurous than I'd expected.

The Uber driver slowed as he drove down a residential street and turned into a broad alley. Several pickups were parked on a patch of brown grass next to a rundown house. The big sign in front identified it as The King Lounge.

"Not what I expected," said Friz, taken aback.

The driver gave him a dirty look. "Blues club, man. Not the Ritz."

Friz tipped him and we got out. The Uber pulled away and we stood a moment, observing a couple approach the club entrance. The doorman checked their IDs and waved them in.

"So what's the plan?" I demanded. After all, this was his idea.

"Plan?"

"To get inside." I tried for a level tone, but my annoyance bled through. "They're gonna card us."

Friz thought for a moment. "Don't suppose you have a fake ID."

I shook my head no. "Didn't think I'd need one for a few more years. You're a corrupting influence."

He ignored that, and moved on to plan B. "How about a pen?"

"Well, MacGyver, amazingly I *do* have one of those." I opened the little clutch purse I'd carried to look grown-up and pulled out a ballpoint. "Certainly hope you're not making a bomb."

"Could, if you have lipstick." I said I didn't, and he tsk-tsked. He pulled the card from his pocket and scrawled something on it. "Let's see if this does any good."

We approached the doorman, a burly bald guy with a scruffy beard, seated on a stool. He looked at us and raised his eyebrows.

"Day of the Dead party," I explained.

"Oh. Thought y'all were trick-or-treaters."

"Candy's dandy but blues're better," said Friz.

"Amen," said the doorman. "IDs?"

"Forgot 'em," said Friz.

The doorman gestured that his hands were tied. "No ticky, no laundry."

"But we got this." Friz showed the man the card. "We're friends of Jackson Greens. Told me to come see him. He signed the back."

The doorman flipped the card over and peered at the back. He shone a penlight on the scrawl. "That's Jackson's mark?"

"Yessir," said Friz with confidence. The doorman looked up from the card and studied him.

"Jackson's on now. He's good people."

"He is," agreed Friz. "Met him when he was playing at a football game last week."

The doorman chuckled. "Yeah, told me he did Thetis a favor. Matter of fact, he said a kid there played 'Little Wing' like—" The doorman broke off and looked at Friz with renewed interest. "*You* that kid?" he asked in a low voice.

"Couldn't have been *me*," Friz said unconvincingly. "*I'm* not a kid."

The doorman flicked the card back and forth, considering. He looked at me.

"*I'm* thirty-five."

He snorted, amused. "In *dog* years. Sit in the back, you two. When the waitress asks what you'll have, you say 'Nothing.' You *do* have cash, doncha?"

"We do," said Friz.

"Good. Tip the waitress ten bucks."

"Ten bucks for *nothing?*" I protested.

"Ten bucks for sittin' at her table. S'how she makes a livin'. *Respect.*"

"Got it," I said. "*Respect.*"

The doorman nodded. "I don't wanta see no liquids in front of you. Not even water."

"Yessir," said Friz.

"All right, now. Go ahead. Band'll break soon, and you can talk to Jackson."

The club would have been unimpressive under any circumstance—but considering we were coming from the mother of all estates—this place seemed especially pitiful. The room wasn't much more than a long, low, stuffy box. The bar on the back wall was inhabited by characters who looked seedier than the pseudo-dead at the party. Guttering candles on the tables dented the gloom, but most of the light came from spots on the no-frills bandstand. The neon sign on the wall behind it that proclaimed "The King" struck me as sarcastic. The place made me nervous. It reeked of stale beer and sweat.

The staff was young—didn't seem much older than Friz and me—dressed in cut-offs and T-shirts, despite the time of year. A trio was playing—guitar, bass, and drums. They finished a number to mild applause from the crowd, which half-filled the place.

Following the doorman's instructions, we took a seat in the back, as far from the bandstand as possible. Friz blew out the candle on the table, making it even darker.

The waitress approached with a lighter. "Let me get that for you," she said.

"Don't bother," said Friz. "We prefer the dark."

"Okaaaaay," she agreed, looking us over. "What would you like?"

"Nothing for now," said Friz.

"Uh...water?"

"Maybe later," I said, with an apologetic smile.

Friz put a ten-dollar bill on the table and pushed it toward her. "We're good."

She looked at him, bewildered, and picked up the tip. "Well, thanks," she said, still confused. She walked off shaking her head.

"So far, so good," I said. "Which one is your friend?"

"Drummer."

I peered at the hunched figure, tapping out a rhythm on the snare. "Looks old."

"Uh-huh." He seemed lost in thought.

"I should have asked this sooner," I started. Friz looked at me. "What exactly are we doing here?"

He gave a little laugh and admitted, "I'm not sure."

"You're not." Friz was acting strange, but he looked confident. Unconcerned.

The band played a slow blues number. The bass player sang lyrics about an evil woman who'd done him wrong, but he didn't look like no angel, himself. His voice sounded like a tumbler filled with grit and rocks trying to wear themselves smooth. The guitarist took a long solo and did a good job convincing he was miserable. Friz had closed his eyes, a little smile turning up the corners of his mouth, as he nodded to the beat.

"Folks, we're gonna take a short break," announced the guitarist.

The house music came up and I looked over, but Friz was already on his feet.

"Be right back," he said, heading toward the bandstand. Before he could reach it, the players went out the door. His friend didn't even glance at him—and if he had, he wouldn't have recognized Friz in his *Día de los Muertos* get-up.

Friz stood next to the bandstand. He looked at where the players had disappeared, looked over at me, looked at the bandstand, looked back at me. I couldn't imagine what he was thinking. Then in a few steps he was on the bandstand, picking up the guitar.

I glanced around at other patrons to see how they would react, but everyone was ignoring him. "*What are you doing?*" I wanted to yell. But I stayed glued to my seat.

I watched him adjust the strap and sling it over his shoulder.

He got comfortable, closed his eyes…and then he started to play.

The lead whined out, competing with the house music, as his fingers raced up and down the guitar neck. It was fast and clean and commanded attention. That's what he got—within seconds, everyone was watching.

Several people exclaimed in surprise. As Friz let the last note hang in the air, I saw the doorman step in and take in the scene. "Kill the house music," he yelled to the bartender. Expectant silence descended on the room.

Friz looked straight at me. When he began again, I realized what we were doing there.

It was the ZZ Top song—the one I'd doubted he could play. I hadn't meant anything by it—but he was sure showin' me. And everyone else in the place.

This was the first time I'd seen him play the guitar. It could hardly have been more dramatic.

The crowd was loving it, murmuring in surprise and recognition.

Friz kept on, adding to the solo, seeing Billy Gibbons and raising him big time.

Then I saw the guitarist pass through the entrance and come to a halt. It was too far and too dark for me to read his facial expression, but his body language was all expletives. Oblivious, Friz played on.

He wound up the solo, and the crowd, small as it was, erupted in applause, cheering and whistling. Friz looked sheepish and attempted a bow. Then he returned the guitar to its stand and exited the stage.

Before he could take a step, the guitar player was at his side. He clamped his arm around Friz and led him out of the club.

Chapter Thirty-Four
Little Willie Reed

THAT GUITAR PLAYER was old and not big, but he was strong. He had my arm locked in a tight grip, forcing me to come along. I didn't resist.

It didn't take long, but still I had time to reflect on what I'd done. How fast I'd forgotten my first lesson: do *not* use a man's axe to cut him to ribbons!

The guitar player pushed me into a bathroom and slammed the door behind him. I glanced around at a toilet and a sink, neither of them too clean. I looked at the guitar player, who was breathing heavily, glaring at me.

"Wash that shit off," he said.

"What?"

"Your *face*. Wanta see it."

I'd forgotten about the makeup. I bent over the sink, turned the water on, and soaped up. I washed with vigor but little effect, like trying to remove a thick layer of crayon. Water wasn't the solvent the job called for.

"Uh…I think you need makeup remover for this."

"*Makeup remover?*" he said, wrinkling his nose. "This look like the cosmetics department? Just rub, dammit!" He ripped paper towels from the dispenser and shoved them at me.

I scrubbed and my reddened face emerged from beneath its ghostly pallor. The guitar player watched over my shoulder, the mirror reflecting his alarmed reaction.

"You just a boy!" I made my eyes woeful, but he hardened. "Still oughta know better'n to shit a man's house."

"Uh…whose house is this?" I asked as politely as possible.

"Son…you can tell 'em was Little Willie Reed who done cut you."

I heard a "snick" and glimpsed the flash of a blade.

The next part happened fast.

Before my adrenalin could surge, Willie had my noose-tie in one hand and the blade at my cheek. The bathroom door swung open. Willie paused and turned to see Jackson Greens enter. Jackson took in the scene at a glance and gave Willie a wry smile.

"Shoulda locked the door."

"Stay outta this, Jackson," Willie warned. "Not your business."

"It *is*," said Jackson. "Boy come lookin' for me."

"Well, he found *me*. Ain't gonna forget me, neither."

"Ease up now, Willie." Jackson gave a little gesture, and I noticed a small pistol in his hand. Willie saw it, too.

"Naw…you ain't gonna pull the rider on me, Jackson." He seemed more disappointed than afraid.

A corner of Jackson's mouth twitched upward. "Don't believe in no fair fights. Do *you*?"

"Um-um."

Neither man moved. I couldn't help asking, "Is that what it means?" I sang the lyric from "Crossroads." "'*Take my rider by my side.*' Is a rider a *gun*?"

Little Willie started chuckling first. The blade closed with a "snick" and the knife was deftly pocketed. Just as fast, Jackson joined him in laughter, and the gun vanished up his sleeve.

Little Willie threw an arm over my shoulder. "You is one green muthafucka, man."

I apologized for my bad behavior. Willie did too, saying he hadn't intended to cut me, just to scare me—which he *had* accomplished. We agreed it was best that what happened in the bathroom, stayed in the bathroom.

When we joined Samantha at our table, Jackson and Little Willie were in the best of moods, taking a trip down memory lane.

"Boy is lucky you ain't the Wolf," Jackson said to Willie.

"Big bad wolf?" I asked.

"*Howlin'* Wolf," said Willie. "Man was big and bad-tempered."

"See that?" Jackson hiked up his shirt to show a scar on his side. "Wolf cut me during a session in Memphis back in '62. Said I was lagging."

"*Was* you?" asked Willie.

Jackson shrugged. "Mighta been."

Willie laughed. "Wolf didn't never cut me, but he knocked me flat one time. Said I was *playin'* flat."

"*Was* you?" asked Jackson.

Willie shrugged. "Mighta been."

They chuckled softly. "Wolf, he had a good ear," said Jackson.

Willie nodded. "Bad temper—but *helluva* good ear."

Samantha was looking between them, trying to figure what this had to do with me. Instead of explaining, I introduced her.

"Willie Reed," said the guitarist, shaking.

The drummer took his turn. "Jackson Greens." He looked to me. "Man you come to see. Best get at it, 'fore the break ends."

Now that it was time, I felt foolish. It seemed an absurd thing to even bring up. But I plunged ahead. "So, that thing you said to me…it's been on my mind. About the devil…"

"Uh-huh."

"Were you serious? Do you think I sold my soul to play the guitar?"

"Is *that* what we're doing here?" exploded Samantha before Jackson could answer. "You told me you were Catholic, but this—! Where are we going next, the *exorcist*?" She took a breath and glared at me. With her spooky makeup, she was intimidating. "The doctors gave you a medical explanation! Why isn't that good enough?!"

"Because…" I struggled to organize feelings and half-formed thoughts. "What happened to me…I don't think it just…*happened to me*. I think it happened for a reason."

Samantha and I looked at each other warily.

"What're the young'uns fussin' about?" Willie asked Jackson.

The drummer considered his partner. "Y'ever hear a kid play like this boy?"

Willie shook his head. "Didn't hear young Stevie Ray, though."

"That ain't the main thing," said Jackson pointedly. "Show him your hand," he said to me. By now I was used to the drill. I extended my left hand to Willie. "Feel it."

He took my palm. "You got some soft hands, honey."

"The *frettin' part*, Willie!"

Willie chuckled and ran his finger over the tips of mine. He tilted his head quizzically. "Hmmmmm."

"Um-hm," said Jackson. "Boy been playing guitar—what—*two* weeks, now?"

"About," I admitted.

"That ain't *right!*" said Willie, thrusting my hand away. He stared at Jackson, his mouth ajar.

"'Member that story about Robert Johnson? Deal with the devil, all that?"

Willie made a face. "Don't much credit that mess. Kinda thing ignorant folk believe."

"Right," said Samantha, thoroughly indignant. "Tell them what the doctors said."

So I gave the medical play-by-play with Samantha doing color commentary. We threw in the part about Blind Tom, though not as hammy as the Dr. Monaghan version.

"Ever heard of that guy?" Willie asked Jackson.

"Naw. Played with a few blind guys, but no one named Tom."

"Maybe because he died, like, a hundred years ago," said Samantha.

"What do you think?" I asked Jackson.

He licked his lips, took a breath to speak, then blew it out in a huff. With the last of the exhalation, he said weakly, "Lotta things I can't explain…"

Then he went on in a stronger voice, "But ain't no call to drag the devil into it. Sorry I ever said that to you." He put his hand on my shoulder and added, "Sure didn't mean to fret you, son."

Willie was eager to weigh-in. "Whatever nonsense they tell about Robert Johnson, wasn't no football and brain injury in the tale. This a different deal." He got up from the table. "Break's over."

"Wanta sit in?" Jackson asked.

"*Me?*" I said.

"Why not?" said Willie. "Crowd like you." I studied his face for any lingering resentment and found none.

"I don't know too many songs," I said, indecisive.

"You'll catch on," said Jackson, hastening to reassure me. "Devil or no, gotta use your gift. Means playing with musicians every chance you get."

I looked to Samantha. "I *know* you didn't drag me here for one measly tune. Go on! Get up there, you silly superstitious savant!" She gave me a shove that left no doubt about her opinion on the matter.

I walked toward the stage with the two men. Willie nudged me with his shoulder. "Had a gal like that once. Made me say, 'I do.'" He gave me a meaningful dip of the brow.

"But you *didn't*," said Jackson.

Willie grinned and spread his arms defensively. "For a while, I *did*."

"For a while, we *all* do," said Jackson. "Until we *don't*."

I pondered what in the world they were chuckling over as we stepped on stage to join the bass player. The crowd buzzed, reacting to me without makeup. Willie took a guitar from a case, plugged it into the amp, and handed it to me.

"So," said Willie. "Reckon you know 'Crossroads.'" I smiled ruefully and nodded.

Jackson counted off and we started.

Performing on stage with another guitarist was a new experience, but it was like eating chips. I sensed when we were going to play together...when it was time for me to lay back and let Willie solo...and when it was time for me to step up and take one of my own. We kept at it after we'd run through the standard verses, until finally Willie brought it back to the original melody. I followed his lead and we finished in unison.

The crowd applauded and Willie introduced the members of the band. When he got to me, he said, "And—*damn*! I don't know this boy's name!"

The crowd laughed and I whispered to him. "*What?*" he said, grimacing. I repeated it, and he announced, "Say his name is 'Friz Collins.' Boy can play a little, huh?" The crowd clapped and whistled. "Say he don't know many songs. But I bet he know a nursery rhyme."

More cheers, and Willie launched into a couple bars I recognized as "Mary Had a Little Lamb." I listened until I got it, then joined in.

This song flowed like a downhill torrent and the house loved it. Willie pointed me toward the rapids and I shot through, visualizing a course my fingers navigated with ease. I had no more idea than anyone what I was going to play next, and we were all surprised together.

When the song ended, I tried to make out Samantha sitting at our table in the back, but the cocktail waitress blocked my view. When she moved, there was Sam, clapping like a crazy dead girl.

But it was the living, breathing person next to her that made my heart hiccough.

That person was Samantha's mother.

Chapter Thirty-Five
Viral

I WAS AWARE of folks hollering for another number, but most of my attention focused on Mrs. Lang, struggling to imagine how she had tracked us down! We hadn't been here an hour, and we were busted. Totally.

I slung the guitar over my head and set it on its stand. I stepped offstage and made my way through the tables to where Samantha and Mrs. Lang sat in back. Dazed, I slapped hands and smiled at people as I passed. A guy held out paper and pen. I looked at him questioningly.

"Slide me your John Hancock, bro!"

"My *what?*"

"Your autograph. Date it, too. Could be my nest egg."

I scrawled my name on the paper and handed it back to him. "Don't quit your day job."

He smirked at the thought. "Ha! *What* day job?"

When I got back to the table, Samantha gave me a mischievous smile. "Please, can I have your autograph, Mr. Clapton?"

"Now don't start."

"I don't know *where* to start," said Mrs. Lang, standing up. "We're headin' home."

She led the way, with Samantha and me following. People were still thrusting paper and pen in my direction. Mrs. Lang caught my eye, so I gave apologetic looks and kept moving forward.

The doorman hit me a gentle pound at the exit. "You done good, man."

"Thanks," I mumbled—but our tender moment ended as a pickup took the turn off the main route at screeching high speed. Kicking up gravel and dust, it ground to a stop in front of us. Watching it, the doorman turned somber.

"Who's that?" asked Samantha, eyeing the truck.

"The owner. Wasn't supposed to be here tonight."

"Neither was I," commented Mrs. Lang. She looked at us wryly. "Neither were *you*."

An enormous man squeezed out of the pickup's cab. He was stretched in all directions, wearing a wrinkled suit with an untucked dress shirt, as if he'd barely had time to throw on clothes. Waves of curly dark hair erupted from under a red Longhorns baseball cap. "Jared, hold that kid!" he hollered.

"Will do," called the bouncer.

"Is he mad?" I whispered.

"Hard to say," Jared whispered back.

The owner was breathing hard when he got to us. He had a large solid head and jowls like a clean-shaved bulldog. His mouth hung open and a big red tongue lolled out as he panted, "Armand... Bab...Babineaux. Own...the place."

"Catch your breath," Mrs. Lang urged. Mr. Babineaux nodded. Hands on hips, he inhaled loudly through his nostrils, like wind rushing through a narrow canyon. I gave him the "hook 'em horns" sign with both hands. He smiled and weakly hooked me back with one hoof.

"Sorry for the trouble," I started. He waved me off, so I doubled down. "*Very* sorry."

Mr. Babineaux exhaled in a rush, and managed, "No trouble."

"No trouble?" asked Samantha, surprised.

His smile was broad. "Best night in months—*years*."

"If you don't have a heart attack," said Mrs. Lang.

"You weren't even here," Samantha objected. "How do you know?"

Mr. Babineaux was breathing more easily. "Bartender called me, told me what was going on. Held the phone for me to listen. Got here fast as I could."

"Obviously," said Mrs. Lang. "But I'm afraid we have to be leaving."

Before we could, Mr. Babineaux extended his hand and I took it. I have large hands for a kid—but I watched mine disappear inside his and wondered if I'd ever see it again.

"I know, I'm part gorilla. Can't even get 'em in my pants." Releasing my hand, he measured his against his trouser pocket to show the misfit. He could just as well have shoved it into a baby mitten. "Why I wear a jacket—so I got someplace to put my keys."

"Very resourceful," said Mrs. Lang. Mr. Babineaux hadn't won her over, but he didn't seem to notice. His focus hadn't wavered from me.

"Listen, kid—you're always welcome. Any time you want to play, do it at The King. *Mi casa es su casa, comprende?*"

"*Sí*," I said.

"*Adios*," said Mrs. Lang, and led us toward the parking lot.

Samantha and I were quiet in the back seat, waiting for Mrs. Lang to make the first move. She weighed her opening gambit as she got on the highway and found her preferred lane.

"So," she said at last, "my daughter tells me you're a savior."

"*Savant*, Mom," Samantha snapped back.

"Excuse me, dear, I'm not familiar with the term."

"It's from the French word *savoir*—to know something," said Sam.

"Well, pardon my French, or lack thereof. I took Spanish in high school. I don't know squat about savants."

"You haven't read about them in a Grisham book?"

For once Samantha hit a nerve. "Don't get snarky, m'dear, when you're the one who went running off to a club you had no business in!"

Before Samantha could craft a rejoinder, I managed to sneak one in. "Yeah, how'd you find us?" I tried for a tone that didn't sound like I was groveling.

"Uber receipt," said Mrs. Lang. "I check my inbox frequently."

"*Neurotically*," said Samantha. She looked at me and whispered, "Didn't think about an email receipt."

Mrs. Lang ignored her daughter. "As I say, I'm not familiar with this topic, Friz. Would you be so good as to enlighten me a bit?"

"Uh...okay," I said. Samantha gave me a long-suffering look. She must've had more than enough of this story, but it was the only one I had.

Mom and Dad invited Samantha and Mrs. Lang in, offering coffee.

"Don't touch it after four p.m.," said Mrs. Lang. "It has a half-life of five hours."

"Wasn't aware of that," said Dad, amused. "How about a glass of wine? Alcohol metabolizes pretty quick."

"Now that'd be fine."

"Red, white...?"

"Red, I guess. It's heart-healthy."

Dad left to fetch drinks and the rest of us took seats in the living room. We regarded one another awkwardly. I didn't know about Samantha, but it had been a while since I'd been in trouble and I wasn't enjoying the feeling.

"So…what happened to your makeup?" Mom asked me.

"It's a long story."

"What we're here for," encouraged Mrs. Lang.

"Yeah," said Samantha. "You know how Mom loves her stories."

It felt like the noose around my neck had tightened and I tugged to loosen it. Relating anything resembling the true bathroom incident was sure to provoke parental panic, but I was poor at lying on the fly. Fortunately, Dad arrived with wine for the adults and sodas for Samantha and me. He distributed drinks and raised his in a toast.

"Not how we planned it, but…here's to Friz's first gig. And many more to come."

"Cheers, I guess," said Mom, and we all drank.

"Mrs. Lang, we're awful sorry for the trouble our son has put you through," Dad continued. "'Specially when you fetched him all the way to Austin for that Day of the Dead thing."

"Oh, that's nothing," said Mrs. Lang with a dismissive wave. "But I coulda used a heads-up on this rock star deal. Caught me by surprise."

"Us, too," said Mom. "You know how children are. One day they won't eat peas—next day they love 'em."

"Hard to stay a step ahead of the little darlings," agreed Mrs. Lang, taking a big gulp of wine. "I'm waiting for Samantha to sprout wings so she actually *can* fly."

Samantha snapped the La-Z-Boy to a full horizontal recline, which felt like a form of protest. "Does this thing massage?"

"Afraid not," said Dad. "It's the entry level model."

Annoyed, she snapped it back upright.

"Tense, dear?" asked Mrs. Lang. Receiving no response, she continued to my parents, "When I saw that Uber receipt pop up, I thought to give daughter a jingle. Went straight to voice mail. Texted her. No response. Hmmmm. Had the address. Plugged it into the nav system and lit out, curious to see where I'd wind up. Tried not to worry."

She took a big swallow of wine, but no one interrupted. Mrs. Lang was on a roll.

"Divey blues joint. Now, that was a head-scratcher, all right. But I went in, looked around, and sure enough, there was daughter, sitting at a table in the back. Alone. Didn't see your son. I just hung there, watching Sam a minute, thinking how I was gonna handle this one. Relieved, y'know, and of course, mad. Taking stock. Trying to figure it out."

I looked out of the corner of my eye at Samantha, who was listening despite herself.

Mrs. Lang swirled her wine and continued. "Here she was, blowing off a billionaire's party to sneak into a club. How did that figure? I wondered how she'd pulled it off. Why she'd do such a thing. No drinks on the table, so she musta had another reason. Never glanced my way—eyes just riveted to that stage. Finally, I looked over at what she was looking at—and it all came together."

Blaring trumpets erupted from my pocket, startling everyone. Then came the cymbal crashes. My NFL Monday Night Football ring tone wasn't an optimal choice for the occasion. I looked to Dad, who pursed his lips.

"Take it," said Samantha, resigned. "Tonight's all about *you*."

I checked the caller ID before answering. "Hey, Jamarie," I said.

"Yo, dude, you're famous."

"Totally," said someone else.

"Who's that?" I asked, confused by the different voices.

"Four-way, bro," said Jamarie. "Me, Zach, and Tyrell here."

"Hey, Friz," they choroused.

"Hi, guys," I answered. "Uh…what do you mean, I'm famous?" I realized Samantha and the adults were listening intently.

"YouTube, man," said Zach.

"Why ain't you tell us, bro?" demanded Jamarie.

"I don't even know what you're talking about."

"Dude, you're at some club and totally shredding! It's sick!" said Tyrell.

"The clip is awesome," agreed Zach. "It's getting like a bazillion hits."

"Naw…"

"Oh, yeah, Friz. You gone viral," said Jamarie.

"I guess I better see this thing."

"Google your ass. It'll pop right up," said Tyrell, laughing like a maniac. My buddies were sure excited.

"All right. Later," I said.

"Call me back," prodded Jamarie.

"Yeah, okay, maybe. Little busy right now," I said, glancing around the living room.

"I imagine," said Jamarie, as I hung up.

"So…what is it we oughta see?" asked Samantha wearily.

Dad was already booting his laptop. "I guess just type my name in on YouTube."

Dad typed and hit enter. "Eureka," he said. The video loaded right away.

We gathered to get a look at the small screen. "Posted tonight, all right," said Mrs. Lang.

Dad gave a whistle. "Over eight thousand views." He refreshed the screen. "Now eleven more." He refreshed again. "Another dozen."

Mom interrupted before he could do it again. "Bill, we get the point. Let's watch the clip."

Dad clicked the play button and the video started. It was tight on the band at The King Lounge, with me in the center.

"I didn't see any film crew in the club," I protested.

"Are you kidding?" said Samantha. She waved her cell in the air. "Citizen journalist. Every person in that place had a smart phone. Any one of them could've shot it."

I nodded, stunned, and watched the rest of the video in silence. It was even stranger to see myself performing than to be doing it. The song wound up and Willie introduced the band. It felt like déjà vu—because it literally *was*—to hear his words. "Say his name is 'Friz Collins.' Boy can play a little, huh?"

Dad stopped the clip and looked at me. He was calm, but very serious. "Thought we agreed to keep a low profile."

I shifted in my seat and examined the carpet, having no words to explain my ill-considered move at The King.

Mrs. Lang beamed at her daughter, "Well, dear, looks like you're the first groupie."

"Mom!"

Mrs. Lang burst into laughter. "Sorry, I couldn't resist." She swallowed the last of her wine and held her glass out to Dad. "Refill?"

"Gladly," said Dad, taking the glass. Our landline rang and he halted in his tracks.

"And so it begins," said Mrs. Lang. She leveled a knowing eye.

Chapter Thirty-Six
Blowing Up I

MRS. LANG WAS SURE RIGHT. If I hadn't used my name at The King Lounge, it might've taken longer for the media to find me. But I'd made it easy. Mr. Babineaux helped, too.

The music columnist from *The Statesman*, Fred Laurain, had grown up with Mr. Babineaux in Port Arthur. Mom didn't want me to talk to him, but Dad argued that was likely to just make a reporter sniff around harder. We agreed on an evasive approach that didn't involve outright lying, but wasn't exactly truthful.

He interviewed me—*us*—at our house. Fred was tall and thin, with a long neck. He was bald, with horn-rimmed glasses and a goatee. I couldn't take my eyes off his Adam's apple, which protruded to an extreme degree and gyrated when he talked. I was entranced by its dance and missed the first minute of our conversation.

"Friz," Mom said sharply, and I snapped my eyes over to her. She tried to glare good manners back into me.

"I know what you're thinking," said Fred good-naturedly. "Does this guy look more like an ostrich in Levi's—or a bearded lightbulb?"

I laughed despite myself. "I wasn't thinking either one."

"Uh-huh. Wondering if maybe I'd been tortured on the rack?"

I couldn't help it: I laughed harder.

"Gregory Collins!" Mom said. But Dad was laughing, too. "*William* Collins!"

Fred Laurain headed down the path of well-known guitar prodigies, such as Derek Trucks, Jonny Lang, and Kenny Wayne Shepherd. They'd caused a sensation years ago, when I was a baby. There were a lot of more recent prodigies—turned out YouTube was chock full. Fred showed us a popular video of ten of them. Most played heavy metal and were lightning fast. Some were so young the guitar was almost as big as them.

"You must've started young, too," said Fred. "Three? Four?"

"Uh, well, I'm a music teacher," said Dad, avoiding the question. "Got a little store in Round Rock."

"How about I mention that?" said Fred. "Maybe give you some extra business."

"That'd be okay," said Dad, and gave Fred the details.

"So…we started on an electric—little easier on the fingers," Dad continued. "But any good guitarist should be comfortable on acoustic, too, so we moved into that right away."

"What kind of guitar?"

"Oh, I've got an old Martin D-28 he's been using…"

The interview continued in that vein, until we got to the topic of how I wound up at The King Lounge on Saturday night. Mom and Dad had decided that I could pretty much tell the truth about this— they thought the ZZ Top connection might intrigue Fred enough to keep him from asking too many other questions. And it did seem to be working. Fred snapped his notebook shut, took a couple of pictures, and got ready to leave.

"Oh, one more thing…why'd you go to The King?" Fred asked.

"Well, I told you," I said. I'd seen enough TV shows to know it was always the last question that you had to watch out for.

"Yeah, I mean, out of all the gin joints, why'd you pick

Babineaux's place? He said he didn't know you."

"Oh," I said. I wanted to look to my parents, but that seemed suspicious. I went ahead and told the truth. "Well, I know one of the musicians. Jackson Greens."

"How do you know Jackson?" he asked, surprised.

"Oh...just met him somewhere."

"Yeah," he said. "Jackson gets around."

Chapter Thirty-Seven
Speed Limit

FOR MOST PEOPLE, learning to play guitar is daunting. I've had students who could type 120 words a minute—perform heart surgery—slice and dice like a food processor. These people were good with their hands, but fumbled frets and strings. Other people have chops but are baffled by music theory. Played by a third group of students, even the simplest songs hardly sound like tunes. These folks lack the rhythm and melody to make music.

Having worked with hundreds like these, I could appreciate the dumbfounding arc of my son's learning curve. He didn't forget *anything*. He struggled with *nothing*.

Yet even he could be intimidated. The video clip Fred Laurain showed him of the young shredders left an impression. Before our lesson, he asked me what I thought about them.

"Yeah, they're fast. But playing the guitar is not a shootout at the O.K. Corral."

"What do you mean?"

"If somebody's faster, it won't kill you."

"Isn't faster *better*?"

"You need a certain amount of speed to play well," I said. "I don't think that's going to be a problem for you. But let's prove it. Time for you to meet the traffic cop." He gave me an inquisitive look, and

I clarified. "Otherwise known as the metronome."

I pulled out my iPhone and dialed up the metronome app. I set it at sixty beats per minute and it started ticking.

"That's the beat," I said. "The beat is *money*." He nodded. "First we count the money. Quarter notes. *One…two…three…four…one… two…three…four*." Friz joined in, counting so that the numbers synchronized with the metronome's clicks.

"Now we're gonna cut up the money. Eighth notes. Double time. *One and two and three and four and one and two and three and four and…*" I counted twice as fast, numbers falling on the beat.

"Same four beats, but twice as many notes. Double again to sixteenth notes. *One-ee-and-uh-two-ee-and-uh-three-ee-and-uh…*"

"Do guitar players ever have to count past four?" he asked.

"Uh…maybe not," I admitted. "Ready for the guitar?"

"Finally!"

"You're gonna play a scale and stick with the metronome."

"The Pentecostal?"

"*Pentatonic*," I corrected. "I guess if you play it in certain churches it might be the Pentecostal. Nice and slow. Just play the scale with quarter notes."

He stayed right on the beat, even though the speed was low. Sometimes playing slow is as hard as playing fast. "Okay, eighth notes," I ordered. No problem. "Sixteenth notes."

"Any more to it than this, Dad?"

"Yeah, skipping fingers, playing with slurs, triplets, different patterns, all kinds of stuff. But first, let's just go faster. I usually increase the speed by five to ten beats per minute…" Friz stared at me incredulously. "But in this case, we'll jump it up. One-twenty. And skip the quarter notes, go straight to the eighth notes."

I ran him through the paces and the scale was flawless. Both the picking and fretting hands were fluid, with good articulation; every note rang clearly, perfectly in time with the metronome.

"Can you do the same thing with the blues notes?" I asked. This required the addition of a couple of extra notes into the pattern. More challenging, but it didn't faze him. I sat a moment, thinking. I had a repertoire of corrections for students who struggled with the drill, but my son had no need for any of them.

"One-forty," he suggested.

"That's pretty fast," I said, setting the metronome. The clicks sounded like a racing pulse. We were still within the limits of what I could do, but just barely. My son handled it with a good deal more grace.

"One-sixty," he called out. The heart on panic attack. I set the metronome and Friz took off. The sixteenth notes were firing at the rate of an assault rifle. He finished and looked at me expectantly.

"Sounds good to me."

"Fast as those little kids?" he asked, referring to the prodigies a few years younger than him.

"Think so."

"Wanta try some of those other drills?" he asked. He sounded concerned he might have tired me out.

"Maybe hammer-ons and pull-offs," I suggested.

I read a biography of Picasso once. Though he's known for abstract works, he first had to acquire the skills of traditional painting. He immodestly said it took him four years to learn to paint like Raphael, one of the greatest masters of the Italian Renaissance. It was Picasso's father—a gifted artist, himself—who helped him do that. But watching his young son progress at a prodigious rate was tough on the old man. By the time Pablo turned thirteen, the elder Picasso had set aside his brushes and vowed to never paint again. Leading my son through the drills, I could sure relate to how Pablo's dad must have felt.

More than that, I felt a nagging worry at the new direction he was headed with the breakneck speed he'd just shown. Talent is one thing, and Friz appeared to suddenly possess that in abundance. But surviving the world—the *music* world in particular—took more than raw ability. There were challenges that would call for emotional resources beyond what he'd developed during a happy childhood chasing footballs. I took a deep breath, forcing myself into the moment, and smiled to reassure the both of us.

Chapter Thirty-Eight
Playing Favorites

"ICE CREAM FLAVOR," said Samantha. "Ben and Jerry's."

I looked at her, weighing the possibilities. "Cherry Garcia?"

"Not even close. Super...Fudge...Chunk."

She drew out the delicious words and I moaned in sudden desire. "Tell me you have some."

Her face lit up at the thought. "Possibly."

Vibrations coursed through the floor I lay on in Sam's bedroom as she pounded down the stairs. We'd been grounded following our unauthorized excursion to The King, yet were still allowed time at each other's house. Hardly a deterrent to future transgressions. Confinement with this cellmate would suit me fine.

The rhythm pounded back up. Samantha burst in with a grin and a pint.

"I *love* your mother."

She plopped next to me, scowling, and leaned against her bed. "That's why you don't get a spoon. Here, lick this." She peeled off the top and handed it to me. "It's your turn."

Guessing each other's favorites was proving that Samantha knew a lot more about me than I knew about her. Or else she was lying, but I didn't think so. After all, her favorite flavor *had* been in the freezer.

"Favorite animals for a hundred," I said.

"Dog. Tell me it isn't."

"It *is*." To reward my honesty, she fed me a creamy spoonful.

"And *my* favorite animal?" she queried in return.

"I'd say dog, but what I think is always wrong. I'm going with cat."

She thrust out her jaw stubbornly. "Don't hedge your bet. Be wrong, but don't be a pussy. Be honest."

"Okay. Dog."

"It *is* a dog. French bulldog, to be precise."

She returned her attention to the ice cream, attacking it like a miner working a claim. Finally, I had to say something. "Please stop digging out all the good stuff."

"Get used to it. Favorite body part."

"Lips," I said, oggling hers.

"That's *yours*, silly."

"You sure you don't work for the FBI?"

"Lucky for transparent you. The eyes give you away." She batted hers and passed me the ice cream. "Okay. What do I want to be when I grow up?"

I went with my first impulse. "Cheerleader."

"*What?*"

So much for honesty. "Well, maybe not forever…" I extended the ice cream as an olive branch. She didn't take it.

"You think I want to be a professional cheerleader? *Seriously?*"

"I could be wrong." I looked at her indignant face. "Extremely wrong."

"Do *you* want to be a professional athlete?" she demanded, making her point. Her first misstep.

"Not anymore. But I *did*." She stared at me with surprise, an improvement over annoyance. "Most guys do. We also plan to be superheroes."

"Which is almost as likely."

"I *am* a very good football player," I objected.

Samantha was quick to dispute the claim. "Good enough for the NFL? Big enough? Fast enough? Tough enough? You're just lucky you got hit in the head. You haven't got anything in it!"

I regarded her a moment. Good thing I'd no longer been harboring *that* fantasy.

"*Please* take the ice cream," I begged. She accepted the peace pint with a laugh. "I'm done guessing your career path. What *are* you thinking of?"

"Getting another chocolate chunk," she said, excavating with the spoon. She looked at me with a gentle smile. "This is *good*, Friz."

"I know you don't just mean the B and J."

"*This*," she said, gesturing expansively to include our conversation. She threw in a chocolatey kiss.

When it ended, I smacked my sticky lips. "I especially like *this*."

"I want to be…" She jumped to her feet and struck a pose with the spoon. "Give me your tired, your poor, your huddled masses…"

"The Statue of Liberty? Isn't that job taken?"

"Not *her*, but what she stands for."

Hmmm. "You want to be a teacher."

"Nothing wrong with being a teacher…"

"Nurse? Doctor?"

"Nothing wrong with the medical profession…"

"Lawyer?"

"Nothing wrong with—" I gave her a look. "Depending."

The loaded bookshelves… "Writer!"

She sighed. "That's as unrealistic as becoming a professional athlete."

"*What* then?"

"I don't know. I want to make a difference." She sat back down and leaned into me. I saw an opening and took the ice cream.

"You're only fourteen," I said. "You've got time to figure it out."

"I'll feel better when I do. You're lucky you've got music."

"Ha! Musicians are a dime a dozen. That's what Dad says."

"*You're* not." She looked at me. "You're going to make a difference."

"Playing the guitar?" Thinking of my father, I couldn't help doubting it. "That's probably no more realistic than being a football player."

"You might have to do some singing, too."

I guffawed at the thought. "That'd require another concussion." I'd always mouthed the national anthem and happy birthday, the only songs to cross my path with any regularity.

"If you can talk, you can sing. Stevie Ray was no great shakes. Dylan."

"Probably some polka singers, too," I conceded the point.

"I'll teach you!"

"Another time, okay?"

She warbled a lyric. It sounded pretty good.

"*The Sound of Music?*"

"It worked in the movie."

"But *you're* not a singing nun!" I objected.

She gave me a lewd smile. "Lucky for you." She sang more of that song about doe a deer and golden sun and needles pulling thread. It was starting to sound like opera now.

I dug out a big spoonful of ice cream.

And when the fat lady opened her mouth for the next line...

I shoved it in.

Chapter Thirty-Nine
Blowing Up II

DAD AND I THOUGHT we'd been careful with Fred Laurain, but we didn't appreciate that journalists are just detectives without badges or guns. Fred wrote his article, which did wonders for Dad's business and generated a few phone calls from newspapers and radio stations. But he was by no means done with the story. Like a sparrow pecking up crumbs I'd strewn on the path, he hopped from Jackson Greens…to a football blog about my concussion…to Dr. Monaghan, savant expert.

Fred's second piece in *The Statesman* attracted a *lot* more attention. Within hours, our phone was ringing with calls from TV shows, publishers, and agents. All the folks who'd already called, called back again. And *again*.

That night we unplugged the landline and had a family meeting to decide how to handle this. Samantha sat in, too. She wasn't stingy with her opinions.

"Just say yes to everybody," she stated with authority, as if that settled the matter.

"Think we're going to rule out that option," said Dad, amused by her bravado.

"What are you afraid of?" she persisted.

Dad looked at me. I considered how to explain my uneasiness.

"You know that saying: 'The nail that sticks out gets hammered down.' I think this would be sticking *way* out."

"No doubt," Samantha said. "But you're not a nail. Might be a coupla haters, but most people are going to be on your side."

"You have a great deal more faith in human nature than I do," said Mom.

Samantha's eyes narrowed. "Aren't they offering money?"

Mom looked at Dad, who rubbed his neck. "Haven't gotten that far."

"Maybe you ought to at least find that out," said Samantha. "Unless you already have all the money you need."

My parents looked at each other. Dad raised his eyebrows quizzically, and Mom nodded assent.

Soon Dad called another meeting. He'd talked to four newspapers, two magazines, two radio shows, an agent, a ghost writer, and three TV shows.

"Ghost writer?" I asked.

"Wants to do your biography," he said, as if it were a reasonable proposition.

"Should be riveting," said Samantha. "'When I was five I went to kindergarten…'"

"Might start slow," I said. "But wait 'til first grade."

"Did the agent have advice?" asked Mom.

Dad nodded. "Said the way to monetize this is to land the big fish—TV shows. After that, you can count on offers for merch."

Mom frowned at the unfamiliar term. "What's 'merch'? Another fish?"

Dad drawled it out, like a cowpoke explaining a jackalope. "Short for merchandise. Apparel, guitars, accessories. He mentioned the big money was in fragrances."

"Perfume?" I was aghast.

"For men they call it 'cologne,' honey," said Mom. "But it *is* perfume."

"*Eau de Friz*," giggled Samantha. "Eet weel heet you upside zee head."

"How could I sell that?" I protested. "I barely use deodorant."

"We're getting ahead of ourselves," said Dad. "Let's come back to the TV show thing."

He said one of the top breakfast shows was willing to fly us out to New York, put us up at a swanky hotel, and pay $7,500 for the appearance. They wanted to do it the following week.

For a moment, no one said anything. It was too much for Samantha to take. "What are you even thinking about?" she burst out. "A free trip to New York, a good chunk of money—and that's a big show! Millions of people will see it!"

"*That's* what I'm thinking about," I said.

Dad nodded slowly. "You'd have to play something."

"How do you feel about that?" Mom asked carefully. She and Dad weren't nearly as enthusiastic about the idea as Samantha. But I was warming to it.

I sucked my teeth, considering. "I like playing."

"It wouldn't make you nervous being on TV?"

"Not until you mentioned it," I joked. "What would I play?"

"'Little Wing?'" Dad suggested.

"I guess. Yeah." Just thinking about the song always made me smile.

"You're sure about this?" asked Mom, giving me one of her x-ray looks. "It's not like ordering sushi you can spit out if you don't like it."

"You're not saying yes to the cologne," Samantha pointed out.

"*Ever*," I said. "But I'm feeling pretty good about this New York deal."

"Maybe you should sleep on it," said Dad gently.

They waited for my final decision. Stars are expected to be demanding, so… "Get them to throw in a ticket for Samantha."

"*And* a hotel room," said Mom.

Dad looked doubtful. "They said just family…" Then his forehead puckered in thought. "But I guess if you want John, you gotta take Yoko."

Mom howled, but Samantha and I didn't get it.

Chapter Forty
Breakfast Show

I HADN'T SEEN a breakfast show before, and now that I was watching one live, I doubted the program would make my cornflakes taste better.

Three people sat around a table and introduced video clips of breaking news. No matter how awful it was, the hosts were unnaturally cheerful. A weatherman made his prediction and they found something philosophical to say about the forecast. Socrates couldn't have done better.

To my relief, they showed several sports clips, a car chase, and a particularly gripping incident of two determined shoppers coming to blows over a deeply discounted vegetable steamer. The last piece repeated several times so viewers could savor every nuance of the bout, the hosts marveling at how the prospect of missing out on a bargain can just set a customer's blood to boiling.

If, after watching a brawl over an appliance, a person still didn't feel informed—well, stay tuned—there were more human-interest stories to come. These clips were shown on a big video monitor like a glorified Skype session, complete with several seconds of awkward audio delay between questions and answers. I could see the hosts had savant ability to make insipid comments about anything.

Then they recycled it several times.

This went on for two hours, though the second hour they changed sets and brought in a small studio audience. Mom, Dad, and Samantha were seated in the crowd.

As the "musical performer," I was the final guest at the end of the second hour. Eventually they got around to doing my makeup.

Technically, this was not my first time "going under-the-brush," as Paula, the makeup artist, put it—Mom and Samantha had painted me up for *Día de los Muertos*. But this was a completely different experience. I guess I'm not macho, because I enjoyed having a beautiful woman pampering me. Made me feel like the Cowardly Lion when he and his pals arrived at the Emerald City and got buffed-up before their meeting with the Wizard.

Paula laughed when I shared the thought with her. "Those guys would've been a challenge. But you're easy. Nice blank canvas. I'll have you done in no time. We could even do your nails."

"Uhhhhhh…"

"Oh, come on! Let's pick out a color for you!" She turned to an array of little bottles and read off the names: "Cranberry Kiss…Portland Square…Rouge Puissant…Pandore…Ring the Buzzer…Lola. How 'bout that one, huh? *Lo-lo-lo-lo-loooo-laaaaa*," she sang.

"I don't even know what language you're speaking."

"*Red*. Those are all shades of red."

"Why don't they just say so?"

"What fun would that be? Wouldn't you rather wear 'Never Tamed' than 'red'?"

I couldn't run away 'cause she was powdering my cheeks. "Rather cut off my fingers."

"Oh, they're gonna love you, honey," she said.

"I don't believe we're going to be having this conversation. At least I hope not."

I was pretty sure about that. The day before, I'd spent time with

LeSean Taylor, the host who would interview me. We didn't exactly work out a script, since they wanted it to feel spontaneous. But we had discussed the basic direction of the questions to avoid a deer-in-the-headlights reaction. LeSean said he'd do his best to help me out. "Might tease you a little," he said with a wink. "Is that cool?"

"Used to it," I answered. "I'll just tease you back."

Finally, it was time for my segment. I avoided tripping on my way to LeSean, we shook hands, and he led me to armchairs for our conversation.

LeSean Taylor, a tall, trim, muscular man in his forties, had been a famous linebacker in the NFL. Now that he was a celebrity, he wore an immaculate outfit that fit him like a wetsuit. He took in my jeans-and-T-shirt ensemble with disapproval.

"Glad you dressed up for your appearance."

"Just keepin' it real, man." To my surprise, as long as I focused on LeSean, it was easy to act pretty normal.

"That you are," he said, and fist-bumped me. "Hear you're a baller."

"Little bit. Wide receiver."

LeSean's eyes bulged comically. "The enemy!" He snorted like a bull about to charge.

I couldn't help laughing. "The *defenseless* enemy. Guy who hit me was about as big as you."

"Got your bell rung, huh?"

"My neurologist doesn't like that expression," I objected. "He'd rather say I injured my brain."

"Point taken." Adept at many roles, LeSean turned serious as an anchorman. "But I understand that after your concussion healed, something strange happened. You had a new ability. Without any instruction whatsoever, you could play the guitar. Is that right?"

It felt weird to claim it on TV, but…"Yes, it is."

LeSean leaned forward in his chair to show how fascinating the next tidbit was. "I'm told you joined a select group of about thirty people who have had a similar experience. You're what's called an 'acquired savant.'"

At that point, a clip of Dr. Monaghan screened on the big monitor, briefly explaining acquired savant theory. LeSean caught my eye and gave me a thumbs-up. I guess I was doing all right so far.

The video clip concluded and the camera switched back to us. LeSean shook his head in mock frustration, again the jester. "I had six concussions, and I didn't get *any* special abilities."

"Least you didn't get brain-damaged."

"Not what my wife says," he joked. "But seriously—are you concerned that some kids who hear about you might *try* to injure themselves?"

"Should I say something to them about that notion?"

"Public service announcement. Be my guest."

So I turned and addressed the camera directly. A little monitor had a script for me to read what we'd worked out the day before. I think I managed to make it sound pretty natural.

"Playing football may not be the best thing you can do for your brain. But it's *fun*," I said. "Now, running head-first into a brick wall or some other jackass stunt doesn't sound like fun to me. Might give your friends a laugh, but it'd be stupid—and probably make anyone who does such a thing even *more* stupid. *Do not do it.*" I turned back to LeSean, who gave me a wry smile.

"Not much of a politician, are you?" he said.

I recoiled at the thought. "*Politician*? I'm a teenager."

That got a big laugh from the audience. It was our cue to head to the climax of the spot.

"All right, you gonna play something for us?" asked LeSean.

"'Little Wing.'"

LeSean began to chew up the scenery. "Jimi Hendrix song. One of his best. *Jimi. Hendrix.*"

"But I'm not gonna sing."

"We'll deduct points for that," he teased. "And how long have you been playing the guitar?"

As if he didn't *know.* "Uh…twenty-four days." Saying it as simply as I could, it sounded like an apology.

The audience gasped. LeSean's eyebrows shot to the ceiling. "*This* I gotta see."

I crossed to a small stage set up for the musical portion of the show. The drummer waited at his kit. We'd rehearsed the day before, and he smiled at me reassuringly. The guitar I'd brought from home rested on a stand.

I hefted it, pulled the strap over my shoulder, and fastened it to the endpin. I played a scale, checked the tuning and audio levels. All good.

I paused a second, looked out at the audience, and saw Mom, Dad, and Samantha. They were smiling at me…so I smiled back and gave them a wave. I closed my eyes and waited for the colors to come.

"Little Wing" is a slow blues ballad. Hendrix's version is just two and a half minutes, because in those days they wanted short songs for their records. Stevie Ray Vaughan's is more than twice as long, which gave him time to stretch out and expand on the themes.

I aimed to split the difference between the two versions. My intro was wistful, exploring the melody—until the drums kicked in after half a minute—which started to accelerate the build of the song. I laid back, letting the tension mount, then began to break free, the notes cascading in riff after riff.

Shapes and colors guided me through the music. Ascending harmonics burst like violet paint bombs, giving way to magenta triplet waterfalls, the path winding through a sonic landscape as majestic as the Grand Canyon.

After the climax, our outro was a gentle return to the melody, accompanied by the drummer's quiet roll on closed high-hats. And...*out*.

The studio was silent—then erupted in applause. I watched, dazed, as LeSean Taylor bounded across the stage to me, a big smile on his face. He threw his enormous arm around my shoulder and turned me to the audience.

"Friz Collins, baby! Twenty-four *days*!" The applause got louder. "Man, I can't wait to hear you after a *month*!"

Chapter Forty-One
Blown Up

THE CROWD WASN'T DONE with me after the broadcast. The audience milled around, thrusting writing materials in my face for autographs. I signed several pieces of paper, a parking ticket, a lotto stub, two copies of *The New York Times*, an arm cast, and almost, the top of a breast.

I was about to ink the last item when I looked for my folks on the periphery of the mob. Mom wagged a scolding finger, so I autographed the girl's arm instead.

Then LeSean Taylor brusquely announced, "Okay, that's it!" He moved people aside and swept me through a door backstage. Mom, Dad, and Samantha followed our path. LeSean grinned at me. "You okay?"

"I guess. What just happened?"

"Ha! You blew up, man!" LeSean seemed delighted.

"Is that normal?" asked Mom, not nearly as enthused.

"Pretty much," said LeSean. "Best fasten your seat belts. Gonna be a wild ride."

"Do you have advice?" asked Dad, dismayed as if he'd been tasked with reassembling a torn-down carburetor.

LeSean held up a giant index finger. "Be nice. Be yourself. But *don't* let those folks chew on you like piranhas." He pantomimed signing autographs like crazy and we all cracked-up. "Give 'em a few nibbles, then get outta there. Otherwise, they'll eat you up. Just too many of 'em."

"Yeah, but…" I started.

"Don't feel bad," he went on. "They'll make it seem like you owe them a drink, an autograph, twenty bucks. You don't owe them nothing."

Samantha started to ask a question, but LeSean ignored her and grabbed my hand, shaking vigorously. "*So* glad to meet you!" He gave me a wink, cocked a finger at me—and was gone, heading out of the room. Before he exited, he turned and looked back at us.

"See how I did that? *You* can, too," he said. "When you've had enough—*before* you've had enough—it's Friz *out!*"

"Yeah, but…you're a giant," I said.

"Oh, that's just flesh and blood," he answered. He tapped his head. "It's what's up here that counts. And you've got plenty of that."

We'd gotten up early and were starved, so we gorged on "dirty water" dogs from a street cart. What colors the cookpot juices is a blend of spices, vinegar, and chilies that gives the hot dogs an addictive zip— along with the onions and mustard that tops them off. Everyone but Mom had a second one, as we took in the scene at Times Square. The temperature was in the low fifties but sunny, so we basked like bundled-up lizards.

Dad's phone rang, interrupting our meal. He handed his hot dog to Mom while he wrestled the cell out of his pocket. She took a big bite, and Dad's eyes grew wide with horror.

"Hello," he said into the phone. We listened to his side of the conversation. "Yeah, this is him." He listened, then interrupted. "Say, Joseph, it's not a good time to talk. I'm in the middle of lunch." Mom pointedly took another bite of his hot dog. "And my wife's eating my entrée, as we speak. Text me your number and I'll get back to you, all right?"

Dad ended the call and stood up, pulling out his wallet. "Finish that one. I'll get another," he said, as his phone rang again. "Told that guy to text me," Dad murmured. He glanced at his cell and reacted. "Different number."

"Let it go to voice mail—and put it on silent, honey," said Mom.

"Yeah," said Dad. He clicked the switch, ending the ringing, and headed for the pushcart.

I watched street musicians set up near us. A fiddler tuned, while a guitarist positioned an open case on the ground in front of them. He saw me watching and caught my eye; I gave him a nod. He nodded back, then his face took on a look of recognition. "Are you that guy?" he asked pointedly.

"Uh, what guy?" I asked.

"He's *not*," said Samantha, quicker to catch on than me.

But it was too late. "You *are*. You're the guy from YouTube." He called out to his friend, "Mark! This is that guy!"

"No way!" said Mark. And they were heading over.

As they did, a little kid being dragged across the Square by his mother recognized me. He tugged her sleeve and they veered toward us.

Later, Mom compared it to a chain reaction. A handful of people was all it took to form critical mass and start everyone carrying on. One second they were minding their own business, and the next second they were all up in ours. After buying his hot dog, Dad could barely get back to us.

Samantha and I enjoyed it the best we could at the nucleus of the throng. I signed autographs and posed for selfies with my, uh, fans. I could hear them quizzing each other, asking who I *was*. As I handed my signature to one guy, he admitted, "I didn't see your clip."

"That's so lame," said Samantha, disgusted.

He grunted. "Whatever. The way everybody's acting, you must be awesome."

Fans abhor a vacuum. As the guy who didn't know me moved out, a dazzling girl who wanted to know me better, moved in. Before I could react, she wrapped herself around me like a boa constrictor and planted a lingering kiss on my cheek. Her lips, which had amazing dexterity, massaged the contours of my bone structure, while her hand raked through my hair. And her *smell*. The merch she was wearing made my knees shaky. By the time she snapped the selfie, I was incapacitated.

"Hey!" Samantha protested. "I'm his girlfriend!"

"For *now*," said the girl, already moving off.

"That's it!" yelled Samantha. "Friz *out*! Statue of Liberty!"

"And Ellis Island!" added Mom.

Dad grabbed my arm and dragged me through the crowd, while Mom opened a path like a lead blocker. Samantha followed behind, protecting my flank. She also gave it a hard pinch.

"Ow!" I said. "That girl was not my fault."

"Maybe not, but you enjoyed it a little too much."

Soon we were into the secondary and it was an open field. Passing a kiosk, Mom had a thought. A moment later we moved on, with me in a NY Yankees hat and a pair of sunglasses.

I'm not sure if I felt more kinship to movie stars or to criminals on the lam. In either case, I was hoping my disguise would hold up for a while. The landscape of sudden celebrity was a far bigger surprise than New York City, like leaving Kansas and winding up in the land of Oz.

We all heaved a sigh of relief once we got on the subway. The seats were filled, so the four of us clung to a pole and hung on as the car lurched to a start.

"Elvis has left the building," said Samantha, and we giggled.

Mom looked at Dad with annoyance.

"*What?*" he said.

"You keep twitching."

"Phone won't stop vibrating. Makes me jumpy as a bean."

"Just turn it off," she said with an edge.

"Yes, dear," he replied sarcastically, and we all started giggling again. We were giddy with the morning's nervous energy.

My disguise worked and we had a great time the rest of the afternoon. Life started to seem like normal. We were debating Italian versus Chinese for dinner, when Dad pulled out his phone to look up restaurants. He checked voice mail and blew out a breath.

"How many?" asked Mom.

It took him a while to count them up.

"Thirty-four."

Chapter Forty-Two
Full Metamorphosis

WHEN WE GOT HOME, Mom and Dad said I had to return to school and carry on with life as normal. As I headed to meet my posse, there were immediate signs that wouldn't be possible. Conversations broke off and heads turned in my direction as I moved through the playground. No one was uncool enough to snap a picture or ask for an autograph—but I sensed a ridiculously heightened level of attention. An internal alarm went off, like a Geiger counter activated by radioactivity. It castanet-clicked to warn me of eager smiles from pretty girls who'd never looked my way before. Even the goth girls were giving me the dark hooded eye.

"Yo, git-tar hero!" Bill Ballard greeted me, giving extensive dap. "You chewed up the Big Apple, homes!"

"Nah," I said.

"Bro, the moms DVRed it. We watched it over and over!"

"For reals," agreed Jack Rucker, though his tone was less delighted. "But I can't believe you never played guitar." He sounded suspicious.

Before I could reply, José Mireles jumped in. "Rucker, where's your faith? Leave it at church?"

"I don't mean nothin'," he said. "Just sayin' Friz's dad teaches music and all. Seems like he musta taught him." He glanced around to see if anyone shared his disbelief.

"Not what Friz says, right?" said Ballard.

"Not 'til after the injury," I said, as if apologizing.

"Word," said Ballard. He looked at Rucker for his comeback.

"Hey, I'm not callin' Friz a liar," he stated emphatically. Then he added, as if explaining his objection, "It just seems like…incredible. Comic book stuff. Superman."

"Wrong dude," said Sam Conner. "He came from another planet. Pretty sure Friz was born on Earth."

"How about Iron Man?" José Mireles suggested.

"High tech hero. No superpowers," said Conner.

"The Hulk?" suggested Rucker.

"Closer. Gamma ray exposure," agreed Conner. "Or Spider-Man. Radioactive spider bite. Daredevil—exposed to radioactive waste. Captain America took the super soldier serum—which was probably—"

"*Radioactive*," said Ballard.

Another nuclear connection. But the one setting-off the Geiger counter was *me*.

"Damn, Conner, you're a superhero encyclopedia," he added.

"I got it!" Conner exclaimed. "You're… *the Savant!*"

"Never heard of that dude," said José.

"I just made him up. His superpower is playing music."

"That's no superpower," José scoffed.

"The way the Savant does, it *is*. He plays music so fine he renders criminals harmless! Maybe it puts them to sleep…"

"Or kills them! Toxic tunes!" said Rucker.

"He doesn't punch them or nothing?" said José, disappointed.

"Doesn't have to. He pacifies them so they can be arrested. They're under his spell."

"Cool," said Ballard.

"I still think he should kick their ass," said José.

"Why?" asked Conner.

"Just on general principles," said Rucker.

"And also, it would be cool," said José.

The bell rang and we headed out. As usual, I'd said almost nothing.

Rushing to science class, I took my seat, opened my book, and pretended to be deep in study. It worked until Rebecca Collard sat on my lap!

"Oops," she said. She smiled innocently and looked deep into my astonished eyes.

Mr. Pennington, a step behind, turned from the board and took notice. "Mr. Collins, thank you for joining us. Would you mind releasing Miss Collard? I believe she has her own seat."

Whoa, talk about blaming the victim! Rebecca's eyes danced with mischievous glee at the misunderstanding. "He's such a bad boy, Mr. Pennington! I can't get away from him!"

"*Mr. Collins!*" said Mr. Pennington. The other students, having seen the whole thing, snickered at the misunderstanding. I tried to back away from the girl sitting on top of me.

"Thank you," said Rebecca, as she wriggled off my lap, using a friction-filled oscillating buttocks dance to dislodge herself.

The class came to order, and Mr. Pennington began to drone about the life cycle of the bald-faced hornet, a particularly aggressive stinger that goes through complete metamorphosis. That struck a chord with my own buggy life. I put my head down to think about it.

Football-player kid. Brain-damaged kid. Savant-guitar-player kid. And...*what?* That was only three stages, and complete metamorphosis consisted of four. Whatever came next, I didn't want it to get any weirder than it already was.

The next days, though, *were* strange. Mom and Dad dealt with phone calls and the media, but it was stressing them. They weren't sure what the right thing to do *was*. We did a couple of interviews with local journalists and put off a decision about anything bigger. As for merch, it was obvious that selling products would be a ticket to sure ridicule.

It seemed I couldn't win, even with friends who'd known me my whole life. I laid low, but they took it wrong. Zach, Jamarie, and Tyrell came to see me one night. I was in my room practicing when they came in. I put down the guitar.

"Don't let us interrupt," Jamarie said sarcastically.

"No, glad to see you guys," I said.

"You are?" Zach challenged. "You ain't called."

"Well, phone works both ways," I said mildly.

"So now it's on *me*?" Zach said.

"Chill, dude," said Tyrell. "Could use you Saturday," he said to me.

"Yeah, I don't know."

"Seem like you're feeling better," said Jamarie. "Good enough to go to New York and hang with LeSean Taylor."

"That's close as he's gonna get to football," said Zach. "Friz is retired—at fourteen."

Tyrell was playing the good cop role. "It's cool, man," he said. "Understand those hands kinda valuable, now. Can't risk them on the field."

"Risk?" said Zach. "I'm the one takin' snaps from Hernandez. Jammed my thumb, then he farted on me. I was laughing so hard I got sacked."

"Bet your dad loved that," I said, smiling at the thought.

"Oh, yeah. Called a timeout to yell at me. Said he's never seen a quarterback lose five yards and think it's funny."

"But it *was* funny," said Jamarie.

"Yeah," said Zach. "You shoulda been there."

I was sorry I'd missed the moment. These guys were still my friends. I enjoyed being with them. I wished them well. I didn't want to let them down…

But since the injury, I'd lost the interest in football that had constituted my entire pre-concussion life. I'd thought it would come back. You know how it takes a while to regain your taste for something you ate just before you got the flu and started blowing chow? Coulda been your favorite food—but after getting the heaves, the very thought of it is nauseating.

Yet, to be honest, what I'd been going through wasn't like that. I didn't find football *revolting*—it just didn't interest me. *At all.*

It was like I'd turned into Zach's mom! To be sociable, she watches the Super Bowl with the rest of the family, but the only part she cares about is commercials and the halftime show. During the game, she *votes* for the team with the best *costumes.*

It confused me to my core, and I lay awake trying to come to terms with my life's before-and-after transformation.

After nights of tossing-and-turning, I decided to follow the notes where they led. That was back to play with Jackson Greens and Willie Reed at The King Lounge. Dad set it up.

Mr. Babineaux publicized the gig—so when Mom, Dad, and I got to The King, it was filled with raucous fans. If football was the hottest ticket in Texas, music was a close second. We had to park blocks away and negotiate a crowd that was frustrated they couldn't get into the club.

People recognized me and the usual autograph-seeking started up. Mom and Dad sandwiched me, and I tried to ignore people pleading for my attention. I waved and smiled, a Rose Queen on her float, nodding benevolently at admirers.

"You suck!" called one disappointed long-haired fan.

"Bro!" his buddy admonished.

"Seriously! Who's he think he is?"

"He ain't Stevie Ray," another guy agreed.

"Or Hendrix, for fuck's sake!" said another.

Still, I took refuge in playing music, and for one night, found peace. Jamming with Willie and Jackson was a comfort, and having folks whistling, stomping, and cheering is loads better than having people hating on you.

However, by Sunday night, several more bootleg videos from the performance had been posted on YouTube. The landline that had calmed started ringing again. We unplugged it, but had no illusions we'd solved the problem.

On Wednesday I went to one of Samantha's cheerleading competitions. Sitting with her mother, I drew those autograph hounds like meat bees on burger.

"Not during the competition!" Mrs. Lang snarled at them. "Leave him alone until a break."

We tried to watch the cheerleading performance, but it was distracting. As many people were looking in our direction as toward the stage. Mrs. Lang muttered to herself and seemed on the verge of making a scene.

When the break came, so did the pests. It seems I was already an ungrateful celebrity, disturbed by my fans' attentions. But Mrs. Lang was a lot more annoyed than I was.

"Stop shoving that stuff in his face," she barked at a middle-aged lady thrusting materials at me. "What're you, a *toddler*? Where're your manners!"

At the end of the competition, Samantha could hardly get

through the crowd competing for my attention. When she did, she angrily grabbed one of my hands. Her mother grabbed the other, and they dragged me toward the door.

The silence on the way home was oppressive. "Are you mad at me?" I ventured.

"No," she snapped. She didn't say another word until they dropped me off at my house. "Bye," she said.

"Bye," I said. I stood on the curb and watched their car drive down the street until it turned the corner.

Chapter Forty-Three
Dr. Feel Bad

FENDING OFF RABID MEDIA was not among parenting issues Marla and I had anticipated. She argued that if we ignored the requests, eventually we'd "extinguish" them, just as she stamped out classroom annoyances. That takes determination and it's important to resist "reinforcement errors." Giving in even once can make the person exhibiting the behavior believe they have to escalate in order to get what they want. That made the appearance on the breakfast show a whopper of a reinforcement error. It convinced other shows that if they only tried harder, they'd have their way with us.

Consequently, the amounts they were offering were getting tempting. Friz's first appearance had generated a tidy sum—but the longer we held out, the more enormous the financial carrot they dangled in front of us. It had now reached well into five figures and was clamoring for a bite.

Marla and I had wondered how we'd afford our son's college tuition. The savings account we'd dedicated for that purpose was sufficiently funded to get him to Christmas of his freshman year—at a state college.

With that in mind, the three of us decided to consider the more lucrative offers coming in—just enough to get the college fund flush. We decided on the *Dr. Jeff Show*. The host was a TV psychologist

who booked guests to explore scientific and health-related topics—
sometimes a bit sensationalized, but far from trash television. It
seemed like a conservative decision.

I'm only belaboring our thinking because of how it turned out.

Marla, Samantha, and I were seated in a live studio audience in the
bowels of Hollywood. They taped three shows a day, an ordeal for all
involved. Friz's segment was the last to film and everyone's patience
was wearing thin. The shows would screen on separate days, so even
though this was the third one we'd all sat through, Dr. Jeff had to
pretend it was the one and only. He began with his usual patter.

"Good afternoon, everybody! Welcome to the *Dr. Jeff Show*." Dr.
Jeff was an avuncular fellow in his fifties, slightly overweight. In his
standard outfit of upscale sweats and tennis shoes, he looked more
like a high school PE teacher than Sigmund Freud. All he lacked was
a clipboard and a whistle around his neck.

"Today our special guest is a young man named Friz Collins. An
unusual name—and a more unusual claim. He asserts that after
sustaining a football head injury, he spontaneously developed the
ability to play the guitar! Not just at a novice level, mind you—but
as well as professionals who have been playing for years! Ladies and
gentlemen—Friz Collins!"

The audience applauded as our son walked on stage with his
guitar. Marla frowned at me. "I don't like the way he put that."

Dr. Jeff gave Friz a cordial handshake. "Thank you for joining us
today," he greeted him, as they took seats in the studio armchairs. "I
understand the last months have been eventful!"

"Some things *have* changed," Friz replied with a smile.

"They tell me you're an 'acquired savant'—a person who has a
traumatic brain injury, and as a result, develops an amazing new

ability." Dr. Jeff said this as if it were the most interesting thing he'd ever heard.

"Apparently," agreed Friz.

"May I ask who made that diagnosis?"

"Well, that'd be the doctor I went to for the concussion—Dr. Sugarman."

"Probably a neurologist?"

"Um-hm."

"Me, I'm just a first name psychologist," said Dr. Jeff with false modesty. "But I do wonder…how did Dr. Sugarman know you'd never played guitar before your injury?"

"Well, that's what we told him," Friz explained. "My parents and me."

"And he took your word for it?" Skepticism was creeping into Dr. Jeff's tone.

Marla looked at me again, pursing her lips. Dr. Jeff was sounding more like a cagey prosecutor cross-examining a witness than a genial talk show host chatting up a guest. Samantha was scowling in disgust.

Friz was taken aback by Dr. Jeff's line of questioning. He gave the man a look, sizing him up, then explained, "One of the things that convinced people was my fingertips. Guitar players develop hard calluses from the metal strings. I didn't have any."

"But if you had gone to a manicurist before seeing Dr. Sugarman, couldn't they have removed any calluses?"

"I don't know," said Friz, repulsed by the notion. "I've never been to a manicurist."

"Well, I haven't either," confided Dr. Jeff. "But I've heard tell." He addressed the studio audience directly. "Ladies, how about it? Could a manicurist take off a few little old calluses?"

The audience chorused agreement, tittering and giggling, heads nodding affirmatively.

Dr. Jeff turned back to Friz, raising his hands in a placating gesture. "Just playing devil's advocate, you understand. I believe your story. But many people don't. How would you convince them you didn't play the guitar before your injury and just kept it a secret? After all—doesn't your father make his living teaching the guitar?"

Friz's brow furrowed in consternation. "He does, but he didn't teach *me.*"

Dr. Jeff adopted an earnest expression, as if he wanted to help. "How can you prove that to the doubters, Friz?"

"It's hard to prove a negative. Can you prove you didn't take clarinet lessons?"

"If you heard me play, I doubt anyone would imagine I had." Dr. Jeff made a face at the studio audience, which laughed delightedly at his self-deprecating wit.

Friz took a deep breath. "Don't you think my parents would know if I was playing the guitar?"

"Certainly. They'd have to be in on the hoax."

"*Hoax?*" exclaimed Friz, now quite sure he was being attacked.

"Just gettin' comfortable here," said Dr. Jeff. It was his signature phrase.

"Just gettin' comfortable," the audience parroted back. It sounded like a taunt.

"*I'm* not gettin' comfortable," Friz said.

Dr. Jeff guffawed and slapped him on the knee.

"We're paying you a large sum to appear today, aren't we?"

"Well, yeah, but—"

"Couldn't that possibly be a motivation to—"

"Are you flat-out calling us liars?" demanded Friz, his eyes igniting.

"Not *me,* you understand, but some might. Some *have.*"

"Well, I'm not on their show," said Friz. "And if you're not going to be polite, I won't be on yours, either." With that, he burst from his chair and headed toward the exit. The studio audience reacted with shock and Dr. Jeff jumped up with surprising speed for a big man.

"I apologize," he said, his tone placating. "Please don't leave. We have another guest joining us."

On cue, a middle-aged woman entered the set, walking toward Friz as if to intercept him. He froze and waited as she approached. Dr. Jeff crossed to introduce them.

"This is Dr. Fielding. She's a neurologist who specializes in juvenile concussions, and she was particularly eager to meet you."

Because our son has awfully good manners—an aspect of his upbringing I was starting to regret—he politely shook hands with Dr. Fielding and allowed Dr. Jeff to guide him back to his chair.

Marla, Samantha, and I exchanged a worried look. "This is the pits," said Samantha, her lips tight with anger. We turned our attention back to the stage, where Friz and the shrinks had taken their seats. Two against one.

At first, Dr. Jeff shifted his attention from Friz, allowing him to cool off.

"Dr. Fielding, are concussions common?"

She nodded soberly. "Every year, somewhere between two and four million sports-related concussions occur."

Dr. Jeff reacted with mock surprise. "That's a *lot*! Are all those people brain-damaged?"

Dr. Fielding smiled at Dr. Jeff's theatrics. "Most of them heal without long term consequences. But getting concussed doesn't do your brain any favors. It is *not* a pleasant experience."

"Good point," agreed Dr. Jeff. "Friz, how did you feel after yours? Tell us about your recovery."

Our son looked relieved to be back on safe ground. As he

described his ordeal, Dr. Jeff listened solicitously.

"That sounds awful! Terrible!" Dr. Jeff paused, then continued with reluctance. "But...do you have any real...*proof*...that you had a concussion?"

Again under attack, Friz rolled his eyes. "Hundreds of people saw the accident."

Dr. Jeff persisted hesitantly. "Yes. But...is there anything that *proves* your brain was injured? MRI? CT? EEG?"

"This lady just said there are *millions* of people getting concussions. Why don't you ask if *she* can prove it? Or is she part of the hoax, too?"

"Just gettin' comfortable," said Dr. Jeff.

"Just gettin' comfortable," the audience echoed.

Dr. Jeff took a different tack. "Dr. Fielding, do you believe there's such a thing as an 'acquired savant'? Could an injury unlock hidden potential in the brain?"

The room seemed to grow quieter with the continued assault on our son's credibility. So did Dr. Fielding. She paused, considering her response.

"Savantism from birth occurs," she stated carefully. "And some individuals—in very rare cases—may experience something similar following a brain injury. Not usually from a concussion, however."

"So you're not buying this story?"

She continued in a lighter tone, as if she were a layman who'd heard something about it in passing. "My understanding is that many of the documented cases resulted from much more severe injuries— being struck by lightning, cerebral hemorrhage, auto accidents, that sort of thing. And usually offsetting deficits occur."

"It sounds like you're skeptical," Dr. Jeff prodded.

"This is not my specialty," she replied with finality. Dr. Jeff would get no more from this witness.

He turned to Friz. "How about that? Have you experienced any negative side effects to your new ability?"

"A couple," said Friz. "The worst is being called a money-grubbing manicured liar in front of millions of people on TV."

The audience gasped, and Dr. Jeff looked sorely aggrieved.

"I'm sorry if you got that impression."

"I didn't," said Friz. "You *said* it."

"No, no, you misunderstood. Look, we're *just…gettin'…*"

This time Dr. Jeff looked to the audience, who finished his sentence in a chorus: "COMFORTABLE."

Dr. Jeff switched direction, saying, "Time for a song. *That'll* help us relax." Friz gave a resigned nod and reached for his guitar, as Dr. Jeff continued, "Ladies and gentlemen—Phil Palmieri!"

Friz looked on in bewilderment as a modest man in his forties came onstage to polite applause, carrying an acoustic guitar.

"If you're trying to place that name, you can stop right now. Phil Palmieri is the most famous guitarist in the world—*that you have never heard of!*"

The audience laughed appreciatively and Dr. Jeff continued.

"Phil plays hundreds of studio recording sessions, as well as touring with different bands. But we've asked him to come here today and play a duet with our young savant, Friz Collins!"

Was that a note of sarcasm when Dr. Jeff said "savant"? His next words made it crystal clear. "What do you think, folks? Would that at least be a test of his musical ability?"

The audience applauded—but not Marla, Samantha, and me. We looked at one another, shaking our heads at the way this whole thing was going south. Samantha buried her face in her hands.

Friz regarded Dr. Jeff as if he'd just bitten into a piece of chocolate candy filled with anchovies. "Something *else* you want me to prove?"

"Why not?" said Dr. Jeff with a big friendly smile.

He ushered Phil and Friz to seats upstage with microphones set up for the guitarists. They sat, tuned, and Friz asked without enthusiasm, "So, what're we playing?"

"Well," Phil said thoughtfully, "do you know an old song called 'Dueling Banjos'?"

Friz glowered, but before he could object, Phil played a tentative line, pausing for Friz to repeat it. This is exactly what my son and I had done in the privacy of our home, but now he was being called-out on national TV.

His playing showed that he didn't like it one bit. While Phil offered graceful melodies, Friz parroted them back as fast as he could with none of the technique of which he was capable. The duet failed to soar. Instead, Friz introduced mistakes, undermining the song. A guitarist might have recognized the sabotage was intentional, but to the audience, it just sounded awful.

They sat in shocked silence when Phil wound up the song.

Like a subject awakening from a trance, Dr. Jeff sprang from his seat. "C'mon folks, let's hear it for our young savant! Friz Collins!"

The audience applauded reluctantly as Friz stalked from the stage.

Chapter Forty-Four
Prodigious Blues

HOLYYYYYY SHIT!

Mom says I've got a long fuse, but a big bang—something I've got to work on. Giving more warning before I go postal, like a rattler shaking its tail. Considering what had just happened, she might have a point.

I was about to escape the studio when the doctor rushed in. Phil Palmieri trailed after him, holding his guitar.

"Young man, wait," Dr. Jeff called.

"What now? You wanta check my birth certificate?!"

"I told you, I was just playing devil's advocate," he protested.

"I'm fourteen years old. I don't even know what that *means!*"

He seemed taken aback. "'Advocate' is another word for lawyer."

I still couldn't get it. "So you're the devil's *lawyer?*"

"It means that, like a lawyer defending an unpopular client—such as the devil—I was speaking in defense of a viewpoint I don't necessarily share," he explained.

My fists were clenched so tight that nails clipped short dug into my palms. "Well, I guess you won your case for Satan. Now millions of people believe my parents and I told a giant lie just to make money."

Before Dr. Jeff could respond, Phil Palmieri interjected an

apology. "I wouldn't have agreed to this if I'd understood what was going on. They said you wanted to play with me."

I forced myself to calm; it wasn't this guy's fault. "Never even heard of you. No offense."

"I should've known better," he said with a smile. "No one's heard of me."

"At the moment, that sounds pretty good."

"At least I thought you could play the guitar," Dr. Jeff said plaintively.

"*That's* your apology?" Phil said, glaring at the host.

I looked at Phil. "Wanta give that song another try?"

He strapped up while I took my guitar from its case. Dr. Jeff backed off a step, a curious look on his face. Several other folks backstage had been taking in the argument and drifted closer.

Phil began with the same phrases he'd introduced in front of the studio audience, but this time I let myself enjoy the experience. Where I'd been brusque and sarcastic, now I was playful.

As our exchanges heated up, I glanced at Dr. Jeff and saw a look of wonder on his face. His mouth was hanging open, and I wished Mr. Pennington's bald-faced hornet would fly into it.

Phil was a great partner and I just went with it. The excitement built until he gave me a slight nod. I returned to the theme and slowed to a lilting pace, to which he played counterpoint. We brought the song to a close.

Phil gave a little laugh and extended his hand. "I don't know if you're a savant—but you're a player."

"Come back on the show!" clamored Dr. Jeff, a foolish grin plastered on his face. "Let's make this right!"

"Think I'll cut my losses," I answered.

Among the listeners beaming at me were my parents and Samantha. I headed into their arms and let them fold me into a protective embrace. Group hug.

"I've never been prouder of you," said Dad, his voice choked with emotion.

"Me, too," said Mom.

"You sure?" I asked. "Long fuse, big bang…"

"Coulda been bigger," said Mom, laughing.

"I'm suing Dr. Jeff for malpractice," declared Samantha, before she planted a big kiss on me.

All's well that ends well, right?

Not…exactly.

The TV powers-that-be decided to screen my catastrophic episode immediately—it aired before we even got home. Worse, anybody who missed it during the regular time slot could pull it up on demand. Bad news goes viral even faster than good.

Every so often we get together with relatives who live in Montana. Since they don't have kids, I'm their lifeline to American youth. They're always eager to hear what the next generation is up to, debriefing me like I'm an undercover operative and they're my CIA handlers.

Someday, I look forward to filling them in on the awesome linguistic creativity of the middle school crowd. It doesn't take much to inspire variations on the theme of "You suck."

You can identify the Neanderthals, 'cause that's all they come up with: "You suck," or "You *suck*," or "Dude, you *suuuuuuuuuuuuck*." Uninspired, but they get mileage out of emphasis, inflection, and body language.

For variety, add a direct object: "You suck eggs, butt, ass, anus, rectum," and all terms for excrement or male sexual anatomy, not necessarily restricted to humans. Special commendation: "You suck multiple orifices."

A Bible-thumpin' bro passed judgement thus: "Thou suckest."

· Armando Lopez went all bilingual on me: "¡*Chupas como chupacabra!*"

Freddy Polkinghorn seemed to make no effort to control his stutter, which gave his proclamation of, "Y-y-y-y-you s-s-s-s-s-SUCK!" a "wait for it…wait for it…" explosiveness. Freddy's rendition became widely imitated. It was a twofer: they could hate on me and Freddy at the same time.

Personal testimonials were graciously submitted, like the one from Allison Jones, who said her dad's playing sucked almost as bad as mine—so her mom "busted the shit out of his guitars and divorced his ass all to hell." Now he lives in a trailer she calls the "Wine-a-bago" in honor of his new relationship with the beverage.

If Shakespeare had been a teenager, he would have written sonnets about how I suck.

Einstein would have come up with a different formula: $Friz = suck^2$.

Descartes would have said, "You suck—therefore, you suck."

Those guys were big time IQ outliers. But what the common herd lacked in genius they made up for in persistence. They were relentless. This did not blow over in a day or two. Like most teenagers, I'd never looked for attention, let alone celebrity. But I'd found *notoriety*, and it looked like it was going to stick. I'd have given anything to go back to being ignored.

Somehow, I had hoped there might be a closing of the ranks—fellow adolescent vs. adult authority figure, Dr. Jeff. Usually kids stick together, right? But, no—it was like they'd bet their last dollar on one of their own, and I'd tanked the fight. Their scorn knew no limits.

One night Samantha came over to hear me complain in person. If crying on her cute shoulder couldn't make me feel better, then nothing could.

"What about your friends?" she asked. "You *do* have friends, don't you?"

"I *did*. Now…" I trailed off. "They don't call me names…but when I join the herd, all the mooing stops."

"Mooing? What kind of school do you go to?"

"I think of kids as cattle." She gave me a look, but I went on. "It gets real quiet. They shuffle their feet and look uncomfortable, like they're smelling something bad."

"So you're a stinky cow?"

"Well, I'm a guy, so…stinky *bull*, I guess."

She brightened with a sudden thought. "Or…*bullshit*." I gave her a look. "Hey, it's *your* metaphor. I'm just working with it."

"At least the media stopped hounding me," I said, moving on.

"Where'd you get *that* word?"

"From the Incredible Hulk. It's his usual complaint about tormenters. 'Why must they *hound* me?'"

Sam shook her head sadly. "You two have a lot in common, especially the limited vocabulary."

I did my best Hulk impression. "Friz SMASH!"

She laughed, and even I had to chuckle. Samantha was quiet a while. Finally, she said, "So when are you gonna start making lemonade out of these lemons?"

"If I had a little sugar…" I said. She picked up the hint and gave me a kiss.

But she didn't let the idea drop. "Isn't that what you bluesmen do—turn misery into art?"

"Like, write a song? The 'Acquired Savant Blues?'"

She snickered. "I was thinking, the 'You Suck Blues.'"

I guffawed.

"Suck is an excellent rhyming word," she insisted.

"Brings to mind the f-word, doesn't it?"

"To *your* four-letter mind. There are lotsa others." She seemed to be serious…

I reached for the guitar. "Well…I've been fiddling around with a little Delta blues melody…"

I don't imagine this is how Son House or John Lee Hooker ever wrote a song. While I noodled, Samantha pulled up a rhyming dictionary. It's a blessing those guys didn't have such a tool. Here's what she came up with:

When he was a boy, his momma, she said
If you play football, don't get hit in the head.
But he was a kid, and kids make mistakes
So now he's savant, and those are the breaks.

Yoooooooooooo suck, yoooooooooooo suck.
Those who speak Yiddish, they call you a schmuck.
Yoooooooooooo suck, yoooooooooooo suck.
To a Canuck you're a puck run amuck.

His fingers they had, a mind of their own.
Without being taught, played songs they had known.
Not natural they said, he couldn't deny.
You must show your gift, how high you will fly.

Yoooooooooooo suck, yoooooooooooo suck.
You're not a C note, you're just a sawbuck.
Yoooooooooooo suck, yoooooooooooo suck.
Not even the wood that the woodchuck could chuck.

Doctor Jeff had a show, on which he did go.
Man called him a liar, and then laid him low.
Went up and went down, the pass incomplete.
His ruin was total, he left in defeat.

Yoooooooooooo suck, yoooooooooooo suck.
The strings that you pluck, the sound is, like, yuck.
Yoooooooooooo suck, yoooooooooooo suck.
You're a bad-tastin' clam, just a tough geoduck.

It was sacrilegious and awful, but a lot of fun, the first laughs in days for me. Samantha was determined to work several words into more stanzas—"roebuck," "aqueduct," "potluck," "dumb cluck," and especially "Starbucks"—but it got late, and Dad had to drive her home.

The next day it was back to the middle school battleground, and I found it impossible to retain a philosophical attitude under enemy fire. The barrage continued, and after getting shelled for several more days, Mom and Dad sat me down and asked if I wanted to talk about it. Twitched my head no. Silence. Sighs. Dad looked at Mom. She gave him one of her looks. So he asked if I wanted to try home schooling.

I could've gone off on them. I was certainly in the mood to do that. But instead, I asked, "What would that look like?"

"Not going to school," Mom said.

"I'm in."

"There'll be more to it than that," Dad added quickly. "But so far we don't know."

So I retreated to my room. The room, the Womb. A safe place to hide away with the music.

My football posters still presided over a realm now dominated by guitars, amps, pedals, picks, slides, capos, and guitar tab. The great players were testimony to a bygone era in my life, a time I felt certain had passed for good. Yet removing them felt like tearing down Roman ruins and denying they had ever existed. So they continued their symbolic reign, relics of a passed age.

At first it was all "home" and no "schooling." Mom and Dad were at work, and to make sure we didn't have problems with the authorities, we hired a housekeeper, Mrs. Enriquez. Our place never looked so sparkling clean, except for my room, which I wouldn't leave. It was lonely, but solitary confinement beat middle school harassment.

This went on for a couple of weeks while Mom and Dad explored options. They cast worried glances my way when I emerged from the Womb. Dad sat me down and told me about Howard Hughes, a famous rich recluse, worried I was headed down that path.

I was concerned, too. I still talked to Samantha, but I'd noticed that some part of me was starting to resent our daily calls as an intrusion. Not *most* of me—but I began to cut calls short to get back to the guitar, as if it were a jealous woman competing with my flesh-and-blood girlfriend.

We'd had classroom visitations to "scare us straight," with counselors telling cautionary tales about folks who sacrificed jobs, money, children, parents—*everything* for their addiction. I'd nodded along with classmates—mostly to reassure the adults, so they'd stop lecturing. I'd never imagined such a thing could happen to me. I didn't have what they called, "the addictive personality." Now, realizing what a force music had become…I wasn't so sure.

One evening I heard a knock on the Womb's portal that I did not recognize as Mom's tap-tap-tap, or Dad's shave-and-a-haircut-two-bits. Puzzled, I put down the guitar and opened the door.

"Whoa," I said in surprise.

Standing in the hallway was Jackson Greens.

"Pack a bag," he said. He tilted his head and gave me a dazzling smile.

211

Part Three

December 2012

Chapter Forty-Five
Trippin'

WITHIN HOURS I was riding shotgun in a shiny black Chrysler 300. Thetis Redford was driving, with Jackson Greens and Willie Brown in the back seat. Bantering and storytelling hadn't paused since we buckled in.

"Yo, Gator," said Jackson. That was me: the navi-Gator. "Keep an eye on the speed limit. Thetis got him a heavy foot."

"My foot just right," said Thetis. "Yours a little light, Jackson."

"Muddy liked it just fine."

"You ain't drive for Muddy," Willie objected, his tone scornful.

"Wrong, Willie. Used to hack a cab, and I picked the Mud up once." Thetis and Willie busted up. "What, *you* drive with him?"

"Naw, but I drove with Wolf. Never forget a trip down to Mississippi. Pass a billboard said, 'You are now entering Klan country.' Got a picture of a muthafucka inna sheet, carrying a torch, whole deal."

"Whole deal include a *lynching*," said Jackson.

"You think Mississippi the most racist state in the union?" asked Thetis.

"Naw," said Willie. "Most racist state the one you *in*."

"*Texas*?"

"Naw, whichever one you in at the *moment*. They all racist, just in fifty different ways."

"You believe that?" I asked. He gave me a sad look, as if the answer were obvious. "Is that why you carry weapons?"

"Thas just parta gettin' dressed," said Willie.

"But this trip we naked," Jackson added quickly. "Gonna be real peaceful."

"Muddy carry a gun?" asked Thetis, reluctant to leave the topic.

"Had him a tonna weapons," said Jackson. "Coulda been a swat team."

"Not Wolf," said Willie. "Thought it was bad for business. He didn't allow nair a pistol. One time, he bought a gun off a drummer—"

"Earl Phillips," said Jackson.

"—paid Earl good money, then threw the rod in Lake Michigan."

"Something 'bout Wolf and drummers," said Jackson. "He had a problem with Sam Lay, once upon a time."

"Oh, that was a good one!" said Willie, eager to tell it. "Sam was drinkin', and Wolf did not tolerate liquor while the band was on the clock. He was strict that way. Buy you a bottle at the end of the night, but no drinkin' while you were playin'. So Wolf, he about to give Sam hell, and Sam, he slam his gun down on the table—POW!—it go off, shoot a big hole in the wall. Ol' Wolf jump like a kitty cat, and a coupla fellas laugh."

"I would've," said Thetis, chuckling.

"Maybe," said Willie. "But that make Wolf hot. He turn to the guitar player, who had him a .38 in his case. 'Shoot that muthafucka, man!' 'Shoot him?' say the guitar player. '*Sam?*' 'Yeah, *shoot* him,' say Wolf. 'I get you outta jail!' Wolf think on it a second and say, 'Don't *kill* him. Just *wing* him.'"

When they stopped cutting up, I asked, "Did he mean it?" The notion of ordering a friend shot fascinated me.

"He might have," said Willie.

"Wolf didn't play," added Jackson. "He'd fine your ass if you

216

wasn't in proper uniform. Run his band like the army."

"Thas true," said Willie. "But don't want you to get the wrong idea, son. Wolf treat his boys right. Had his bookkeeper take out unemployment and Social Security from paychecks. And they didn't steal your money—held it right and turned it over to the government."

"I'd rather get alla my money and keep Uncle Sam out of it," said Thetis.

"You think that now," said Jackson.

"But when you an old man, you be glad for that Social Security," said Willie. Thetis had his eyes on the road, so Willie's meaningful look was directed at me.

I turned my attention to the navigational tools—Google maps on my iPhone and an actual paper folding map. The phone app was great for idiot-proofing my job, but I liked the old school method for seeing the big picture.

We were headed for Chicago, though I did not know why—it was a surprise, was all anyone would tell me. I was going to meet someone—somebody important, the way everyone was acting. After three hours on the road, we'd just passed Dallas, making the transition to Route 30, which we'd ride out of Texas, then cut a diagonal through Arkansas to Memphis before turning north. Thetis would drive all night. While he caught a few winks after daybreak, Jackson and Willie were each good for a few hours behind the wheel. Apart from pit stops, we would be on the road nonstop to the Windy City.

It had only been six hours since Jackson had told me to pack a bag. "Wait—*what?*" I'd said. We'd gone downstairs to sit with Mom and Dad. They said that the first step of my home schooling was to *leave* home on a "field trip." "Places to go and people to meet," was how they put it.

"These folks gettin' old," Jackson explained. "Ain't gonna wait 'til you grow up. You already done missed a bunch of 'em. Muddy, Wolf, Lightnin', Son House, Willie Dixon, John Lee. Seem like every day, another one of 'em pass."

The plan for the trip had evolved over meetings between my parents and Jackson, who had suggested that my dad come along. But after discussing it further, they decided I'd grow up faster without a parent in the back seat.

Mom wavered. Later they told me that, to close the deal, Jackson looked Mom in the eye and promised, with utmost conviction, "I'll take care of your son as if he was my *own* son."

"Do you *have* a son?" Mom asked.

Jackson maintained his sober look, considered, then answered, "*Probably.*"

When they stopped laughing, Mom agreed to the plan, if I reported in every day.

While they trusted my care to Jackson, they had less faith in Thetis's pickup, which was too small, anyway—so Dad volunteered to spring for a rental and gas. Jackson said they'd have friends to stay with and they'd pay for my meals, but Dad slipped me cash and told me to pick up a check or two. We planned to be gone only a few days—but we had to make haste, since whoever we were meeting in Chicago was on a tight schedule.

I'd barely had time to call Samantha and tell her what was happening. She listened quietly and I tried to read her mood through the ether. Finally, I just asked her, "What do you think?"

"I expect Chicago beats the hell out of school." She sounded wistful.

"Wish you could come."

"Off the top of my head, I can think of twenty objections my mom would make."

"I can't even believe *mine* is letting me go."

"She probably doesn't love you anymore."

"Could be," I agreed. It was a good sign when she started teasing me. "She might just be getting me out of my room so Mrs. Enriquez can clean it. Jackson said, 'Smell about three weeks funky in here.'"

"*Gross!*"

"She's making me take a shower before we leave."

"Put on deodorant, too."

"Thank you, Miss Manners."

"No one likes a smelly savant."

"That's harsh!"

"If the stink fits…"

We were laughing now, and I was starting to feel better, when she blurted out, "You're getting too big for me. I'm just a little cheerleader girl, and you're all famous and stuff—"

"—Everybody hates me," I broke in.

"They're just jealous. That Dr. Jeff junk will blow away with the next news cycle."

"So will I. I'm the flavor of a three-day month."

"I'm not the flavor of *any* month."

"You're *my* favorite flavor."

The line went silent. Then she said quietly, "For *now*."

I didn't know how to reassure her. I told her I'd miss her and call when I could. When we hung up, I hadn't felt good about it, and I doubt Samantha had, either.

With a sigh, I listened to Willie and Jackson argue about who was a bigger star, Wolf or Muddy. Thetis gave me a look, like a big brother commiserating when the parents get to bickering. He turned up the radio a notch. Before long, I drifted off to sleep.

"Boy, wake up," said Jackson. He gripped my shoulder hard. "Wake up!" he said urgently.

"What's happening?" I was groggy. It was dark and we were rolling on the highway.

"Gettin' pulled over. Need you alert."

Flashing red lights strobed through the car's interior. Thetis cut off the radio. A bullhorn blared, "Chrysler 300, take the offramp and pull to the shoulder."

"Was you speeding?" Willie asked Thetis accusingly.

"No, man. Cop pulled next to us, took a look, dropped back. Then he lit me up."

"Shit," said Jackson.

"Three black men and a white boy," said Willie. "Probably think we done kidnapped you."

"Don't say nothin' lessin' you have to," Jackson warned me.

"You carrying any shit?" Willie asked Thetis.

"Hell, no!" Thetis was getting annoyed by Willie's tone.

"Fuckin' Arkansas," said Jackson. "Klan headquarters."

"Thas up north. Worst part of the state," said Willie.

"Where we at?" asked Jackson.

"Comin' up on Little Rock," said Thetis.

"Oh, yeah," said Jackson. "Round here they *liberals*."

Thetis took the exit and pulled to the shoulder. He turned off the engine, rolled down the window, and flipped on the interior cabin lights. I took registration and rental papers from the glove compartment and handed them to him. He pulled his license from his wallet.

"Now stay still," he said. "Keep your hands where they can see 'em, and don't no one move." We sat and waited. It was in the thirties, and the engine ticked as it cooled. Frigid air rushed in through the open window, amplifying my nervous shiver.

The patrol car had stopped close enough to hear its radio squawking. A door slammed and an officer walked deliberately to the driver side window.

"Evening, boys." He was a big, middle-aged white man, wearing a crisp uniform. His black necktie was tucked neatly into a blue dress shirt with epaulets, studded with metal buttons. He had a badge, and another on a broad-brimmed hat like the Canadian Mounties wear. I think they look ridiculous.

He took a careful look at each of us. "Nice car," he remarked. "Gangsta."

"It's a rental, sir," said Thetis, his voice measured and respectful. He carefully offered the paperwork. "License, reg, and rental docs."

"Fella who knows the drill. Be with you in a minute. Y'all can roll up the window. Little nippy tonight."

"Yessir, it is."

The officer walked back to his car. We heard the door open and close as he got in.

"What's he doing?" I asked.

"Calling it in," said Thetis. "Make sure the car isn't stolen. Runnin' my license for warrants."

"You got anything?" asked Jackson.

"Naw, I'm clean."

"Then…we're fine?" I asked.

Willie shook his head. "It ain't that simple." The words were weighted with menace.

"Got a letter from the boy's father, if it come to that," said Jackson. "Your folks sleep with the phone next to 'em?" he asked.

"Yeah," I said.

"Call 'em if we have to." He didn't sound reassured by the thought.

After waiting nervously for several minutes, we heard the officer's door open. Thetis rolled down the window and put his hands on the steering wheel. The rest of us hadn't moved.

The officer handed the paperwork back to Thetis. "This appears to be in order," he said tentatively. "Y'all from Austin. Where you headed?"

"Chicago," said Thetis.

"Ways to go. Mind if I look in the trunk?"

"That'd be fine."

"Pop it for me and stay put."

Thetis found the release and the trunk opened with a click. The officer strolled to the back of the car and returned within moments.

"What is all that stuff?"

"Instruments. We're musicians," said Thetis.

"That a fact? Him, too?" he asked, indicating me.

"Yessir. Plays the guitar."

The officer frowned. "He's just a boy. Is he your…son?"

"Nossir. Just a friend. Another musician."

The officer seemed to be choosing his words carefully. "You understand this looks kind of odd." His eyes swept the cabin, and Jackson spoke up.

"His parents give me a letter in case anybody ask." Jackson carefully extended the letter to the officer, and added, "Can also reach them on the phone."

The officer illuminated the letter with a flashlight, read it carefully, and looked up at me.

"I was on TV last month," I offered. "*Dr. Jeff Show.*"

I could have picked a better name to drop. The officer's voice was low with scorn. "Dr. Jeff. What a jerk."

"You got that right," I said.

"But my wife likes him." He had a sudden thought. "Wait, are *you* that kid? She told me about that! Said you had a concussion and when you got better, you could play the guitar."

"That's what happened." Even I was starting to think it sounded like a hoax.

"She said you didn't play too good on the show…" he added, though not in a mean way.

"He ain't feel like it, way that Dr. Jeff did him," said Jackson. "But he can play good."

"*Real* good," added Willie.

The officer smiled at me and said, "Would you mind giving me your autograph? I mean, for my wife?"

"Sure thing."

He extended a pen and a notepad. "Make it out to Mary."

"M-a-r-y?" I spelled, an old hand at the routine.

"Right. Man, she won't *believe* this." His attitude had brightened, and he was smiling like he'd found a twenty dollar bill on the ground. "I'll be a hero for a day."

"Happy wife, happy life," said Thetis, as if he were also married.

"Too true," said the officer, retrieving the pad and pen. He asked, "While we're at it, any more famous people here?"

After a moment, Willie replied, "Nobody your wife woulda heard of."

"All right, then," the officer chuckled. "Let's keep it that way. If you head through the intersection, the on-ramp'll take you back to the highway."

"Good deal," said Thetis. "I'm gonna let you go first. Ain't comfortable having the law on my tail."

"Understood," said the officer. "And screw Dr. Jeff," he added in parting.

The officer walked back to his car and Thetis rolled up the window. We sat a moment, waiting. "Is it over?" I asked.

"Naw," said Willie.

"Never over," said Jackson sadly. But a moment later he was laughing. "Nobody your wife woulda heard of," he taunted, giving Willie a shove.

"You sure about that?" laughed Thetis.

"Pretty sure," said Willie, smiling slyly.

Chapter Forty-Six
White Privilege

WE RELIVED the encounter with the patrolman, the unexpected outcome, and Willie's deliciously irreverent line. Spirits were high. Then they changed.

"He was pullin' the tiger's tail," said Jackson.

"How you mean?" asked Thetis.

"Willie know how I mean," said Jackson, looking at his partner. Willie scowled, but didn't respond. "Ain't many years a line like that get you killed."

"For *what*?" I said.

"Naw," said Thetis. He couldn't believe it, either.

This was something I had to make sense of. "He was saying the cop's wife wouldn't know him. Why isn't that okay?"

Jackson pursed his lips. "Way he said it, sounded like she *might* have. Why it was so good—line had more than one meaning. Cop knew it, too. Just lucky he wasn't no good ol' boy."

"Fuck them good ol' boys," said Willie, but he wasn't smiling.

"And they wives, too," said Thetis. "*The men don't know, but the little girls understand.*" He laughed, but the mood from the back seat was dark.

"Just lucky he ain't call for backup," said Jackson. "We be cuffed and on the way to lockup now."

I was still unconvinced. "What could they arrest you for?"

Jackson guffawed. "Y'all so young."

"And white," added Willie.

"DWB," said Thetis, explaining.

"What's that?"

"Driving while black."

"There's no law against that," I argued. "They can't take you to jail for that."

"Stop you, though," said Thetis. "Once you stopped, anything happen."

"Why you let him check the trunk?" demanded Willie hotly. "Coulda tossed some reefer in there and we'da been fucked."

Thetis was indignant. "What if I tell him no? You think he just gonna take that?"

"Thetis right," said Jackson. "Man wanta look, you 'twixt devil and the deep blue sea. Pick your poison."

"Have you guys...been arrested?" I asked.

"Once," said Jackson.

"Twice—no..." said Willie, recollecting. "Yeah, twice."

I looked to Thetis. "Not me."

"You do time?" Jackson asked Willie.

"Two years. Parchman."

"*Parchman?*" Jackson was taken aback. "Why ain't you never tell me you was in Parchman?"

"Musta done."

Jackson's jaw clenched grimly. "Not the kinda thing I'd forget."

"What's Parchman?" I asked.

"Mississippi state prison," said Jackson. "We ridin' with a celebrity, boys."

"'Cause he was in Parchman?" asked Thetis.

"Naw," said Jackson. "'Cause he come *out*."

His words hung like a judge's sentence, until Willie ordered, "Turn the car around, Thetis."

"*What?*"

"Goin' home. I'm too old for this mess…"

"We halfway across Arkansas!"

"Drop me at a bus station." Then he muttered, "Can't be playing Uncle Tom to no kid with his white privilege and whatnot."

"Aw, that ain't cool," said Thetis.

"White privilege?" I asked, not understanding the words.

"See?" said Willie, as if I'd proved his point. "He don't even know."

"He just a boy," said Thetis. "Cut him some slack."

"Seriously, what are you talking about?"

Willie gave me a long look, considering whether he wanted to say more. He made up his mind. "White privilege what get us outta that jam with the cop—'cause you was white and give him an autograph. It's what keep white folks from gettin' pulled over in the first place, even when they *breakin'* the law. Your daddy drive this car, ain't no one call him gangsta!"

I didn't say anything—heck, I had no idea *what* to say. Willie's anger had seemed to come out of nowhere, but he had deep grievances. And he was just getting started.

"Y'all live where you want, no harassment from neighbors who mad you move in. When you go shoppin' in a nice store, don't nobody follow you 'round. You in trouble at school, your folks know it ain't causa your color. You grow big and tall, people *respect* you, 'stead of *fear* you. When you a man, you can look a cop in the eye without he ride you down. You gettin' the idea?"

"Yeah…" I said, not sure I really was. Though I knew prejudice existed, I had never considered how it played out. "But what you're calling 'white privilege' is just basic rights."

Willie snorted in disgust. "You got 'em and we don't."

I had to admit he was right, but something rubbed me the wrong way. "I guess it's the name that bothers me," I said. "It makes me feel like *I* did something wrong."

"'Scuse me for offendin' you."

"Willie…" Jackson started.

"Naw, he asked! It's white privilege not to even know you *got* white privilege! It's white privilege to be put out when a man tell you what you *got*! And he got 'savant privilege' on toppa that!"

"Oh, come on," said Thetis.

But trying to settle him down only threw fuel on Willie's fire. "Hell, no! The blues is black. Music come from sufferin', come from pain—*deep* pain—four-hundred-*year* pain."

"He play 'em good," insisted Thetis.

"Um-hm," said Willie, his eyelids drooping. "But they ain't his."

"No black, no white, just blues," said Thetis.

"Seen that one—on a T-shirt a *white* man wearin'. Yeah, *now* he wanna be color-blind. Done took everything else. Coulda left us the blues."

Willie's words lit me like a brilliant searchlight from a police helicopter. I froze as I finally identified the nagging sense of shame I'd felt since I started playing the guitar. My ability wasn't acquired by theft, but I *had* come into possession of something extremely valuable that I hadn't earned. In one concussive stroke, I'd been granted a skill beyond what dedicated musicians achieved after twenty-five years of hard labor. An ability so special a man could suggest I'd made a deal with the devil to obtain it. To make it worse, I was playing music that didn't even belong to me.

But I was a teenager: after a moment I rallied and tried to mount a defense. "So if I stop playing the blues, will that make a difference?" I asked. "What about Stevie Ray?"

"*He* earned 'em," said Willie. "*You* ain't."

"What you think, Jackson?" asked Thetis.

Jackson chewed his lip. "Willie got a point."

"You agreeing with him?" exclaimed Thetis, shocked.

"Naw. That boat done sailed."

"But the bus *ain't*," said Willie. "Y'all can drop me at Greyhound in Memphis."

"Uh-huh," said Jackson. "Right after breakfast." He gave me a wink and added, "Gator, get on that smart-ass phone an' find us some good-ass food."

Chapter Forty-Seven
Buddy

THE CAR WENT SILENT as Jackson and Willie slept. I was left to think about what had been said.

Under stress, Willie had spoken his mind, revealing a chasm I hadn't known existed. My mind turned to football friends—Jamarie, Tyrell, and others. Did they experience the kind of prejudice that Willie had referred to? And was that how they saw me—not just as a friend, but as a white kid with advantages? I thought back to experiences together, conversations. I couldn't come up with anything to answer one way or the other. But these were awful thoughts, and I felt ashamed they had never occurred to me.

We detoured in Memphis to try early breakfast at a spot I located online. The menu was in the form of a fake newspaper. Along with food offerings, it featured rules to live by and quotes from famous people. After ordering, we sipped coffee and orange juice and studied the "wisdom."

"They good rules, far as they go," said Jackson.

"Boring, though," scoffed Willie. "No wonder people don't pay them no mind."

"We can do better," said Thetis. "I got one. 'The only reason to look down on someone is to pick them up.'"

"Good line," said Willie. "But Jessie Jackson the one who said it."

"Didn't claim it was original," said Thetis.

"'I have decided to stick with love. Hate is too great a burden to bear,'" quoted Jackson.

"Brother Martin?" said Thetis.

"Always a good guess," Jackson replied, nodding.

"'Resentment is like drinking poison, and hoping it will kill your enemies,'" said Willie.

"Oh, thas good," said Thetis. "You oughta remember that one."

"Just did," said Willie. "Nelson Mandela."

"Um-hm, he would," said Jackson. "Man had plenty to resent."

"'Don't look back. Something might be gaining on you,'" I offered.

They looked at me in surprise. "Boy know his Satchel Paige!" exclaimed Jackson.

When food arrived, proverbs gave way to groans of satisfaction. We debated whether the flaky biscuits were better with butter or bathed in country gravy. The bacon was thick, lean, and chewy; the omelet was fluffy; and the cinnamon raisin pecan pancakes were breakfast dessert delicious.

"Eat a lot," said Jackson. "Gotta hold you 'til dinner."

"We're not stopping for lunch?" I asked.

"Our friend like his food," he said. "Gonna wanna have an appetite."

When the meal was over, Willie cleaned his teeth with a toothpick and looked over. He gave me a little smile.

"Sorry about that earlier," he said.

"Nigga, you should be," said Thetis, quick as a shot.

I was shocked, but Jackson and Willie roared, particularly amused by my reaction. I looked to Thetis.

He cocked an eye at me. "I can say that, but you can't. *Black* privilege."

"*Black* privilege," said Jackson. "Why not?"

"I'm *not* sorry about what I told you," Willie clarified. "Good for you to hear them things, whether you like 'em or not. Didn't have to be mean about it, though."

"World's fucked up, but it's not Gator's fault," said Thetis.

"An' he made a good point," said Jackson seriously. "Word 'privilege' make it sound like something oughta be taken *away*. But that's *wrong*. 'Stead, all the things Willie said are rights *everybody* oughta have. Boy had that dead on."

The men chorused agreement, nodding.

"We good?" asked Willie.

"Yeah, but...what about the blues?" That was the part that bothered me the most. I didn't want to give up the music, but Willie had a point. "I haven't suffered compared to a lot of people."

"No limit on sufferin'," said Willie, looking to the ceiling and beyond. "We all get the blues. I had 'em 'fore breakfast."

"So...next stop Greyhound?" asked Jackson, his eyebrows raised.

"Aw, man...I hate buses," said Willie, smiling in defeat. "Best roll on."

The waitress brought the check. I slapped bills on it and handed it back to her before anyone could move. She nodded and walked off to get change.

My friends looked at each other, startled. Willie frowned at Jackson.

"You gone let him do that?"

"I ain't have a chance to stop him," said Jackson.

"Least you oughta look at it, make sure you payin' for what you got," Thetis said to me.

"Shit, Muddy study his tab like a lawyer goin' over a contract— and he couldn't read a lick," said Jackson. He did a comical impression, scrutinizing his dirty napkin as if it were the bill.

"Couldn't hardly write, neither. Had him a stamp for autographs," said Willie.

"Oh, you lyin'," said Thetis, laughing.

"Um-um," said Willie, shaking his head. "If you got a handwritten autograph from Muddy, that was somethin' special. Most times he just stamp 'em."

Jackson looked at me and explained, "We was all sharecroppers. Had to take care of the cotton—plant it, chop it, pick it. City kids got full nine months of school. We didn't get but three."

"If *that*," said Willie. "Not that we *liked* school…"

When we returned to the car, Thetis asked Jackson, "You take the wheel a spell?"

"Sure thing. Get us back to Arkansas and I take over."

Thetis gave him a look. "Arkansas just the other side of the river."

"Yeah. I don't drive on no bridge," said Jackson.

"Okay," said Thetis with the lift of a brow.

We buckled in and I navigated back to the highway. Within a moment we were crossing a span over the Mississippi. I felt a tap on my shoulder and turned to look. Willie pointed at Jackson, whose eyes were shut so tight the crow's feet were puckered into brown hills and valleys. I gazed down at the water, wondering what there was to fear.

"The Mississippi sure doesn't look blue," I said.

"*Muddy. Waters*," said Jackson.

"How would you know?" said Willie.

"Don't have to see 'em to know. Been like that a good little while."

I navigated through the interchange to I-55 North which would head us toward Chicago. After a couple of miles, Thetis pulled over. He and Jackson switched places and Jackson buckled in. He adjusted the seat, adjusted the mirrors, adjusted the volume on the radio. He studied the dash and the console. He tried the electric windows: down...up...down...up. We waited.

Finally, Willie broke the silence. "You *can* drive, can't you?"

We busted up. "This just foreplay, man," said Jackson.

"Lemme ask you," said Thetis. "Which you done more recently—drive a car or get with a woman?"

"Don't answer that," said Willie quickly.

"Take some thought," admitted Jackson.

"Well, you *can* do one of them today," said Thetis. "If you hurry."

"Hopin' to do 'em both 'fore we get home," said Jackson. With a chuckle, he put the car in gear, and carefully maneuvered off the shoulder and into the slow lane. Traffic was light, and within a few minutes he had worked his way to the fast lane and was whistling happily.

"Feel good, don't it?" asked Willie.

"Yeah, it do," said Jackson.

"Keep an eye on the speed limit, Gator," Thetis teased. "I'mo catch a few winks."

"We in no hurry. Man we seein' take him a long afternoon nap, an' we can't show up early."

We drove for a couple of quiet hours, the route carving through the last of Arkansas and into the southeast corner of Missouri. Most of the time we couldn't see the big river, but the map showed it writhing not far to our right, a giant, mysterious water snake. Like the state named for it, the Mississippi was inseparable from the blues, and had assumed mythic status in my mind.

When we left I-55 for I-57, I looked ahead on the map. "Uh-oh."

"*What?*" said Jackson.

"Bridge coming in a few miles."

"Pull over. I take it from here," said Willie.

Jackson drew to the shoulder and they switched places. A few minutes later we crossed a short span across the windy Mississippi, which was not at its mightiest.

"Shit, I coulda done that one," said Jackson.

"Umm-hmm," said Willie skeptically. I looked back and noted that Jackson's eyes were again clenched tight.

We stopped for gas a few hours later and Thetis woke up. He climbed out of the car, stretched like a big cat limbering up, and got back behind the wheel.

It was getting dark as I navigated the route to a suburb outside Chicago. Following my directions, Thetis turned into a long driveway that led to a mansion set well back from the road. It was surrounded by forest, threadbare in the early December weather.

As Thetis turned off the ignition, the front door of the house swung open and a man stepped out, waving. Smiling broadly, he seemed about the same age as Willie and Jackson.

"Hello, boys!" he called, as we piled out of the car. "Jackson, Willie—it's been a minute! Thetis, I've heard of you and glad to meet you. An' I guess this the young man you told me about."

Jackson elbowed me and said, "Boy, shake hands with Buddy Guy."

"Oh, no way!" I blurted. I'd only been paying attention to music for a couple of months, but even I knew Buddy Guy was among the greatest living guitarists.

Buddy laughed and took my hand. "Last I checked. What do you go by?"

I sighed. "No one likes it. Friz."

Buddy winced.

"Been callin' him 'Gator,' 'cause he the *navigator* on this trip," said Jackson.

"Naw," said Buddy, "sound like a cracker. We come up with something. Let's get your bags."

We took our luggage inside and Buddy said, "Drop 'em here. Show you to your rooms later."

"Aw, Buddy, we ain't the Rollin' Stones. 'Spect we can sleep on the couch," said Jackson.

"Speak for yourself," said Willie, his jaw set.

Buddy chuckled. "B'lieve that's where Keith wound up, after he done drunk everything in the house."

"Uh-oh," said Thetis.

"Restocked since then," said Buddy with a wink. "Hope you ate on the road, though."

"*What?*" said Jackson. "You ain't cooked nothin'?"

"Naw, I gave that up," said Buddy. "But we can order a pizza."

"I like pizza," I said, and Buddy burst into laughter.

"Boy, you can't invite Jackson without you fix some greens," said Buddy. "How he got his name. While the rest of us reachin' for ribs, Jackson always after collards."

Willie was looking over the premises like a realtor. "This some house, Buddy. How many rooms it got?"

"'Bout twenty," he answered off-handedly. "You want a *tour*, or you want a *drink*?"

In a rough chorus, three men said, "Drink." Buddy cocked his head at me and smiled.

The kitchen was filled with good smells. Buddy had a soda for me and glasses of corn liquor for the others. He poured a beer over ice for himself.

Willie took a swallow and smacked his lips. "Ummm! This from home?"

"Yeah, they send it up to me," said Buddy, lifting lids and stirring pots.

"Thetis, you ever drink this?" asked Jackson.

"First time. Won't be the last." He poured another finger in his glass.

"Go easy," said Jackson. "Little stronger than the usual. Can't have you passing out 'fore supper."

The house had a dining room with a big table, but instead we ate in the kitchen, which was warm and cozy. I set places and everyone helped carry platters of steaming food. When we sat down, Buddy looked over at Jackson. "You say anything?"

"Not in the habit. But this is special, ain't it?"

So we joined hands. I lowered my head and closed my eyes, holding the strong, weathered fingers of Jackson and Thetis. "Lord, thank you for keepin' us alive long enough for old friends to see each other again. Thank you for our new friend. You'll take care of us all, won't you? We've got music to make and need as many years to do it as you see fit to give us. Thank you for this food, and our friend, Buddy Guy, who cook good as he plays guitar. Amen."

"Amen," we echoed. We parted hands to pass platters, respectfully silent after the prayer. Then Willie turned to Jackson.

"I thought you was never gonna stop!"

"Longest grace I ever did hear," said Buddy. "You done become a Texas preacher."

Jackson reached for our hands. "Wait, I forgot a few things…"

"Naw," said Willie. "You ain't forgot *nothin'* but to pass the ribs!"

As I took a bowl from Buddy, I said, "I like your shirt." It was a flowing, long-sleeved, black shirt, with big white polka dots.

"This old thing?" he said in a high-pitched voice like a woman. "Story behind it."

"When you an old man, they's always a story," joked Willie.

"If you lived right," said Jackson.

"Polka dots are kinda my thing," Buddy explained. "My trademark, like. See, my momma had a stroke when I was still down south, so I didn't want to leave her and come to Chicago. But my daddy, he knew this is where I had to be for the music. He urged me to go. I told Momma I was gonna make it big and buy her a polka-dot Cadillac. Still bothers me I couldn't get Momma her car before she died."

"Best take care of your momma while you can," said Jackson, stabbing a fork at me for emphasis.

After dinner Buddy got up and declared, "Boys, I got to go to the club. Y'all must be tired from the road. Why don't you sleep tonight and come down with me tomorrow?"

"If I was a young buck, I'd come *tonight*," said Willie.

"Yeah, but you only half a buck," said Jackson.

"Well, *you're* two-bits," said Willie.

"I'll tag along, if I can," said Thetis.

"Glad to have you," said Buddy.

"Y'all go on," said Jackson. "We'll clean up."

We cleared the table and did dishes after they left. On our last legs, we got our bags and trudged upstairs to the third floor.

"Think if Buddy so rich he'd get him an escalator," said Willie.

"You mean an elevator?" said Jackson.

"Either one," said Willie tiredly. "I'm about done in."

The third floor had several bedrooms, one of which was obviously Buddy's. We put Thetis's bag in one of the empty ones, and each of us took one of the others.

"You got what you need, son?" asked Jackson.

I told him I did, and we said good night. I closed the door to the room, slipped off my shoes, and lay down before getting ready for bed. Not twenty-four hours had passed since I'd left Texas, but it felt like much longer. Life on the road happened at a different pace, with new experiences coming so fast and furious that one day felt like a year. It had been frightening, exciting, upsetting, startling, thrilling. It left me feeling and thinking, trying to sort out the events of the day.

I thought about calling Samantha.

I thought about calling Mom and Dad.

But I was too tired to talk. I shot my parents a quick text to keep them from panicking.

And then, as my eyes drifted shut, I thought about what might happen next year.

Tomorrow.

Chapter Forty-Eight
Legends

"WAKE UP, SLEEPYHEAD," said the voice. I opened my eyes to see Buddy sitting on the edge of the bed. His big hand gently shook my shoulder.

"Is it late?"

"Been up for hours."

I pulled myself out of bed in a rush.

Buddy chuckled. "It's only seven. What say we let the old men sleep while we cook up some breakfast? Let's see can you make a biscuit."

"I can't."

"We gonna fix that."

I threw on some clothes, brushed my teeth and hair, and went downstairs to the kitchen. It was warm and smelled like coffee.

"When did you get up?" I asked Buddy.

"Four-thirty."

"*Four-thirty*?" It was an inconceivable hour.

"Been doin' it my whole life."

"But now you don't have to," I argued.

Buddy's voice was like my grandfather's, gently confiding the secrets of a lifetime. "Don't do it 'cause I *have* to. Do it 'cause I *want* to. Something feels good about being awake while other folks asleep—whether it's the middle of the night or early morning."

"Yeah, but when do *you* sleep?"

"I get me three, four hours at night, another few in the afternoon." He turned to give me a knowing smile. "That feels good, too— *sleepin'* while everyone else *workin'.*"

Graceful as a ballroom dancer, Buddy plucked pans from a rack, cartons from the fridge, canisters from the cupboard. Soon he had everything he needed.

"Now, let's see can I teach you to make biscuits. First thing, freeze the butter. Always did wonder why winter biscuits were better. Gotta keep the dough cold as can be…"

If you ask me, Buddy could have his own cooking show, and I'd be glad to be on it. Along with biscuits, we fried eggs and bacon, and assembled the best breakfast sandwich I ever had. Mouth too full for words, I widened my eyes to convey how delicious it was. He gave me the smile that has won over the whole world.

"Better than McDonald's?"

All I could do was nod.

"Thetis told me how y'all met. Can't believe he played a football game—and it wasn't no halftime at the Super Bowl."

"Texas Youth. I was supposed to be in the game."

"But you had the concussion," he said gently. "He told me you watched him play 'Little Wing,' then you played it better than him. And that was the first time you heard it?"

"He played it twice…"

"Oh. Well, then," he said, as if that settled the matter. "Suppose you play it for me?"

"Won't it wake up the guys?"

"Naw, they way up on the third floor. Got a little practice amp here you can plug into. Go grab your axe—still in the foyer."

I swallowed the last of my sandwich, wiped my hands on my

jeans, and rushed to get my guitar before I had time to think too much about playing for Mr. Buddy Guy. When I got back, he had a small amp and handed me a cable. I plugged into the jack and strummed a few chords. He adjusted the volume. I checked the tuning.

"No clip-on? You tune by ear?" he asked, intrigued.

"More like by *eye*. I see these shapes and colors and…I just know when the notes are right." I played the open strings, and he nodded.

"Yeah, you do. All right, then."

I took a moment to gather myself…to think about all that had happened in the last few days…last few months…then the shapes took flight and I began to play.

When I finished, I looked at Buddy. He gave me an approving nod.

"Ain't nobody could play that song like Jimi or Stevie. But they gone." He heaved a sigh, and let the sad words hang. "Now nobody can play that song like *you*, young man."

"Thank you," I mumbled, relieved and embarrassed.

"Would you mind telling me the whole story?"

He listened as I took him through my concussion and treatment, his brow furrowing. He didn't ask questions until I explained what Dr. Monaghan had told me.

"He said what, you got a computer in your head?"

"Sort of. He thinks the brain may be like a hard drive—the part of the computer that holds tons of information. When you buy a computer at the store, it comes with lots of programs already installed on the hard drive. Most of them you never use, but they're there."

"And that knock on the head opened up those programs?" Buddy sounded amazed.

I shrugged my own doubt in Dr. Monaghan's theory. "He said that, in some cases, people know things they never learned—could not *possibly* have learned. He said this information must be coded into our bodies. It's like an inheritance we normally can't touch."

Buddy sat a long while, thinking. Finally, he said, "'Inheritance' is a fine way to put it. You been given a mighty big gift. How you feel about that?"

"Jackson says I've got the blues," I said.

Buddy gave me a knowing smile. "Welcome to the club. Tell me about 'em."

I explained about Dr. Jeff and Samantha and football and my friends.

"My team's in the playoffs. This week is the semis. If we win—I mean, if *they* win—they go to the state finals."

"They want you to play?"

I bit my lip, thinking about all the times the guys had urged me to get back on the field.

"*You* wanta play?" Buddy asked softly.

My shoulders slumped and I bowed my head. "Not like I used to. Before the concussion, it was all I cared about." I took a deep breath and admitted, "Now I feel different."

"You ain't who you were," he said simply. "Now, who you *are*, you just gonna have to find out. But a man gotta be who he is. Can't be nothin' else and have no peace. It's simple. But it don't come easy. Bein' who you are in this world…man, that'll give you the blues."

He flashed that dazzling grin. "Little secret, though. Playin' the blues, *chase* the blues."

"Is it…" I started. He waited patiently. "Is it even okay for me to play the blues?"

"You just *did*."

"Yeah, but… I'm white."

"Someone tell you only black folks can play the blues?" I nodded, and Buddy frowned, annoyed. "Like we got extra fingers white folks *ain't*?"

He displayed his wiggling fingers, and I had to laugh.

"Son, you caught in the middle of an old argument. If you got to be a certain color to play a certain music, that mean only white folks can play Beethoven? Maybe just Germans? Sound ridiculous, don't it? Where would it stop?"

I nodded, not really agreeing. "But the blues are different. They're special."

After reflecting a moment, he said, "If you want a slice of '*bluesberry* pie,' does that take away from me? Do I have to give *my* piece of pie to *you*? Naw—'cause the pie just keep gettin' bigger. Plenty for all of us. Ain't no one goin' without."

I didn't say anything. Buddy studied his fingernails, as if he didn't like the way they looked. Then he went on.

"But you're right—the blues *are* special. Ought not take 'em for granted. Respectful to know the history. Where they came from. How they happened. Who played them. And what they mean. Why you're goin' to the Delta. That's the right way to do it."

He gazed into space, as if seeing words where I saw colors and shapes. "Somehow, though…you already *do* know. Blues is in you, maybe the way the doctor said. They been passed on to you from somewhere. Else you couldn't play them like you do. Not just the right notes, but the right feeling."

He looked at me with a little smile. "That put your mind to rest?"

"No," I said, smiling back. "But thanks for trying."

Buddy laughed and clapped me on the shoulder. "Boy, you got the blues about the blues! C'mon, let's do a little woodshedding in the studio. Couple things I might could show you."

The next hours passed like a dream. Buddy's enthusiasm was infectious. He stopped jamming frequently to point out a setting on the amp, to explain choices of pedals, guitars, strings. Everything reminded Buddy of a story. He told me about growing up in the

South, about music, and how he'd learned to play it. He even got out a one-string diddley bow guitar and showed me how poor Delta kids got their first taste of the instrument.

Buddy finally put his guitar on the stand. "Man, you wore me out. Believe it's time for a nap before we hit the club. You up to sittin' in for a couple songs tonight?"

"With you?" I asked, stunned.

"Uh-huh."

"Well, yeah. Sure," I said. It was an *amazing* offer, but… "Am I, you know…good enough?"

"You been plenty good enough last few hours. Kept right up. You ain't gonna freeze onstage, are you?"

"I don't think so. I was okay with Jackson and Willie."

He cocked his head, considering me with narrowed eyes. "Legends a little bigger house than The King."

Buddy wasn't kidding. His place, Legends, was one of the last blues clubs in Chicago, and it was cavernous compared to The King. As we entered, my eyes swept the wall behind the bar, hung with glittering electric guitars donated by great players. We stopped to admire a mural that showed a mountain range studded with the heads of four men. Placards in the painting identified them as Muddy Waters, Sonny Boy Williamson, Little Walter, and Howlin' Wolf.

Buddy put a hand on my shoulder. "How you like my Blues Mt. Rushmore?"

Before I could respond, Jackson said, "Notice Muddy in the place of Washington, the *first* president."

No way Willie could let that go unchallenged. "Yeah, but Wolf in the place of Lincoln—the *greatest* president."

Thetis heaved a theatrical sigh. "I'm just glad Walter and Sonny

Boy betwixt 'em to keep the peace. Sorta like me and Gator."
Laughing, we continued inside and took a table. Buddy ordered a
lavish spread, and we sipped drinks until the food came.

"It's good," Willie said to Buddy, his mouth full of gumbo. "But
not good as *you* make."

"Yeah, I can hardly choke down these greens," said Jackson. "Pass
me more of 'em, Thetis, and I'll keep tryin'."

An acoustic guitarist entertained the dinner guests. When he went
on break, Buddy wiped his hands on a napkin.

"Y'all ready?" he asked, and I nodded.

Buddy stepped onstage and the diners reacted. Even though it was
Buddy's club, most nights he didn't play.

"How y'all enjoying your dinner?" Buddy asked the crowd.
Shouts of encouragement, a few whistles.

"That's good, so are we. Some friends visiting from Texas. Like
to show 'em a little Chicago hospitality."

"Break their legs!" yelled a big guy.

Buddy laughed. "Not *that* much hospitality." The crowd laughed,
too. "They *old* friends. Come up here 'cause they wanted me to meet
someone *new*. Just a boy, fourteen years old. Got hit in the head
playin' football, and next thing you know, he could play the *guitar*.
Imagine that? Just happen, like a miracle. Once I heard him, thought
y'all oughta hear him, too."

The crowd cheered encouragement. "Jackson, y'all sit in on
drums, and Thetis, maybe you take bass, huh? Willie, you play a little
keyboard, don't you? Come on, boys, let's have a go."

It was one giant step to the stage, with a big Legends logo on the
brick wall behind us. Thetis and I plugged in, and Willie took a seat
at the keyboard. Jackson settled himself at the drum kit, checked the
bass kick and high hats, and Buddy turned to the mike.

"Y'all mighta heard it said that once upon a time the blues had a baby and they called it rock 'n' roll…" Cheers, and a couple of boos. "Well, some babies ain't *planned*, you know…" Buddy noodled on the guitar and enjoyed the banter.

"Still, in the way of the world, little fella grew up and started taking care of his parents." Buddy chuckled. "Returned the favor, you might say. Gigs got better, and I didn't have to keep drivin' a tow truck. By the way, anybody here I towed, back in the day?"

A guy in the back raised his hand. "To the *impound!*"

Buddy winced for show. "Sorry 'bout that, man. Hey!" he called out to a waitress. "Get that fella a drink—on me." Instantly several other hands shot up. "Oh! I towed you, too, huh?" Then everybody in the place was waving at Buddy, laughing and carrying on. "Oh, I towed the whole house, did I? Y'all weren't even *born* back then!"

Buddy laughed along with them. He was great with the crowd and enjoyed the interaction as much as they did. When it settled down, he continued. "Anyway, we were talking about rock 'n' roll. Lotta British cats led the way. One of them you mighta heard of. Eric Clapton." Cheers and clapping for one of the greatest ever. "This a Robert Johnson song, but Eric showed how you can make them 'old things new again.'"

Most people knew what was coming: "Crossroads." When Jackson laid down the pounding beat, all doubt vanished. But we held back, Buddy deferring to me, as I opened with a moody intro that worked the crowd up until they were mad with anticipation. They were urging me on with shouts like you'd hear when a Baptist minister gets to preaching, though more off-color: "Do it, man, do it!" and "Give it to me, baby!" They exploded when we hit the signature riff that drives the song.

I took the first solo and didn't look back. Playing onstage with Buddy was just as easy as jamming in his studio, and the crowd did its best to encourage me. When we transitioned into another song, they dropped their forks and leaped out of their seats.

"Folks, let's hear it for my friends. Jackson Greens on drums, Thetis Redford on bass, Willie Brown on keyboard, and the young man I was telling you about—Gregory Collins. I call him 'G.' Believe you'll be hearin' more about him," said Buddy. The crowd applauded long and loud, whistled, stomped, and pounded tables.

"Don't break nothin'!" yelled Buddy on the mike, grinning. Several people sprang up for selfies with me. Then we sat back down to finish dinner.

"Thank you, Buddy," I said.

"You're welcome, son," he said. "Think they liked you."

"Yeah," said Thetis. "Oughta put that stupid Mr. Jeff thing to bed."

"*Dr.* Jeff," I corrected.

"He ain't no doctor," said Thetis scornfully.

Willie looked over at Buddy. "Ain't you got another prodigy under your wing?"

Buddy nodded and chuckled. "Good thing I got *two* wings," he said, flapping his elbows like a chicken.

Chapter Forty-Nine
Homecoming

WE WATCHED the first set after dinner, then headed home. Buddy had to catch an early flight for shows on the west coast. Even at his age, he still played over a hundred concerts a year.

"Shouldn't you be slowing down?" I asked.

"That *is* slowing down," said Jackson.

"Buddy getting lazy, what it is," said Willie with a smile.

"I mean…you don't need the money," I persisted.

"Oughta know by now, son…"

"Don't do it 'cause you *have* to. Do it 'cause you *want* to," I said, imitating him.

"You're learning," laughed Buddy.

We trudged up two floors to the bedrooms, then paused as the old men caught their breath. "How early do you have to leave?" I asked Buddy.

His mouth twisted in amusement. "Even before *my* normal. Best say our goodbyes now."

There were hugs all around, but I held onto Buddy for extra seconds. "Play them blues, an' *chase* them blues," he whispered into my ear.

Finally, I let go. "I hope I see you again," I said.

"You know the way." He looked at the others and turned serious.

"Goes for alla you boys. Our age, can't be waitin' no five, ten years, y'hear?"

"Do that, you'll be seein' me at my funeral," said Willie.

When we got up the next morning, the door to Buddy's room stood open and he was gone. The maids had arrived, changing linen and dusting furniture. Thetis made coffee and we sat around the kitchen. The mood reminded me of the letdown following Christmas Day.

"Don't feel right here without Buddy," murmured Jackson.

"Yeah. Feels sad," agreed Willie.

"Why you have to say that about funerals?" Jackson complained. "Believe a goose walk over my grave."

"Let's get goin'," said Thetis. "Eat on the road."

"Good idea," said Willie. We agreed to take showers, pack, and meet downstairs.

Forty-five minutes later, we loaded the trunk and left Buddy's castle to the sounds of vacuuming. Thetis put the car in gear, and I returned to my job of navigating our way to Mississippi.

"Son, tonight you get a taste of an old juke joint. That'll make you perk up," said Jackson.

"Make us all perk up," said Willie.

Our route to the Delta consisted of retracing the road to Memphis, then driving another hundred miles down to Clarksdale, Mississippi. I navigated interchanges to get us back to I-57 South, and then we had downtime.

I'd just had a few minutes after my shower to slip in calls to Mom, Dad, and Samantha. The calls to Mom and Samantha went to voice mail, so I tried to put all I was feeling into the messages and resolved to call them later.

But Dad picked up, and I had a chance to fill him in on the

amazing things that had happened. I left out the part about getting stopped by the Highway Patrol, and focused on Buddy Guy and Legends. Dad asked for details and laughed when I told him the things Buddy had said to the crowd.

"Are you writing this down?"

"Uh, no…" It hadn't occurred to me.

"Well, you should. These are memories you're making."

"Okay…"

I must have sounded unconvinced. "It's an assignment, bud. Daily journal," Dad insisted. "Then go back and write about all that's happened since the injury."

"You're serious?"

"Why not? Maybe someone'll want to read about this. Least your mom and me."

Though I didn't have a notebook, I had my trusty iPhone. I opened a page in the notes app and started typing away with my thumbs. I could go a lot faster than I could write longhand.

"Whatcha doin'?" asked Thetis.

"Homework."

"On your *phone*?"

"My dad gave me an assignment this morning. He wants me to write down everything that happens."

"Sounds like evidence to me," said Willie.

After breakfast, we got back on the highway and I continued typing on the phone. Outside, plots of farmland streamed by, gone depressingly dormant for the winter. They didn't change for miles.

After a bit, Jackson said, "Leave off a while, G. Promised your folks I'd teach you some history while we on the road."

Willie bridled at the notion. "What do *you* know about history?"

"Lived a lot of it, same as you. Ain't nothin' but a buncha stories."

Willie grunted skeptically.

I stopped typing and closed the app. "I like a good story," I said.

"This one pretty sad," sighed Jackson. "You may not know what happened to our people after the Civil War. Textbook probably say slavery ended with proclamations and amendments, but takes more'n the law to change a man's heart. And it ain't change down South, or lotta other places."

"You right," said Willie. "'Fraid I *do* know this history." His nose wrinkled, as if he were trying to identify a foul odor. "Them Southern white men had all kinda tricks to keep a black man down. Sharecroppin' one of the big ones. Work the plantation owner's land in return for a bit of food and cash money. The 'furnish' they called it. Furnish barely enough to keep a family alive."

"That wasn't better'n slavery?" asked Thetis.

"Somewhat," Jackson allowed. "Dependin' on which plantation you was at. Muddy, he come from Stovall Plantation. Me, too."

"Was lots of 'em," said Willie. "Dockery's Plantation another one. Charlie Patton spent time on it. Howlin' Wolf, too."

The mention of plantations recalled the savant slave who predated the bluesmen. I watched the landscape flick by, and thought of Blind Tom filling concert halls with audiences who considered him a curiosity, like a trained bear, rather than a remarkable musician.

"Overall, things *was* better in the Delta," said Jackson. "Them plantation owners didn't want nobody messin' with their workers. They kept the worst of the Klan outta there."

"Who's the Klan?" They'd used the word several times, so I finally asked.

"Shit," said Thetis. "*KKK?*"

"Boy, ain't you learn *no* American history?" asked Willie. His disgusted tone reminded me of his words a few nights earlier. I suspected it was a prime example of white privilege not to know who the Klan was.

"We're only halfway through the year," I said. "We haven't even gotten to the Civil War."

"Ain't gonna teach you this, anyhow," Jackson harrumphed. "Folks get all worked up 'bout Middle East terrorists crashin' planes into buildings—but sure don't want to talk about no American terrorists, running around in sheets, burnin' crosses and killin' folks."

"Well, nine-eleven *was* pretty bad," I challenged.

"So was this, son," said Willie. "And been goin' on for more'n a hundred years."

I blinked hard but didn't say anything. During a lesson on immigration, we'd come across a sentence in the textbook which stated that "millions of workers" had been brought from Africa to cultivate Southern plantations. That had struck Barbara Richardson's mother as a pretty repulsive way to describe the slave trade. She raised a fuss on social media and the publisher took fast action, issuing stickers we all pasted into our books a couple of weeks later to cover the offending passage. It hadn't bothered me at the time. Now I realized this couldn't be the only thing the book got wrong. And you couldn't put stickers on all the stuff you left out.

Jackson picked up the thread. "See, right after the War, things did improve for a while—just long enough to give false hope. With the North ridin' herd on the South, black folks treated somewhat better. Black men got the vote—and they put some of their own in office."

"Crackers *despise* that," said Willie. "Fought a war to keep the black man down, now they see him dressin' in suits, goin' to Congress, and makin' laws. Give 'em *fits*! Klan rose up to stop black folks from votin', even if it had to kill 'em."

"That's so," said Jackson. "Soon as the North pulled out and went home, South made it legal, too. Mississippi give itself a new Constitution, say you only vote if you pay a tax and can read and write. Had to come up with somethin'. State was more'n half black folks, and they sure wasn't gonna elect no white men used to *own* 'em, body and soul."

"But I don't understand," I protested. "You just said black men *could* vote."

Jackson slashed at the air, trying to diagram the bewildering US system of governance. "Feds pass a law say they *could*. State pass a law say they *can't*. Went to Supreme Court to sort it out. Supreme Court say, 'fair is fair.' Won't let no illiterate poor white people vote, neither."

"How'd that work out?" asked Thetis. He didn't know this history, either.

"Was white people give the test," said Willie. "And *grade* it. How you think it worked out?" His tone was bitter as green olives fresh off the tree.

"Illiterate white people passed—and black people who *could* read failed," I guessed, hoping I'd be wrong.

"Um-hm," said Jackson tiredly. "Then come Jim Crow laws. Last almost a century. 'Separate but equal.'"

"You *know* wasn't never equal," said Willie. He was plunged into deep gloom, slumped in the seat as if he were part of the car's upholstery. He seemed to have shrunk.

"Course not," said Jackson. "Separate bathrooms, drinking fountains, schools, place on the bus…"

"Musta heard of Rosa Parks," said Willie. Thetis and I were glad to finally say, "Uh-huh." The annual school "celebration" of black history in February pretty much consisted of paying homage to Rosa Parks and MLK. Teachers wrote their names on the board and read us a picture book or two. Then it was on to the rest of the year.

But it was finally paying off. This was something I could talk about. "Rosa Parks didn't want to sit in the black part of the bus," I stated confidently. "So they arrested her."

"*Shit*," said Willie, appalled.

I glanced at Thetis and he gave me a confused look.

"That ain't it at all, G," said Jackson, disappointed. "Was *worse* than that."

"Not only did we have to sit in the back of the bus—when wasn't no *white* seats, black folks have to give up *theirs*," Willie explained, trying hard to be patient.

"*That's* what she was protestin'," said Jackson. "Miss Rosa wasn't playin' that. Would not get out of a *black* seat for nothin'. *That's* why they arrested her. They had *theirs*—and they take *ours*, too."

The one thing I thought I knew—I *still* didn't know. Thetis and I exchanged a look of shared frustration at this crowning injustice. It was starting to feel like state, local, and federal statutes were all trumped by Murphy's Law.

"Let's leave off, Jackson," said Willie tiredly. "Can't take no more of this."

"Why?" I asked.

"'Cause you probably think things is better, now," he said.

"Aren't they?" The alternative seemed *impossible*.

He sniffed and sighed. "They *different*. Musta heard King's line about the arc of the moral universe bein' long, but bendin' toward justice?"

I hadn't, but Thetis had. "You don't think so?" he said.

"If Martin could see the shit goin' down now," said Willie carefully, "comin' up on fifty years after he got shot—he'd take that one back."

"Time for a nap," said Jackson. "You okay at the wheel, Thetis?"

"Um-hm," said Thetis. "But I be waitin' for another lesson when you wake up. Shames me not to know all this about my people."

"I don't know it, either," I said.

"Yeah, but you white," he replied, excusing my ignorance.

"They say everybody's got some black blood in them," I objected.

"You play like you do," Jackson agreed.

"Seem like everybody got some black, everybody got some white, too," said Willie.

"Don't nobody ever look at it that way," said Jackson. "Sleep it off, Willie."

Willie's voice was heavy with resignation. "Been sleepin' it off my whole life."

Thetis drove for hours, with Jackson and Willie snoring in the back, leaving me to reflect on the conversation. My massive history textbook, whose bulk should have accommodated the truth, neglected topics like these. I guess they didn't make some people feel proud to be a Texan or an American. But like Mom always says, that's why it's called "history," not "propaganda." You don't get to cherry-pick the past. Still, she and Dad hadn't taught me this history, either. I thought if we'd been a black family, they probably would have.

Eventually, old bladders woke old sleepers, and we pulled over for gas and rest room relief in south Illinois. With the next few hours free of bridges, Jackson took the wheel a spell. Being back in the driver's seat seemed to lift his spirits.

"Willie, how long since you been back to the Delta?" he asked.

"Ummm…could be twenty years. You?"

"Same. You know what Muddy said?"

"Well, no, Jackson, I don't. What *did* Muddy say?" said Willie, hamming up the straight man role.

"'I couldn't *wait* to get out of Mississippi. What I want to go *back* for?'"

"But now we goin' back," said Willie softly.

"Um-hm," said Jackson. He paused, then said, "G, you ain't gonna see it. But try to imagine the old days, even before me 'n' Willie. Delta was a wild place—bears, panthers, snakes. Rivers was liable to flood and wash it all away."

"I knew a man, had him a heavy wire tied from the roof of his shack to a big tree," said Willie. "When the water come, it'd lift the house off its foundation—but the wire'd keep it from floatin' away. Only go so far, then the wire stop it, like a boat tied to a dock. Water'd go down and he'd buy a coupla bottles of corn. Buncha fellas'd come have themselves a drink and lift his house back on the foundation for him."

"I'da been one of them," said Thetis, smacking his lips.

Jackson abruptly changed the subject. "Place we stayin' ain't like Buddy's," he warned. "Ain't no palace."

"They do have beds, don't they?" said Willie.

"Said so. They sisters. Love the blues. And musicians. Frisky. *Young*, too," he said with enthusiasm.

"Oh?" Thetis's voice rose with interest…

"Um-hm," said Jackson. "Ain't but *sixty* or so."

"Ooooh." …and dropped with understanding.

Willie and Jackson chuckled at the joke.

Chapter Fifty
Po' Monkey's

LUCILLE AND VIRGINIA were twin sisters who looked a lot younger than sixty. One had prepared a feast for our arrival and the other served it, doling out caresses, pinches, batted eyelashes, and suggestive comments, along with the food.

Lucille—or Virginia—I couldn't tell them apart—ran her hands through my hair. "How you like that corn bread, sugar?"

I swallowed hard. "Yummy."

"Put a lotta butter on it. And honey. It's go-o-o-o-d with honey." Her voice oozed the condiments she recommended.

Jackson watched with disapproval. "Why don't y'all sit down and eat some of this?"

"Oh, no," she said. "I like to wait on a man. See he has what he needs."

"Are you Lucille or Virginia?" I asked.

"Can't you tell?" she crooned. "I'm Lucille. Virginia the dirty one. Don't know how she got that name. She may be a queen—but she sure ain't no virgin."

"We shared Mama's uterus, Lucille," said Virginia, scowling. "But since then, *you* the sister been so generous with your own female parts."

"Leave off that talk," said Jackson sharply. "And ain't none of this goin' in the notes," he warned.

257

An hour later we were back on the road headed to Po' Monkey's, the last of the Delta juke joints. Lucille and Virginia followed in their own car.

Po' Monkey's given name was William Seaberry, and he was a few years younger than Jackson and Willie. They hadn't known him growing up, but by now, Po' Monkey and his club had become famous. For more than fifty years he'd been opening at least one night a week, and the club had earned an international reputation.

I didn't know whether to call him "Poor" or "Monkey." They both sounded awful.

"Just don't be callin' him '*Mr.* Monkey,'" advised Thetis, and got us all to snorting at the thought.

Jackson suggested, "I expect if you called him 'Mr. Seaberry,' he'd think you were a polite young man."

"Then he probably tell you just call him 'Monkey,'" laughed Willie. "He's regular folks."

"Last I heard, Monkey still sharecropping cotton on a piece of land next to the club," said Jackson. "Got him a tractor, though, and a cotton pickin' machine. Don't do it the ol' way, by mule and hand."

"Who'd wanna do that?" said Willie. "Pushin' a plow behind an old fartin' mule's be-hind ain't no way to spend a day."

"Do they really fart?" I asked, fascinated.

"Worse'n my first wife," said Willie. He gave me a playful look. Since confronting me, things hadn't been relaxed between the two of us, but maybe he was trying to bridge the chasm.

We got our instruments from the trunk while Lucille and Virginia parked, and we all walked toward the club together. Several cars and pickups were arranged haphazardly in front of an old wooden shack. Flat dirt fields stretched into the distance, barren in December, with an occasional spindly tree poking up to break the monotony.

The exterior of Buddy's Chicago club had not been impressive— and Po' Monkey's was less so. But it *was* colorful. The weathered walls were covered with blue, green, and yellow hand-lettered signs. Most of them advised what *not* to do. *No* loud music. *No* dope smoking. *No* drug products. Especially *not* to bring in any beer. Oddly, the warnings were offset by a big picture of a beer bottle, which looked like an advertisement.

"Ain't changed none I can see," observed Jackson.

"Nope," agreed Willie. They both seemed pleased with the fact.

"I like the signs," I said dubiously. Not sure what I'd been expecting. But, certainly, *more.*

Jackson gave me the frown of a disappointed teacher. "The place called *Po'* Monkey's, not *Bling* Monkey's. Wasn't never much money in the blues. Not like rock or hip hop." The thought was so vile, it took a moment before he could continue. He drew a calming breath. "Was survival music for folks struggling to do the same—like this shack's done. Place was standin' before me and Willie was," said Jackson emphatically.

But Thetis was still not impressed. "Big bad wolf woulda took care of it with a couple huff-puffs, look like."

"Um-hm," said Willie. "But the Mississippi ain't got it yet. It's built up high, like on stilts, so's it can survive a little flooding."

As we approached a rickety set of steps that led to the entrance, I asked Jackson, "How much is it?"

"Like it say—five dollars on Thursday."

"But…today's Saturday."

He nodded, getting my meaning. "Monkey do it tonight for the beer sales. Ain't need no band 'cause *we* playin'. Some friends sit in, too."

We clambered up the stairs and entered another world. The space was lit with strings of Christmas lights. Stuffed monkeys hung from the ceiling, along with sparkly tinsel and a rotating mirrored ball that flashed colored lights all over the room. The walls were decorated with pieces of reflective foil and memorabilia celebrating Po' Monkey's legacy. Maybe a dozen people sat in plastic chairs at simple tables. Several more were on a plywood dance floor, shakin' it to a Marvin Gaye song playing on the sound system.

A tall man with a moustache and a big smile took turns folding Jackson and Willie in his arms. He was dressed in a crimson suit with a white cowboy hat, broad white tie, and white shoes. An unlit cigar dangled from his mouth.

"Jackson, Willie," he murmured.

"Long time, Monkey," said Willie.

"Been here waitin' on ya."

"What *is* that mess you playin'?" asked Jackson, his face screwed up in distaste.

Monkey had the diplomatic air of a country gentleman. "R and B. Meet 'em halfway. But don't allow no rappin', no saggin' an' baggin'."

"You got standards," said Thetis.

"Damn right. Hello, ladies," he said, greeting Lucille and Virginia.

"Hi, Monkey," said Lucille. "You lookin' go-o-o-o-d." He gave her a little bow. "Miss Virginia." He took her hand and kissed it like a courtier.

"Who this young man?" he asked, smiling at me.

"Guitar man," said Jackson. "Name's 'G'."

"Nice to meet you, Mr. Seaberry," I said, extending my hand. The palm and fingers that took mine were creased like the furrowed fields they had worked their whole life. No manicurist could ever produce a hand like that.

"Mr. Seaberry was my daddy," he laughed. "Y'all call me 'Monkey.' Everybody do."

I glanced at Willie and he gave me an I-told-you-so look.

"We gonna set up," said Jackson. He handed bills to Monkey. "Let's buy everybody a beer and get things rollin'."

"'Spect they'll like that." He looked over at me. "Not for G, right? Don't need no troubles with the a-b-c-d-e-f."

"Who's that?" I asked.

"Rev'nuers, used to call 'em. Gov'ment. Can't have no underage drinkin'."

"I'll take care of him," said Lucille. "I don't drink beer, either," she added, making a conspiratorial grimace.

As we were setting up on the bandstand, she brought me a cup of brown liquid. I looked at it suspiciously. "What is it?"

"'Sippi cola," she said innocently. I tasted it cautiously. "Got a little tang, don't it?"

I took another sip and nodded. "It's good. Thank you."

"Oh, sugar, you ve-e-e-e-ry welcome." She gave me a dazzling smile, then walked back to a table, swinging her hips like a runway model.

We opened with one of Howlin' Wolf's greatest songs, "Smokestack Lightnin'." It started with a simple guitar lick that let everyone know what was coming. They hooted approval.

Jackson is no Wolf, but he did his best to sell the vocal. Soon the whole club pitched in to help, howling 'til they were hoarse.

We wrapped up the number to applause. I drank half my soda while the others tugged on beers. Jackson pulled out a handkerchief and mopped his brow.

"Warmin' up, ain't it?" said Willie on his mike.

"Wouldn't know it to look at them," Jackson said on the mike, hitching his chin at the crowd. "Tell me, why this place called a 'juke joint'? Ain't no juke box."

"You got it ass-backwards, man," said Willie, feigning annoyance. Several folks chuckled, enjoying the byplay. "Juke *box* named after the juke *joint*."

"That don't make no sense," protested Jackson.

Willie pretended impatience with his foolish partner. "*Damn*, Jackson, must be yo' Alzheimer's kickin' in. You done forgot juke an *African* word. Means actin' up—misbehavin'. Every plantation had a shack like this where folks could hear music, drink corn, and cut loose."

"Why, these folks ain't doin' that..."

"Maybe think they in church," said Willie.

"Yeah, must be they thought that last one was a hymn," said Jackson.

"Let's see can we fix that," said Willie. "Coupla y'all boys play harp. Get on up here an' let it hang out."

We launched into our next song, one of Willie Dixon's hits, "Spoonful." I played the twangy hook, then laid back as three old men clambered onto the stage. Willie surrendered his mike, and they took turns blowing harmonicas and grinning at each other. Between the three of them I think they had about a dozen teeth—which made it easy for them to fit harmonicas entirely inside their mouths and play with their hands clasped behind their backs. The crowd cheered them on and I just hoped they didn't swallow their instruments.

I finished my soda and soon Lucille had a fresh one to replace it. We played for the next hour and I tried to sip my drink—because I realized that's what it had to be—but I was thirsty. It made me think of another Wolf song, "I Asked for Water and She Gave Me Gasoline." Every time I got to the bottom of the cup, Lucille had another one ready.

"Now, ladies and gentlemen, this boy G, he somethin' special. We gonna show you what he can do with this git-tar."

That was my cue to launch into "Pride and Joy," one of Stevie Ray's catchiest songs, which I'd been working on since I stopped going to school. Thetis handled the vocal and I stretched out on the lead. The shapes were swimming in my mind's eye, and whether I was drunk or not, I think I played it pretty good. I guess the crowd thought so, too, 'cause when I finished, they carried on like crazy.

Thetis took over the lead and women led me to the dance floor, where they taught me a slow blues shimmy. Jackson must have seen me swaying, because when the song ended, he came out and took my arm. "Believe Lucille slipped you the mickey, G."

"He can lie down where I sleep in the back," said Monkey. He was now dressed in a bright yellow suit with a navy shirt. I hoped this wasn't a figment of my drunken imagination.

"I'll put him to bed," suggested Lucille.

"No, you won't, neither," snapped Virginia, leading her sister away.

Between them, Jackson and Monkey helped me to the back onto a large unmade bed. I slipped off my shoes and lay down. Monkey set an old kitchen pot next to me.

"You got to throw up, use this. Don't vomit in my bed, y'hear?"

I laughed weakly.

"This door lock?" Jackson asked Monkey.

"You worried about him goin' off somewheres?" Monkey asked, astonished.

"Naw. Gotta keep them ol' gals *outta* here."

Monkey laughed softly. "Ain't *never* had that problem. Sure ain't no lock on that door."

"Well," said Jackson resignedly, "Just hafta let nature take its course."

Chapter Fifty-One
When the Levee Breaks...

I WOKE the next morning. Undressed.

But I wasn't in Monkey's bed. I saw my bag, so I must have gotten back to Lucille and Virginia's place. I couldn't recall anything that had happened after Jackson and Monkey had laid me down in the bedroom back of the juke joint.

Sitting up, I assessed my condition. Actually, I didn't feel too bad. I pulled on some clothes and went downstairs.

Jackson was alone at the table, drinking coffee. He gave me a meaningful smile.

"How you doin', G? Headache?"

I shook my head no. "Did I throw up?"

"Um-um. Hold your liquor just fine for a fourteen-year-old. This don't go in the notes, neither."

I nodded, thinking we'd probably all be better off leaving it out.

"Did anything…else…happen…last night?" I asked tentatively.

"Sure *did*," he said, pleased. "But not to *you*. Let's say I accomplished *both* my objectives this trip."

"Congratulations," I offered. "What're we doing today?"

Jackson sipped his coffee thoughtfully before answering. "Willie got with Virginia. They still…occupied. Thetis found his own gal and gone back to her place. We catch up with them later. You and me, we got a free mornin'."

"Are we going to the blues museum?"

"It's real good. You *oughta* see it." He stopped and sighed. "But I can't. That museum a sad place for me, G. Feel I oughta bring flowers, like goin' to the graveyard. All them old friends, dead and gone. Pretty soon, I be joinin' them."

"Maybe not so soon."

"Maybe, maybe not." Jackson put down his coffee and stood up. "Let's just drive. Plentya places to show you."

Half an hour later we walked out of a donut shop on the other side of Clarksdale. The day was grey and bitterly cold; even with two shirts and my heaviest jacket, I still hunched my shoulders against the chill. I took a donut and passed the sack to Jackson. He pulled one out, then we chewed and walked thoughtfully up the street.

We reached a triangular island at the intersection of old US Highways 61 and 49. A pole marked the spot, topped with highway signs above a little sculpture of three electric guitars. A placard below proclaimed, "The CROSSROADS."

Several other travelers paid their respects, snapping photos. I rotated in place and surveyed the terrain. Amid a sea of asphalt and concrete, what stood out were mini-marts, fast food outlets, and banks. I took in a U-Haul dealer on one corner and a barbeque spot on another. Down a ways were a furniture store and a grocery store. Their signs all played up the connection to the famous "crossroads," trying to drum up business. The commercialization cheapened the romantic legend.

"You think it happened here?" I asked.

"That's two questions—did it happen—and if it *did*, was it *here*."

"Okay."

After a moment, he said, "Coulda been here. But many folks say was Rosedale, like it mention in the song."

"Does Rosedale look better than this?"

"Probably not no more."

"*Did* it happen?" I persisted.

Jackson sighed, then met my gaze. "Come right down to it, I *do* believe in the devil."

We got back in the car and cranked up the heat, as Jackson guided us out of town along Stovall Road. A few miles later he hit Highway 1 and pulled onto the shoulder. We got out and walked over to a blue sign that announced, "Muddy Waters's House." We read the information and looked over the shack nearby. Almost nothing else was visible on the barren landscape, save several withered trees.

"This ain't the real thing," said Jackson. "But back in the day, it look pretty much like this."

"You saw it?"

He nodded, peering into the past. "Lived in one just like it. Willie did, too."

We returned to the car and headed south on Highway 1. Fallow black fields lay on both sides of the road as far as the eye could see. The land was unimaginably flat.

"'Causa how it came to be. This all the work of rivers overflowin' their banks, leavin' soil fifty, hundred feet deep. Happen for thousands of years 'til they built the levee."

During a lull in the conversation, I blurted out, "Does Willie not like me?"

"*What?*" He glanced over at me in surprise. "This 'causa what he said, 'bout that white privilege?"

"Well, yeah…" Willie's angry words had stayed with me, like a catchy song your mind returns to whether you want it to or not.

"Didn't sound too friendly, did it?"

"Uh...I don't know..." I'd brought it up, but I felt awkward talking about it.

"Willie like you a lot. You probably the first white person he spoke his mind to his entire life."

"It didn't seem like it. He knew exactly what to say."

"Oh, he done it many times before. But in his *head*. Not to no white person in the flesh."

I laughed. Jackson looked over and chuckled, too.

"Why'd he pick me to say it to? Did I do something especially wrong?"

"Naw! Thought you understood. He said it to *you*—" He glanced over. "'Cause *you* the first white person he trust enough to say it to. To be real with." He waited a moment. "'Cause he care about you."

"Even though I'm white," I said, wiping my eye.

Jackson laughed. "Yeah! Even though." He turned on the radio, scanned a couple of stations, then turned it back off. "See, it's like this. Some white folks think like we all the same—same rights, same opportunities. What's past is past. We startin' fresh, even-steven. That's fine—big improvement over how it used to be." He paused and shook his head. "But it ain't real. Stay on the surface. We friendly, but we ain't *real* friends. We...*acquaintances*."

Abruptly, Jackson turned the car around and accelerated. "Where are we going?" I asked.

"Opened up a canna worms. Now we gotta go chase 'em down."

Twenty-five miles down the road we pulled in front of a billboard. Though it was an official government sign, it was oddly reminiscent of the hand-lettered notices outside of Po' Monkey's club. At the top, in red capital letters, was the word "WARNING"—not once, but three times. I scanned a bulleted list of forbidden items until I got to the punchline: "ANY AND ALL PERSONS GAINING ADMITTANCE TO MISSISSIPPI STATE PENITENTIARY—"

"*Parchman?* We're going into Parchman prison?!"

"Naw," said Jackson, amused at my reaction. "Just gonna drive around it. Thought you should see the place. But hell no, we ain't goin' *in*."

"Good. Otherwise I'd have to get rid of my saws, axes, hacksaw blades, chisels, picks, and knives," I said.

"They had to tell you that," said Jackson, tickled.

"Also the explosives."

We navigated side roads around the periphery of the grounds. It wasn't like prisons in movies. "It looks like a farm," I said.

"It is. Well, it *was*, don't know about now. Prisoners worked the cotton."

"Like a plantation?" There it was again.

Jackson nodded. "But much worse. They had guards—baddest, most dangerous prisoners in the place. Murderers, some of 'em. Gave 'em rifles. 'Trusty shooters,' they called. Shooter who kill a man tryin' to escape get himself set free in return."

"Wait—if a murderer killed a prisoner trying to escape, they'd set the *murderer* free?"

"Yeah, sometimes. Think about it the way you said, don't make much sense. But it gave a powerful reason to shoot a man makin' a run for it."

I gave him a doubtful look. "Then why would anyone try to escape?"

Jackson's eye twitched. "Was terrible inside. Even lock up kids, 'most young as you. Some of the convicts were bad men, use those boys hard. And was the whip. 'Black Annie.' Could lay a man open, kill him if they give too many strokes. They'd lash a man for *anything*—look at a trusty wrong, break your shovel, ain't pick enough cotton. Just the start, son. Take a man who live through it to give the whole story." We knew who that man was, but we wouldn't be asking him to tell it.

We drove on. "One thing I don't understand. Slaves picked cotton. Sharecroppers picked cotton. Prisoners picked cotton. So...why does Monkey pick cotton? Think it'd be the last thing he'd want to do."

Jackson nodded thoughtfully. "Wasn't cotton was the problem. Monkey, he got a choice, and he *choose* cotton. He like the work, like the field, sky...sun...rain...plants growin'. Long as it's *his* choice, he's happy."

I never raised my hand in class, but now I couldn't stop asking questions. "Didn't sharecroppers have a choice?"

Jackson's bitter expression told the tale. "Little, if any. Hard to leave your plantation for another if boss didn't want you to. They had many ways to prevent that. Most of 'em cheat you on your share, keep you in debt. No matter how good the crop, break even at best. Didn't never get a stake to move on."

"So nobody left?"

"Sure we did. Me and Willie, lotta others. Wasn't easy, but found a way. Go north, go west. Anyplace but the South."

Jackson navigated away from the prison, staying to back roads. He muttered to himself, as if he were looking for something.

"Ah, this it," he said at last. He pulled onto a frontage road and we drove down a short way to a shallow river. He opened his door and got out. I did the same.

The cold hit with a slap. He led me to the riverbank, and as we passed a stand of ragged trees, a decrepit bridge came into view. It had eroded to geometric basics, a framework of steel girders without even a roadbed. Massive concrete pilings supported it above dark, stagnant waters. Despite the ravages of time, the skeleton had an air of stubborn permanence.

"This?" I said doubtfully.

"Not the exact one, but it'll do. You know how I don't drive on no bridge? Account of what I seen."

"*What?*" I prompted after several moments. "What did you see?"

Jackson plunged his hands into jacket pockets, hunched his shoulders against the cold. He frowned, sucked his teeth a moment, and shook his head, trying to deny the memory.

"Bodies. Hanging off the bridge. They lynched them boys." He gazed at the rusty span as if witnessing the victims, still. "Most times was trees they used, an' I seen that, too. But that bridge…"

We lingered, the chill penetrating deeper, but Jackson explained no more. His eyes were fixed on the old steel scaffold in front of us. It didn't seem right to prompt for details or to intrude on his thoughts.

At last we walked back to the car. We got in and Jackson turned the key, but he didn't put it in gear. After a moment, he cut the engine and looked at me. He took a breath and began.

"I was a rascally little kid. Always up to somethin'. And the planter, he wanta make an impression on me. Teach me a lesson. Was maybe five, six years old. One evening, already dark, he tells me come with him. I do, and he tells me get in the car. I ain't know what's goin' on, so I hesitate. He give me a look people give, say they ain't gonna hurt you *now*, but they sure will if you don't obey. So I get in.

"He drive for hours, but I don't say nothin', just keep my mouth shut. He even give me a sandwich. Finally, I ask him where we going, and he say one word: 'Shubuta.' I ain't heard of that place."

Jackson stared out the windshield, slipping back through time, the weathered old man becoming a frightened boy, taking me along for the ride. "Coulda been hell," he murmured.

He rubbed his forehead and went on. "At last, seem like middle of the night, we pull up to a bridge like this one, but not old. We get outta the car and stand, lookin' up at that bridge. Was a dark night. No moon, just stars. No cold to speak of, but I was shiverin'.

"Not long 'til three, four cars come along and pull onto the bridge. 'Good timing,' say the planter. 'Good timin' for *what*?' I say. He just look at me and say, 'You'll see.'

"Up on the bridge, cars stop and leave the lights on, so they can see what they doin'. We can see, too. Buncha white men. Some of 'em got ropes. An' two colored boys. 'Colored' what they call us, those days, if they bein' polite."

Jackson turned to look at me. "Polite or not, they call us 'boys.' Grown men, old man like me—we all 'boys.' Way of makin' you small, no matter your size. But *these* boys—they *are* boys. G, they weren't no older than *you*. Got their hands tied behind their backs. 'What'd they do?' I ask. '*Enough*,' say the planter.

"I know what was comin', so I make a move to run. But the planter was a big man. He grab me tight, force me to watch. 'Don't you look away,' he say. 'I will *know* if you close your eyes.'"

As if prompted to do the opposite, I turned my head, unable to meet Jackson's gaze as he continued the story to its dread conclusion. "Lord, was they fast at the work. Had the rope 'round those boys' necks just like that, t'other end tied to a girder. Next thing I know, those poor souls droppin' off the bridge, one on either side of it. White men shinin' lights so we can see it all. Seem like those boys fallin' and fallin'. Fallin' so far, I think maybe the men just throw 'em offa the bridge into the river, maybe just scarin' them, way the planter scarin' me. Sure they can't hang boys so young! *Naw!*"

Jackson's voice broke with the memory of that vain hope.

"But they *did*. Boys come to the end of the rope. Hear a sound when their necks break, or maybe was the rope itself snappin' taut. Then bodies swingin', but every moment, less. And comin' to rest, just hangin', well above water they had *no* chance to reach. Those boys dead, sure 'nuff, heads cocked, like they listenin' at somethin'. After a bit, white men cut off the light, leave 'em in the dark. Maybe leave 'em in *peace*."

Jackson paused, and I thought he might be finished. But he had more. "Voice come up on the bridge then, first since they started. 'Boys, that was a real neat lynching. Best I ever seen.' They very pleased, laughin', gettin' in cars, drivin' off. When it was over, the planter, he spin me 'round to face him, grab me by the shoulders. He say, 'Son, iffen you don't straighten up and fly right, *that's* what'll happen to *you*.'

"On that long drive home I got time to think 'bout it all—I didn't drop off a wink. Think me a lotta thoughts. Think I best do as he say, or most like, I wind up at the end of a rope like those boys. He ain't lie about that. But I make up my mind, then an' there, I'mo leave this place with these white devils. Ain't no doubt 'bout *these* devils—they real as could be. Let you know every day—your soul belong to *them*. They do with it as they please. Kill ya soon's wring a chicken's neck."

We sat a long time. I felt Jackson's arm come around my shoulders. I still couldn't open my eyes, knowing if I did, tears would pour out. "You okay, G?"

I bowed my head and didn't answer. After a moment, Jackson said, "I shouldn't have done told you all that. Sorry I did."

My eyes snapped open and I faced him. "*No*. I'm glad you told me. I *needed* to hear it."

Jackson laughed sadly. "Well, you the first one. Ain't never tell that story before."

"Not even to your parents?"

"'*Specially* not to them." Jackson scrubbed his face with his hands, as if trying to wash away the horror. "Was a hard burden to bear. Tell the truth, sharing with you ease it some."

I extended my hand. "Friends?"

Jackson took it. His eyes were moist and warm. "*Real* friends."

After a moment, I asked, "Did they ever catch the men—the white men, I mean?"

He blew out a breath of resignation. "Far as I know, never brought no white man to justice for a lynching. An' there was thousands."

"*None?*"

Jackson's voice grew softer, as if reluctant to tell me. "No jury convict a white man for killin' a black man. Or woman. Simple as that. Yeah, they have a trial now an' then, but everybody know goin' in what the verdict gonna be."

I was stunned as I absorbed this revision to "with liberty and justice for all." I was not completely ignorant, nor completely naïve— but the blunt specifics of history were overwhelming. I grasped for questions to make sense of the past.

"Do you know what the boys did—or were *accused* of doing?"

He grunted tiredly. "Most times, was just look at a white woman wrong. Say somethin' wrong. Don't drop your eyes to a white man. It didn't have to be no big thing. Or...*anything*."

Finally, overcome, I arrived at the emotional bottom line. There seemed no way out. "How can you not hate us *all?*"

"Was times I *did*," he confessed. "But my mother, she teach love and kindness. Even back then, not all white folks like that. Was a bad system, propped up by fear. Even good white folks scared to go against it."

"I understand that," I said. "But still..."

Jackson's shoulders slumped resignedly. "Think about it, even that planter wasn't no bad man for the day. Might say he did me a kindness, drivin' all night to teach me a lesson."

"Maybe he just wanted to see the lynching," I objected.

"Maybe," he admitted. He turned to look at me. "Maybe."

Finally, Jackson started the engine again, turning the heater on full. "Let's get outta here, G. 'Nother river to show you."

We found the highway, drove it for a while, and turned west onto a smaller road. A few minutes later, Jackson took a turn south.

"I don't know how you can find your way without a GPS," I said. "My dad uses one to even get to the grocery store."

Jackson laughed, the mood lightening a touch. "Had me a good sense of direction since way back. And ain't nothing changed since I left, leastways not the roads."

We drove for a few minutes, then he pulled over. We got out of the car, hiked through trees and up a rise. When we reached the top, I was surprised to see a river flowing in front of us.

"The Mississippi?"

"Um-hm," Jackson said. "Look inspiring?"

The waters were brown, broad, and slow. An island with scraggly bushes broke the dark expanse of water.

"Not really." It was as disappointing as the crossroads had been.

"Different in spring, when everything green and river running high."

I surveyed the terrain and frowned. "Where's the levee?"

"Standing on it," he said, amused. "This wall is man-made. Was dangerous work, too, didn't nobody want to do it. Without it, river'd flood most every year."

"Does it ever break?"

"Yeah, and it's bad. Worst was before my time, 1927. Busted in over a hundred places. Lotta folks lost all they had. Lotta folks died."

We headed back to the car with that melancholy thought hanging in the air, which seemed to be growing colder by the minute. Jackson paused to face back up the slope we'd just descended.

"Imagine hundred years back. Sharecroppers down here choppin' cotton, hear a whistle. *Oooooo-oooooo.* Look up and wipe the sweat

274

away. Rest a minute—and watch a riverboat sail by, stern wheel churning, water dripping—on a Mississippi River they can't even *see* from down here. Look like it just sailin' through the sky."

We stayed a moment, scanning the gloom above the levee, searching for the Delta Queen. Shivering, we returned to the car. Jackson pulled onto the road and we headed south alongside the river.

I had a thought and pulled up a song on my iPhone. I punched a Bluetooth setting, and Led Zeppelin's "When the Levee Breaks" boomed through the speakers.

The lyric started and Jackson exclaimed, "Why, that's an old song. Kansas Joe and Memphis Minnie done that one."

"I thought it was Led Zeppelin…"

"The one you playin' *is*. Do it over."

I restarted the song. It opens with a pounding, surging, insistent drumbeat. A wailing harmonica and a screaming guitar come in, laying down a swinging rhythm that builds and builds like the rising waters of the swollen river. A soaring slide guitar riff comes next, punctuated with cymbal crashes—which hush for a rest—and Robert Plant's vocal begins, warning, "If it keeps on raining, the levee's going to break." From there the song rocks on for seven incredible minutes.

When it ended, Jackson smiled at me and said, "Again. *Louder.*"

I cued it and turned it up. This time Jackson and I were pounding the dash and the steering wheel in delight, our blues chased by Led Zeppelin's majesty.

As the final notes died, an alarming wail erupted from the sound system. I looked at Jackson in confusion. This was not part of the song.

Jackson flinched away from the dash. "What the hell…"

Rattled, I looked at my phone, which vibrated insistently. An emergency alert was pasted on the screen. I read it in disbelief. "It's a warning for a—"

My words were lost in the high-decibel shriek of an air raid siren nearby.

"Oh, shit," said Jackson. "I *know* what that is."

Chapter Fifty-Two
13 Minutes

"*TORNADO*," SAID JACKSON.

"Yeah," I confirmed. I scanned three hundred sixty degrees, but didn't see anything.

The screaming phone and shrieking siren were making it hard to control my racing pulse. I shut off my cell, and the siren grew less shrill as we headed away from it.

It was starting to rain. Hard.

During our Led Zeppelin interlude, Jackson had maneuvered back to Highway 1 and was heading south to Rosedale. We'd passed few houses and the road was desolate.

"What do we do?" I asked.

"Get in the storm cellar. If we had one."

From behind, two cars flew by on our left, doing about a hundred miles an hour.

"Shit!" I exclaimed, startled.

"Storm chasers." Jackson pointed out in front of the car. "Uh-oh. Look."

Lowering clouds loomed in the distance and spread across the limitless horizon. Fingers reached to the ground, grasping at the earth.

"That ain't good, G. Headin' our way."

Jackson slowed to the shoulder, then executed a careful about-face. We headed back north, away from the storm. I turned to keep an eye on it.

"How we doin'?" he asked nervously.

"It's gaining on us."

"Gotta find us a hidey-hole. But ain't nothin' out here 'cept dirt."

The siren got louder as we returned the way we'd come. Its alarm sounded more and more urgent as it increased in volume, screaming at us, "Get away! Get away!"

The two cars that had passed had reversed course, too. They were behind us, closing the gap as if we were standing still. "Here come those guys again," I said. "Watch out."

Once more they passed on our left, going even faster this time. Our car shuddered in their wake.

"Guess they ain't complete fools," Jackson said. We watched them pull away, putting more space between themselves and the storm.

I thought of suggesting Jackson drive faster—but when I looked over, his fingers had the steering wheel in a death grip, and they were trembling.

We drove like this for tense minutes, Jackson gradually accelerating. I searched the map for possibilities. "Them clouds are in my rear view, and both side views," he said. "It's big and it's closin'. Can't outrun it."

The storm had stayed behind us and seemed to be moving directly north. We had no chance of escaping it on this course—but maybe we could evade it at an angle. There was a turn-off ahead for a road heading east.

"Take the exit."

Jackson took the turn at speed and the wheels squealed on wet pavement. Once the car straightened, he punched the gas harder. I snuck a glance at the speedometer, which was pegged at more than sixty.

A funnel had appeared, now more pronounced. As I watched, it dissipated—and another formed to its right. It was a hypnotic display of nature's terrifying power. I forced myself to focus on the task at hand—making sure the funnel didn't get to us.

"I think this is working," I said.

"Good," he said. Then, "Oh, *shit!*"

I spun to face forward. Straight ahead a short bridge crossed a narrow river.

"I got the wheel!" I grasped it with my left hand and took control as Jackson relaxed his death grip. "Stay on the gas and close your eyes!"

I held it steady and we were across the bridge in a few seconds. "Clear."

He opened his eyes and dragged in a breath. After a moment, he said, "Okay, I got it." I removed my hand as his took charge. He gave me a tight smile. "Helluva trip for you, G. Now you done drove a car." After a moment, he added, "You can put *that* in the notes."

I turned back to the storm. It had changed course and seemed on a path to intercept us, though that might have been an illusion, like a creepy portrait whose eyes appear to follow wherever you go. The funnel was closer, and I thought I could see rotation. I knew I could hear the wind speed picking up. The tornado felt like a living creature.

"Bad news," I said. "This twister wants us."

"Got that feeling myself," said Jackson. "Member what I said about the devil?"

"Yeah. I do."

I allowed myself a moment to wonder if somehow… someway…Satan was coming to collect on a deal I didn't know I'd ever made. Poor Jackson might be collateral damage to the transaction.

Something banged on the roof, and several more on the hood. "Damn!" said Jackson, and I jumped in my seat.

It sounded like we were inside a popcorn popper with small explosions going off all around us. Hail assaulted our car, and I watched the icy missiles grow from grains to golf balls. Ice thudded into black fields, rebounding into the air when it hit a hard patch. Within moments it looked as if the Easter bunny had hidden thousands of large white eggs in plain sight.

The road turned bumpy as hail covered it, like driving over rough gravel. But this surface was slippery and the car lost traction, sliding out of control.

"Slow down!" I yelled, as the wheels on the driver's side plowed the shoulder.

"If I do, it'll get us!"

"If you don't, you'll kill us!"

Jackson laughed nervously, slowed a touch, and pulled the errant wheels back onto the pavement. "We gotta find a house, G."

I scanned forward, to the sides—and saw a farmhouse off to the left. I pointed. "There!"

He glanced in the direction, nodded, and took the turn onto a narrow track. He had to slow on the dirt road, but the house wasn't far away.

Neither was the tornado. The wind howled and roared. I could feel it rocking the car. Spindly trees bent grotesquely, branches snapping and flying through the air. The sky was thick and dirty with clouds of soil from the fields.

Then, as abruptly as it started, the hail ended and it began to rain again. Driven by the gale, precipitation came directly sideways, thudding violently into back and side panels of the car.

Sturdy phone poles lined the road, bringing a power line to the house. As we approached, one of the poles teetered, then toppled like a felled tree, blocking the road in front of us.

"Stop!" I yelled, but Jackson was already braking.

The power line snapped and the severed ends sparked and whipped in the wind like Air Dancers advertising a sale on tires. The tornado was breathing life into inanimate objects just as it was threatening to take our own.

"Get out!" he yelled. I shoved my shoulder hard against the door, fighting wind that seemed determined to keep it shut. I pried it open a few inches and wedged my body into the gap. Pushing hard with my back and arms, I got leverage to force the door further—then the wind caught it and finished the job, springing the hinges and snapping the door open. I helped Jackson wriggle out my side. He was spry for his age, and terror limbered him further.

The noise outside was incredible. We clambered over the power pole and tottered down the road to the house, maybe fifty yards away. Normally I could have run this distance in a few seconds—but fighting winds and debris, our progress felt infinitely slow. Every moment the funnel got closer.

We reached the house and I tried the knob. Locked! Jackson rang the bell and pounded the door, though we knew it was in vain.

Then the atmospheric pressure shifted, and my ears popped like they'd never popped before. I doubled up in pain. Next to me Jackson did the same. With mouths open, we worked our jaws like dying fish, trying to equalize the pressure.

We weren't the only ones suffering. The house groaned from the pressure drop—then windows burst outwards, shards of glass flying as if shot out of a cannon. By chance we weren't in their path, and I had a moment to reflect on the irony of good fortune amid disaster. One cataclysm hadn't killed us, though the next might.

But the problem of gaining entry had been solved. I dove through a busted-out window and rushed to open the front door for Jackson.

"Storm cellar?" he asked. I looked back out the door. It was even darker and the funnel was almost upon us.

"No time to find it!"

The entry served as a mudroom, with a rack holding shoes, boots, and cleats. Heavy jackets hung from pegs on the wall, along with a couple of football helmets. Jackson grabbed the helmets with one hand and me with the other.

"C'mon!" he yelled, pulling me farther into the house.

The windows were blown out of the kitchen and the gale howled through. The cupboard doors banged open and shut, as if spirits terrorized a haunted house. Off the kitchen we saw a windowless bathroom, an island of relative calm.

We rushed into it and slammed the door—like that would do any good. "Put this on," he said, handing me a football helmet. I looked around as I did. Wash was hung to dry over a tub on a length of rope hooked to the walls. I ripped the clothes down and grabbed the rope.

"Down here!" I yelled, huddling under the sink. Without a cabinet, pipes and fixtures were exposed. I wound the rope around the pipes and around myself. Jackson got the idea. When I passed it to him, he did the same, and passed it back around the pipe. I tied it off the best I could.

"You a boy scout?" he asked. Jackson was plucky to the end.

"Never been. Hang on!"

It sounded like a jet engine revving up, rattling the house like a tremor. It was dark in the windowless room, though a sliver of light crept in beneath the door. That blew out like a candle and it got darker. My synesthesia was running a cavalcade of ominous shapes in my mind's eye like nothing it had ever shown me before. Jackson and I hunched low, holding the drainpipe hand-over-hand, two kids choosing up on a baseball bat to see who would take the plate first. At my side I could hear him whispering a prayer.

"Lord, thank you for the bounty you bestowed on me last night. If you take me, I'm ready to go."

"*I'm* not," I thought.

The house screamed in pain—*and the entire roof ripped away.* Light burst in, filtered through dirt and debris. Wind filled the room, turning bathroom objects into projectiles. My body levitated off the floor, its upward lift halted by the sink above me. The rope cut into my stomach like a garrote. A mirror shattered and I felt a tremendous impact on the football helmet.

Then the walls fell and we were outside, still clinging to our freestanding drainpipe.

The house had been no more than a shell. The tornado had cracked the nut, peeled the husk, and now it had arrived at the meat. In a moment, it would consume us.

Yet, even as Jackson and I waited for the end to come, it never arrived. The storm passed, the roaring winds ebbed, and the noise abated.

Like a faithful dog who dies defending its master, the house had survived just long enough to save us.

The knots had pulled tight and were hard to undo. Also, my hands were shaking. Next to me, Jackson chortled.

"Wasn't our time, G. Um-um, not yet, uh-uh, nossir…"

I started to giggle. My hands calmed, and I got the knots.

"Free at *last*, free at *last*," sang Jackson, as the rope fell away and we rose to our feet. He did a little dance step and I laughed harder, a little hysterical. He grinned at me, then reacted with surprise.

"Still got your phone?"

I felt in my pocket and pulled it out. He had me pose while he snapped shots.

"You ain't gonna believe this. Look."

I opened the photo gallery, flipped through pictures he'd taken, and stopped on one. I pinched-out to zoom on my head. A dagger-shaped mirror shard protruded from the football helmet at the back of my skull.

I removed the helmet and looked at it. The embedded knife was six inches long—yet no part of it had penetrated the plastic shell.

"Second time a football helmet save your life," he said. Then his face fell.

"What?"

"Just thinkin'…wondering…"

"*What?*"

He met my eyes. "Can you still play the git-tar."

"I don't know," I replied. "One way to find out."

We made our way through the remains of the house, knocked flat by the storm. It was now dead calm, and a patch of blue sky offset the grey heavens. The sun peeked out hesitantly. We gaped at the countryside in awe.

The twister had cut a path of destruction, as neat and thorough as a mower sweeping through an overgrown lawn. The house, garage, and surrounding trees had been shaved to the ground. Yet a hundred yards away, a barn and another stand of trees stood unscathed.

Our car was among the casualties. The tornado had picked it up and flung it into the fields, smashing it onto its roof. The trunk lid flapped open and our instruments were gone. After a search, we located one of the guitars—my father's prized Martin acoustic.

It was lying in the field. The case, though dented and gouged, was intact. I flipped the latches and took out the instrument.

"Damn, G, think it's all right," said Jackson with wonder.

I turned the guitar over in my hands, checking for damage. I turned it over again. Jackson gave me a look but said nothing.

I was stalling, as I had been since Jackson raised the question of whether my musical gift might be gone with the cyclonic wind. It would seem like a kind of justice: God giveth, God taketh away. I sure hadn't earned my skill—and the shame I felt over that had yet to resolve.

But now, faced with losing the miraculous ability, I was afraid. Dread had been lurking since the power first appeared. I hardly even called it "mine"—who knew when, or if, the uninvited guest in my body might depart without warning? The tornado seemed like the kind of thing that might shake it loose. That's how it worked in comic books and in fairy tales. But I hoped not.

In the last few days I had turned a corner. The road trip had taught me that, whether this musical aptitude made my life different—in some ways, harder—it made it richer. All the knobs had been turned up to eleven. I liked it that way. I wanted to continue as the person I was becoming—and I couldn't do that if I couldn't play the guitar.

Hardly daring to breathe, I closed my eyes and waited for shapes to materialize. The colors of the spectrum emerged, light and satin-bright for high notes, dark velvet shadows for the lows. Following their lead, I played the intro to "Stairway to Heaven." The exquisite melody traced a path that I hoped to travel the rest of my life.

When I opened my eyes, Jackson was smiling.

Chapter Fifty-Three
Chasin' the Blues

THERE'S NOTHING like a little life-threatening encounter with the awesome forces of nature to put your existence in perspective. In point of fact, it hadn't been a "big" tornado, and no one had been killed, though Jackson and I *had* come pretty close. We were among the few who had found themselves in the tornado's path, since it had missed cities and blown itself out pretty fast.

Supposedly, thirteen minutes is the average warning before a tornado hits. Had we truly had that long after the sirens sounded? The search for shelter had seemed to transpire at breakneck speed, lasting the briefest of moments—yet time slows when your head is on the chopping block and you're awaiting the death blow.

Save for minor cuts and scrapes, Jackson and I were unhurt. Cell service had been knocked-out and our car was obviously undrivable. We could have hiked to the road and maybe hitched a ride, but we were in no hurry to leave the scene of the miracle. I played guitar and Jackson tapped a rhythm on a board from the wreckage.

After a bit, an SUV turned onto the dirt road and drove slowly down the path, halting at the downed power pole. A man, woman, and two teenaged boys, dressed in their Sunday best, emerged from the vehicle. They stared in awe at the two strangers deposited among the rubble that had been their home.

We introduced ourselves to the Taylors and told them what had happened. Our hosts concluded that God had spared them since they were piously attending church instead of watching Sunday NFL games. Jackson and I saw no need to debate, though in fact their house had saved the lives of a couple of sinners, with an assist from a football helmet. Perhaps the Lord does indeed work in mysterious ways.

The Taylors generously took us into town, and our friends were relieved to see us. They made us repeat the story of our storm encounter over and over, as if subsequent retellings would make the incredible believable.

The least we could do in return for the life-saving assistance their house had rendered was to treat the Taylors to Sunday supper. Along with Lucille and Virginia, we made a large party. The Taylors seemed scandalized—but also fascinated—by Lucille's risqué behavior, as she picked right up where she'd left off.

I caught Jackson smiling indulgently at her antics. We had decided to fly home, but first needed to meet with a representative from the rental agency to evaluate our totaled car. I expect Jackson was looking forward to one more night with the woman who'd prepared him to meet his maker.

Escaping death is a strange feeling. As you'd imagine, life tastes sweeter when you've come that close to losing it. Jackson and I ate supper with the realization that our last meal had very nearly been a donut. These may not have been the best biscuits on the planet, but they tasted like they were. I wondered how long we could live with this kind of appreciation.

If you think about it, the end is always out there. For some it arrives sooner. In the music world, the names come easily to mind: Jimi, Janis, John, and Jim; Buddy, Stevie, Otis, Elvis. The list goes on and on.

After the Taylors left to find shelter, the rest of us returned to Lucille and Virginia's place. Over a long, liquor-filled evening, we processed our brush with mortality, and the premature deaths of others who had not been so fortunate. It was another sobering history lesson.

Many blues musicians had been poisoned, stabbed, shot, or had their throats cut. One was bludgeoned with a hammer. Small plane crashes claimed the lives of others. Suicides were rare, but a good number drank themselves to death. Later, drug overdoses became commonplace among rock stars. Expiring of natural causes seemed a rare victory.

Perhaps something in the psyche of artists inspires them to fly too close to the sun. Or maybe they experience the anguish of life more acutely than others. These were theories offered that evening. I listened, checking for the fit with my own turbulent emotions. I could imagine how, like a river swollen by storms without end, such feelings could burst the levees of your life and wash you away. Would that happen to me?

But then I thought of Buddy Guy, and how he'd taught me that playing the blues, chases the blues. His example showed that creating art can be a survival mechanism for life, helping a musician endure the most blues-inducing heartache and pain.

By evening, phone service had been restored and I could call Mom and Dad. The tornadoes in Mississippi hadn't made the national news, and they were unaware of the peril I'd survived. I saw no need to cause them retroactive worry, so I limited my account and filled them in on our changed travel plans. Then I called Samantha.

What boy can resist bragging to his girl about a brush with death? Since it was impossible to use voice and data simultaneously, after a few minutes I hung up and sent her the footage I'd shot of the destruction. When my phone rang moments later, it seemed I could hear Samantha's urgency in the shrillness of the ringtone.

"I can't believe it! Where were *you*?" she demanded.

"You see the sink that's still standing?"

"Yeah…"

"Me and Jackson were roped together, holding onto the drainpipe under it." The other end of the line was silent so long, I finally asked, "Sam? Samantha?"

"Yeah, I'm here," she said with annoyance.

"Awesome, huh?"

"That's not the word I was thinking of."

"You sound kinda mad…"

"You should've been more careful. You could've *died*!"

"We weren't chasing the storm, or anything," I protested. "It chased *us*."

"You *should've* read the weather report."

"Well, we didn't. But there wasn't anything about a tornado, anyway. Surprised everybody." I was disappointed: this was not the dazzled response I'd expected.

The line was silent a moment, then Samantha replied weakly, "I guess I'm just worried, and that gets me riled up. That's what my mom does. I *hate* that."

"So…you're acting like your mom?"

"Now, just a damn—"

"Well, you said—"

"I'm *over* it. Don't care if you wanta juggle chainsaws."

"It's only natural. You *are* her daughter."

"Wrestle alligators. Go on."

I pressed my advantage. "You've inherited genetic traits."

"Swim with the sharks. Run with the bulls. Bungee jump off Mount Everest. Shit, *I* don't care."

"We were just driving around," I protested.

Samantha snorted derisively. "Pussy."

I burst out laughing, and she kept going.

"Real man woulda stood outside and fought that tornado with his bare hands. That's what Pecos Bill did."

I couldn't stop.

"It's just wind, is all it is. A *breeze*."

"It was *hailing*…"

"Don't try and make yourself sound tough. What a wimp. Call me when you survive a volcanic eruption. And not a little one. *Pompeii*, or stay away!"

And she hung up on me!

Chapter Fifty-Four
Mustang Stadium

IT HAD NOT BEEN two weeks since Friz—or "G," as we all called him, now—had come home. But since I'd seen him every day, it felt like longer.

How could he have grown so much in just a few days on the road? It was hard to fathom, but there was no denying the trip had changed him. I hoped he wasn't outgrowing me. Instead of wrestling with his future, he was now rushing at it with open arms. I figured he'd catch it in stride, like a pass on the numbers. G's not one to drop a toss in his direction, especially with nothing in front of him but green and glory.

Mustang Stadium is in Manor, on the way to Austin. It's a high school stadium with a capacity of 6,000. Overkill. That's just how we do it in Texas. The crowd filled only a small portion of it, though the weather was delightful for early December. With temperatures in the high seventies, I was in shirtsleeves, along with G's mother and father. The other players' families were all there, as well as lots of friends.

Everyone was keyed-up for the Texas Youth Football Championship, pitting G's team, the Round Rock White Tigers, against the Fast Camp Eagles. Just like the pros, it would start with a coin toss to determine who'd kick and who'd receive. That was minutes away—when the band started up.

They were on the sidelines, facing the bleachers. Jackson sat at the drums, with Thetis and Willie on guitar and bass. They launched into "La Grange," a catchy, up-tempo ZZ Top song that everyone knew. Thetis took the vocal—just about the only part of which you can actually understand, is this knowing sneer—"*A-how-how-how-how! A-how-how-how-how!*"

The tune set my foot tapping to the driving beat. With lots of people sneering along, Thetis dragged it out, milking the crowd. Then he pushed the lyric forward and they got to the guitar solo.

It exploded from the bank of speakers, fast and deft. Thetis and Willie threw hands in the air to show they weren't playing it. The audience buzzed in confusion, trying to figure out who *was*.

That's when G, seated next to me, rose up. His Strat transmitted to the amp with a hundred-foot cord. It was something Buddy Guy taught him. When the old bluesman was getting his start, he'd use this trick to make dramatic entrances to the Chicago clubs, strutting in from the street, playing all the while.

Without missing a note, G swaggered out of the stands and headed to join the rest of the band at the sidelines. Thetis and Willie picked up the boogie groove to accent the lead, which just kept coming. G started with the Billy Gibbons solo, then he took it further. The crowd jumped to its feet, urging him on.

No art form can match music's ability to inspire a high-octane response. It activates the primitive brain, calling up emotion beyond memory. It connects us to cavemen.

Under G's spell, the crowd broke loose, freeing pent-up feelings, their excitement given joyous expression in the music. They danced, they yelled, they whistled, they clapped. G played on, taking them higher.

The music reached a crescendo and the band brought it down, down…to gracefully transition into the national anthem. Bodies stilled and hats were dragged off as the crowd stood to attention. We lifted our voices to the patriotic hymn, the plaintive notes soaring above us.

The song came to an end, and a moment of reverent silence followed. I could hear sniffling, because the experience had been moving.

But young men are not much for sentimentality. Respectful moment observed, the Tigers rushed G, high-fiving and clapping him on the back. Grinning and laughing, they mobbed him as if he'd just won them the championship—and then, celebration concluded, they headed onto the field to play for it. G's three closest friends lingered with him a moment longer. Then, pulling on their helmets, they ran to join the rest of the team.

I watched G help Jackson break down his drum kit. With volunteer roadies lending a hand, they carted speakers and instruments to Thetis's old pickup, parked just outside the stadium. Final fist bumps between G and his friends, then Thetis, Willie, and Jackson squeezed into the cab of the pickup and drove off. G watched them pull away.

There'd been something odd about that farewell scene—a fourteen-year-old boy on equal footing with men generations older. Yet it had looked comfortable, and no doubt they'd be doing it again. Jackson and G had passed through fire and lived to tell about it by binding themselves together. The four had travelled through a time machine to Chicago and Mississippi, an experience that bonded them forever.

G walked slowly into the stadium, head down. On the field, the coin had been tossed and the players were lined-up, ready for kickoff.

Coach Two Bob caught G's eye and patted the bench next to him. G gave a friendly wave, but veered to the bleachers to take a seat with his parents and me.

"Go sit with your friends," his dad urged.

G shook his head. "Not part of the team."

"Sure you are, honey," said his mom. "If you hadn't made that catch, they wouldn't have gotten this far."

"Few other things wouldn't have happened, either," said G with a little laugh.

"Like meeting me," I said.

"Maybe Dr. Sugarman will be best man," his mom teased.

G and I looked at each other, embarrassed.

"You missing football any?" his dad asked, helpfully changing the subject.

"Some," he admitted. "But me and Tyrell are gonna play tennis when it warms up. Challenge Zack and Jamarie to doubles."

"*That* I gotta see," I said.

G's tone brightened. He was gonna start something... "Oh, you will. You'll be the cheerleader."

"Toldja I don't do that kinda cheerleading."

"Gonna get you pompoms for Christmas."

"Might as well have Two Bob spit on 'em. I'm a flyer or I'm a liar."

"Maybe I'll find another cheerleader."

"Yeah, right," I said. "Maybe I'll find another savant."

"They don't grow on trees, you know."

"Neither do cheerleaders."

"Better quit, bud," his dad advised. "Oughta know by now. *Dos—*"

"Don't *even*," his mom interrupted.

To make sure he *didn't*, she silenced his lips with her own.

Effective. Worth remembering.

I tried it myself.

Yeah...

It *worked*.

The Thrill Is *Never* Gone
May 30, 2015

AFTER THE MEMORIAL, I located my friends in Buddy's suite, digesting their lunch with belches and farts. Having sworn off funerals in their old age, they'd skipped B.B.'s service—but now they wanted a thorough account of what had been said. Their interruptions during my eyewitness report gave me a chance to attack the leftovers they'd thoughtfully fetched back.

"They say anything 'bout his children?" asked Willie.

Mouth full, I shook my head.

"Naw, they wouldn't. Fifteen children by fifteen different women!" said Jackson. "Johnny Appleseed couldn't do no better with *his* seed!"

"Amazing," said Thetis. "Book of World Records stuff."

"Sure is," said Buddy. His face lit up in amusement. "*Miracle*, more like. Way I heard it, B was shootin' *blanks*. His two married wives never had *any* kids."

"*What?*" I managed.

"That's true," Jackson concurred. "B never asked for no paternity test. He *knew* he'd slept with their mothers—least, I *think* he did…"

"Wooooo! Man had him a *lotta* women!" said Buddy.

They cut up about the notion that perhaps B.B. couldn't even remember *who* he'd been with.

"Man on his deathbed an' they still showin' up," said Jackson. "Eighty-nine years old—and B finally tell 'em he wasn't takin' on no more kids!"

"They mentioned how generous he was," I mumbled, mouth full of brisket.

"Say *that* again," said Willie. "Now he's gone, I 'spect they'll fight over money and complain he ain't left enough of it."

"What about his guitar playing?" asked Thetis. "They talk about that?"

"Not too much. Awards and stuff."

"Man revolutionized the 'lectric," said Buddy. "Things he did with his left hand, mighta been the first. Now days, they just press a button and call it good."

The purists in the room were roundly offended by the thought.

"I used to say his initials stand for 'Blues *Bird*,' 'cause that's what he look like to me," said Willie, demonstrating the best he could. "His left hand a big old flappin' wing, gettin' vibrato like nobody else. Was a thing of beauty."

"When I first started, I was impressed by fast players," I confessed, shoveling beans and potato salad onto my plate.

"Shredders," said Thetis. His tone was scornful.

"B.B. showed me that less can be more. He made every note count."

My friends chorused their agreement.

"You notice how he play out of tune?" asked Jackson.

"Yeah! Thought he couldn't hear it."

I could hardly have said anything more absurd! My friends guffawed.

"Couldn't hear it!" said Willie. "Like maybe the man gone deaf!"

"I know, I know!" I protested. "Dumb kid. It took me a while to understand the emotion of coming up on a note, but not quite reaching it—or overshooting it just a hair. How that makes you *feel*."

"B was all about the feel," said Jackson.

"Your defense, son, most people don't *never* understand it," said Buddy.

"So, G," said Thetis. "You find what you were lookin' for at the service?"

They quieted and looked at me. I kept chewing, expecting them to interject. But they remained silent.

We'd not been strangers since our trip to the Delta more than two years before. Jackson, Willie, Thetis, and I got together often, and we'd managed to rendezvous with Buddy when he was playing Texas dates. I'd been blessed to play with more great guitarists when they came through Austin, curious to experience the acquired savant for themselves. Dad and I travelled to see others, such as B.B., and the trips broadened my perspective.

Strangely, injuring my brain had opened my mind—but not just to music. I'd never returned to school, and as a result, I'd begun to learn something. I had come a long way from my lighthearted days of chasing footballs, when ignorance had been bliss. Through my new friends I had become painfully aware of our country's brutally racist past—even worse, its racist present. There was no escaping it on TV or on the Internet.

As for old friends, in time I got the nerve to open-up to Jamarie and Tyrell. At first, they found talking about black and white as awkward as I did. But we pushed through the uneasiness and became closer because of it. *Real* friends.

It frustrated me that America fell short of its ideals. I had a notion I was to play a role in pushing it forward, though I didn't know how. Perhaps I'd developed a "superhero complex"—a belief that with great power comes great responsibility. Or, maybe the burden I felt spread beyond me and Peter Parker. Samantha felt it, too.

I'd been stewing over these thoughts since our last trip to Mississippi. Now my friends regarded me as if I were some teenage sage. What *had* I learned?

"You remember that last time we went to see Buddy, up in Dallas?"

They nodded that they did. Buddy smiled encouragement.

"Between songs, you told the audience, 'You may *hate me*—but I *love you.*'"

When he'd said it to the crowd, he'd cocked his head, eyes twinkling, as if to win over an imaginary enemy. And of course, he'd given them the smile.

"You remember that, huh, G?" said Buddy, surprised.

I nodded slowly. "Seems like that was B.B.'s way, too." I hesitated. "Could it be that simple?"

"It *could*," said Thetis, delighted. "Yes, it *could*."

"You don't have to be a musician to do that, though," I said. "Anyone can live that way."

"They can—but the music *help*," said Jackson.

"Oh, it help a *lot*," said Willie. He waved his hands expansively. "You think white folks be throwin' open doors to B, Buddy, Wolf, Muddy, rest of us, without the music?"

Jackson added, "How B woulda played all those benefits for prison reform without the music?"

"How white kids get to know black kids back in the fifties without the 'race records'?" said Willie.

"It's a bridge, what it is," said Buddy. "The Stones roll all the way 'cross the Atlantic Ocean on that bridge."

"Now white kids taking the bridge to hip-hop city," said Thetis, cocking a disapproving brow. "Don't know that's so positive."

"Don't matter," said Willie, shaking him off. "Better to bring folks together than to divide 'em."

"That's so. Hafta *build* our bridges, *share* our bridges," said Jackson, giving me a meaningful look. "When folks get together, bound to find we got a lot in common."

As usual, Buddy pulled it all together. "We born lovin'," he said. "It's *hate* that's unnatural. You have to *learn* it."

"If you can learn to *hate*…" said Thetis, leaving the rest of the thought unspoken.

"Thetis right," said Willie, tapping his head with a finger. "Was a miracle what happened to your brain, G. But shouldn't take no miracle to change a man's heart."

The End

If you are among the many readers who publicly
expressed enthusiasm for my first novel
—*The Book of Moon*—
thank you, thank you, thank you!
It means the world to me,
and has brought new readers to my little book.

So now...
IF YOU'VE ENJOYED *THE ACCIDENTAL SAVANT*,
PLEASE CONSIDER REVIEWING IT ON AMAZON.
I'd appreciate it immensely.

My books are not for everyone.
But if this one was for *you*—
—just a brief note expressing your thoughts—
—would help potential readers decide whether it might be for *them*.

Then come visit me at my webpage:

www.georgecrowder.com

Acknowledgements

ONE OF THE CHALLENGES confronting an independent author is to assemble a team capable of creating the technical equivalent of a conventionally published work. I am fortunate to have found a tremendous group of people to work with: my gifted cover designer, Dane Lowe; my eagle-eyed proofreader, Helen Baggott; the typesetting wizards at Polgarus Studio; and, above all, my brilliant, insightful editor, Tim Parolini.

A marvel of writing is the process by which a novel assumes a life of its own, beyond the original conception of its author. Written during enormous social and political turmoil in the United States, this book morphed into a deeper, more serious coming-of-age story than I had contemplated. The story and the times demanded it.

I am indebted to Tim, who agonized long and hard over my first draft before arguing that Friz's story required more direct and honest exploration of the topics of racism, white privilege, and cultural appropriation. It has been a daunting and profoundly rewarding experience for this sixty-five-year-old white man to imagine what that would look like for my cast of characters. If I have somewhat succeeded, it is in no small part due to the efforts of Tim. If the reader finds fault, it's mine alone.

Thanks to real-life acquired savant Derek Amato, who generously walked me through the ups and downs of his post-concussion life experience.

Thanks to my friend and terrific guitar teacher, Drew Buzzell. Again, any mistakes in the text are mine, not Drew's.

Thanks to my wife, Liz, who by now is familiar with my writerly labor pains and mustered her customary patience, insight, and enthusiasm through multiple readings of the manuscript.

About the Author

To the IRS, he has been known as a bartender, a waiter, a restaurant manager, a window washer, a grocery clerk, a delivery driver, a telemarketer, a bead stringer, a teacher, an elementary math specialist, a tutor, a lecturer, a screen-writer, and a novelist.

He also frequents his garage woodshop, tennis courts, cyberspace, and the trails of Southern California. Tai chi and qigong counteract the ill effects of everything else, along with four wonderful grandchildren and a frisky cockapoo convinced he's the fifth.

He is the best-selling author of *The Book of Moon*.

Follow George on Facebook and at www.georgecrowder.com.

Made in the USA
Middletown, DE
26 February 2021